Café de Paris

CAFÉ DE PARIS

Nicholas Wollaston

Constable · London

First published in Great Britain 1988
by Constable and Company Limited
10 Orange Street London WC2H 7EG
Copyright © 1988 by Nicholas Wollaston
Set in Linotron Palatino 11pt by
Rowland Phototypesetting Limited
Bury St Edmunds, Suffolk
Printed in Great Britain by
St Edmundsbury Press Limited
Bury St Edmunds, Suffolk

British Library CIP data
Wollaston, Nicholas, *1926*–
Café de Paris
I. Title
823'.914[F]

ISBN 0 09 468580 0

1

The band was playing *Oh Johnny!* at the time of the bomb and the little dance floor was thick with people. Among them a girl was wearing a soldier's tin hat. She pushed it to the back of her head, letting her red hair float from under the brim, and laughed at her partner laughing at her.

'*Oh Johnny, oh Johnny, how you can love!*'

Other dancers laughed with this lovely girl in a tin hat, shuffling round the crowded patch of parquet. She tossed her head and the hat nearly fell off. She caught it and put it on her partner. A fighter pilot in a tin hat. Together they danced on. She loved him in her hat, she would give him anything tonight.

'*Oh Johnny, oh Johnny, heavens above!*'

As the couple danced in front of the platform the band leader, conducting with his back to the musicians, lifted the tin hat from the fighter pilot and crowned himself with it. People cheered and stamped with the music. After a dozen bars he took it off and laid it on a girl with a huge gold key on a ribbon round her neck. She wore it briefly before giving it to her own partner, a young captain of the Irish Guards, who gave it in turn to a tall thin woman with green eyes and a soft smile, who slipped it on top of the rabbitty sun-tanned little man in a white tuxedo she was dancing with, who reached up to place it on a woman with a fussy heap of curls, who shrieked and let a South African naval surgeon snatch it for his Australian nurse, who surrendered it to a colonel of the Polish cavalry. First bestowed like a sacrament on her lover by the red-haired girl, the tin hat was passed on casually, promiscuously. It went to a bald dome, a greasy scalp, a blue rinse, a permanent wave, a temporary blonde, a probable wig; to white strands and black tresses and golden ringlets and scurfy locks; to heads from Norway, New Zealand, Belgium, Denmark, Newfoundland. A pale unhappy woman with a double chin put it on a laughing wounded marine with no chin at all, who put it on a girl in a crêpe de Chine dress, who put it on a boy in a blue suit, who put it on a fat man in a velvet dinner jacket, who put it on an officer in Free French uniform, who put it back on the red-haired girl where it belonged, the heroine of the dance who . . .

It was a child's game – Old Maid or Musical Chairs. Who would be wearing the tin hat when the music stopped? When the bomb dropped?

'*Oh Johnny!*'

2

The eighth of March 1941, eighteen months into the Second World War. This is the Café de Paris in Coventry Street, between Piccadilly Circus and Leicester Square. A balcony runs in a circle round the inside of a beautiful underground chamber full of people. From the dramatic lighting and theatrical shape and from a whiff of anticipation – though nobody here knows what is about to hit them – you have a feeling that an event is going to happen. This must be more than just a restaurant, it was designed for a show. Tonight being Saturday you can expect something spectacular.

The balcony overhangs an arena, so you are suspended between the glittering ceiling and the crowded lower floor with a view of whatever goes on in the middle. It is wide enough to be set with tables for people who haven't got a place downstairs and still to leave room for you to walk round and see who else is here, or be seen. Or you can stand between the potted plants and gilded lamps along the edge and look into the pit below.

The pit indeed. Once there was a bear pit down there, deep under the London street. Lean over the rail and with luck, among the spotlights that cut the smoke and shadows, you may see a dark figure groping about, lumbering and swaying from foot to foot in a torment of perplexity – a vision from above of a scene in hell. The bear's performance, neither dance nor duel, is ringed by excited faces. Dogs bark and snap at its flanks. Bets are laid, shouts and laughs fill the room.

In its different style the present entertainment is noisy too. The trumpet and saxophone can even sound like the cry and moan of a tortured animal. But when the nightly cabaret begins the scene will turn into something unrecognizable to anyone from the old bear pit days.

From the balcony a wide staircase falls and divides and curves in two gold and crimson arms to the floor below. At the bottom, clasped in those arms, is a platform on which a Caribbean dance band plays. Already the dance floor in front of the band, under the balcony circle, is thick with couples. The edge is lapped by a flood of light that tosses over musicians and dancers. Waves of it reach the second row of tables, striking a wine glass, a polished spoon, a hand with jewelled fingers. Drops of brilliance splash outwards from the centre as from a fountain or a firework, a gorgeous Roman candle. But further back there is only darkness. Behind a row of pillars supporting the balcony nothing is visible from where you stand by the rail.

Upstairs, beyond the top of the staircase, the balcony

opens into a foyer with a cocktail bar where Felix Bayne and Guy Ronson sit drinking dry martinis. The barman is Harry who ran a famous place in Paris till the Germans came along last summer. You can see the foyer receding to the foot of another staircase which rises out of sight. You know, because it is the way you came in, that it leads in one straight flight up to the entrance and out into Coventry Street where you were greeted by the doorman, Leo Robb.

At the balcony rail the feeling is insistent: this place isn't what it seems. It was meant for another purpose, not just for eating and drinking and dancing. You are in the middle of something that has been adapted from something else. You have strayed into an illusion, you are caught up in an elaborate spectacle manipulated by someone in the wings, surrounded by scenery for an act which is somehow familiar though you can't remember why. And the other people won't help you, they are no wiser. Perhaps it is a dream you once had. Or the start of an old movie, the opening number of a Hollywood musical. They all begin the same way, you can't tell if you have seen this one before. In a moment the title will appear in yellow letters across the entire technicolor chorus as the music swells and a thousand voices burst into song. Clearly a drama was intended here. There is an element of staginess, of make-believe.

Suddenly you know what you are reminded of. You are on board one of those glorious transatlantic liners, at sea somewhere between Europe and America before the war. The weather is calm, the voyage can't last for ever, the ship will be docking in a few days, but till then you have no cares. From the rail you look down on the first class dining-room where dancing will shortly give way to the cabaret. Passengers in evening dress and officers in uniform pass up and down the companionway. Stewards bustle, corks pop, a foxtrot thrums in pleasant harmony. Out of sight but distinctly close are the kitchens, corridors, cabins, lounges, the boilers and engine-room and the captain's bridge. All round in the huge mirrors you can see baffling images of luxury and passing gaiety. The deck itself seems to rise and fall. As the picture grows, as the eye circles the balcony and passes over the shimmer of glass and gilt, you may catch sight of the four pale trunks of a White Star liner's funnels and a row of lifeboats backed by the blue ocean. The ship is far from land, the water is three miles deep.

The picture isn't all fantasy. When the old bear pit was converted into an underground restaurant much of the decoration, famous for its glass and ornate woodwork, was copied from designs for the greatest liner of the age, then being built. She was the *Titanic* and said to be unsinkable. On her maiden voyage to America she struck an iceberg in the middle of the night and went to the bottom with fifteen hundred lives lost. That was thirty years ago. What you see now in the Café de Paris is overlaid with detail added in the nineteen-twenties and 'thirties, and the music and clothes are modern. None of the people here is aware of any connection with the *Titanic*.

Just as well. By tomorrow morning thirty-four of them will be dead and a hundred injured, many very badly. The chorus girls who are still in the dressing-room, squeezing flesh into blue rayon and dabbing at false eyelashes, won't be called tonight. The famous cabaret, supplanted by a more dazzling show, will never begin.

3

'Have another martini,' Felix Bayne says, sitting beside Guy Ronson at the cocktail bar but looking beyond him to the balcony. It is nine-thirty, twenty minutes before the bomb.

'D'you think,' Guy asks, 'that in Berlin they're doing the same? – watching the war, wondering how much longer –'

'Exactly the same.' Felix lived in Germany for four years before the war. 'But with more style there. Cheaper gin for one thing.' He pays for the drinks. 'Prettier women for another.'

'I don't know – these aren't bad.'

Felix can see the Germans he used to know – sun-loving, fun-loving, prosperous, indifferent: 'God knows why they let themselves be swallowed by the Nazis.'

'But these people wouldn't?'

The two are getting on well. You may think they are old friends, but they met for the first time at a party earlier this evening and came on to the Café de Paris together. Friendships, like affairs and marriages, are made and broken easily in these wartime days. This is to be one of the shortest, cut off after a few hours by the death of one of the men, sitting at the bar a yard from the other who will survive unscathed. You can't tell which of them is to die. Neither deserves it more than the other. They are on to their third martinis.

Felix says, 'We're amateurs at this. We can't convince ourselves, we're ashamed of anything home-grown. The Café de Paris –' He traces a finger line in the dew on his glass, seeing in it the brief promise of tonight in this lovely place. 'We give it a foreign name and pretend it's naughty.' Then, as if Paris and Berlin evoke the lost delights of Europe before the war and remind him of something that by midnight will be too late to mention, he says, 'It's my birthday – thirty-four today.'

'Happy birthday!' Guy lifts his drink and holds out the other hand to shake his new friend's.

'Eighth of March, St Felix's day – my father loved the English saints.'

'Who was he?'

'Never got further than vicar. Shepherd of the Surrey suburbs. Fancied being made a saint himself, but he'd have settled for a bishop. All his friends became bishops. My mother died when I was born and he was done for. Forty years with the same suburban flock – saintly enough.'

'I meant, who was St Felix?'

'A figure from the Dark Ages – the Bishop of Dunwich. A great city on the Suffolk coast. Now there's nothing there, hardly a village. The sea took it away, it was built on cliffs of sand. Once there were nine churches, big medieval Suffolk churches. The last one fell in when I was a boy. My father took me there for holidays. Each year there was a little less till only the tower was left, then one summer we came back and it had gone. It's still a marvellous place – I chose it for my honeymoon. Stand on the beach on a rough day and you hear the bells ringing under the sea.' Felix would like to believe it. In his youth he wrote endless poems in the styles of endless poets on the town beneath the waves – his Lyonesse, Atlantis, Xanadu – and tore them up. But the lines aren't lost, they still sometimes ring in his head in stormy weather.

'Church bells are banned till the end of the war,' Guy says. 'Only to be rung if there's an invasion.'

'The idyll of the English countryside. Bells pealing from the church tower down the centuries, ringing for joy, St George for ever, peace and happiness, for thine is the

[11]

kingdom, the bride and the bridegroom, world without end. Now they ring for a German parachutist. Dropping out of the clouds with his arms up like a crucifix, pretending to surrender, with a grenade in each hand. And Dunwich is a minefield. Pillboxes, tank traps up and down the beach –'

Felix Bayne seems both older and younger than he is: a tall neat figure – mobile shoulders, legs curled round the bar stool – that would be dapper if the flannel suit were newer, the woollen tie less loosely knotted, the socks better hoisted, the suede shoes not so shiny at the toe. Pale skin, long nose, wide mouth, thick hair lightly oiled and brushed – a touch of youth lingers in his eyes and slanting smile, or else it is the first theme of middle age, a bright new one being tried out, tested for the future. He looks a happy man. You may take him for an actor with a part in a long run, or a university lecturer with another income above his salary, or a journalist trying to pass as a diplomat. But he is a poet with a wartime job at the BBC. At the Café de Paris he is one of the few not wearing uniform or evening dress, or at least a dark office suit. He can thank the war for being allowed in.

'D'you come often?' Guy asks. By contrast Guy Ronson looks less than his twenty-four: a young army lieutenant, fresh and boyish with a face as smooth as his new uniform. He makes a convincing officer, without the flair of a regular. Infallibility is something he may acquire in time. Till then a moustache or even a medal ribbon would clinch his rank, but he has neither.

'Most Saturdays.'

'To eat?'

'Just drink.' Felix swills his martini round the glass as if to conjure an olive into it, though none has been seen in London for months. 'I play cards if I'm alone. Harry keeps a pack behind the bar. I play for luck. The way they fall, the signs – I picked it up in Berlin.' He looks sideways at Guy, wondering how much to tell: 'Also, I've got a friend in the band.'

You may wonder what sort of friend. You can see that Felix isn't married, though he mentioned a honeymoon. He has the indefinable buoyancy of a single man, aloof and derisive for a moment before the generosity returns. His eyes, tired of looking into himself, are fixed beyond you at a scene you have no place in.

The Caribbean dance band down on the lower floor, which has been playing *Somewhere over the rainbow*, breaks into *It's a hap-hap-happy day*.

Guy smiles at Felix: 'Specially for you.'

The musicians are from the West Indies. The band leader is Johnson, known as Snakehips from an artful wriggle of the pelvis as he stands in front of his men. Leslie Hutchinson plays the piano – the great Hutch. There is a girl too, the vocalist, a delicious Jamaican called Violet, very black and considered one of the hottest singers in town. Violet has brought extra fame to Snakehips Johnson's band, which has brought customers to the Café de Paris. Tonight she is in a silver dress, scaly like a fish. When she isn't singing at the microphone, pressing it between her speckled mermaid breasts, she sits on a small gold chair beside her brother, Baxter, who plays the alto saxophone. He is less black than his sister but just as beautiful. If Violet is lustrous and shimmering, Baxter is iridescent and velvety.

You may guess that Felix's friend in the band is Violet, and be half right. It is to sleep with Violet that he comes here on Saturdays, the only night that she can spare, but he loves Baxter too. He drinks at the bar till long after the kitchen has stopped cooking dinner and begun on breakfast, talking or dealing cards to himself, waiting for the signature tune, *The last time I saw Paris*, and a solemn *God save the King* before the band packs up. Then he has to sit another half hour while Violet and Baxter eat bacon and eggs. Often it is dawn before they take a taxi to the

[13]

Jamaicans' flat in Pimlico where the three spend the whole of Sunday. Felix calls it 'holding the Empire together'. With old friends he is never reticent about his private life, but with Guy he isn't ready for such a confidence. Probably it will come, perhaps tonight with more martinis.

'Have you known Eunice long?' Guy is asking all the questions. It was at a party in Eunice Fancourt's flat in Bayswater that the two men met this evening.

'We're practically twins,' Felix says. 'Born and bred in the same Surrey suburb.'

4

Felix Bayne was always surprised by his affection for that tight-pressed suburban parish. Till he was eighteen he never left it except for summer holidays at Dunwich with his father. Some of his friends had itinerant childhoods, he was glad of the constancy of his own. It gave his life a pulse which, though later he tried to suspend it, he could never stop.

Eunice Fancourt was there from the beginning. Her father was the Revd Bayne's churchwarden, the parish tycoon who started the first garage before anyone else thought of it, then the first cinema, then a boarding-house known to everyone as the local brothel. Eunice said her father only joined the church as a cover. Her mother – half French, half Egyptian and believed to be a whore brought back by Mr Fancourt from a Cook's tour up the Nile – was manageress of the boarding-house. There was a lot of both her parents in Eunice, and something more.

Felix was first aware of her at a fancy-dress pageant to celebrate George V's coronation in 1911, when they were both four years old. To please his father he decided to dress

up as someone in the Bible. To annoy him he settled for
Adam. But even after the Fall, with a fig leaf from the
garden strung in front of him, he was censored by the vicar
who tore an old shirt into rags and turned him into John the
Baptist. Eunice had to be converted too. She was meant to
be Marie Antoinette in honour of her mother's French half,
but at the last minute she sicked up her pudding over the
dress. A quick substitute was needed and Mr Fancourt
raided the vestry for a choirboy's surplice while Mrs Fancourt, summoning her Egyptian half, hung some borrowed
bangles and watch chains over her. With cork black on her
face instead of powder, little Eunice became Cleopatra.

'How far can you *spit*?' she asked when she saw Felix,
ejecting the word like a gob between her scarlet lips.

Not as far as she could, was the answer. For the next ten
minutes they had a spitting match on the vicarage steps till
the Revd Bayne, disguised as Thomas à Becket, intervened
with his crozier. As they were being separated, Cleopatra
picked some snot from her nose and flicked it through a gap
in John the Baptist's rags where Adam's fig leaf showed.

They ran neck and neck through childhood. Eunice won
the prize for reading the lesson in the children's service,
Felix came second. It went on for years – variations on the
first encounter, heats in a contest that lasted till 1925 when
they both left home at eighteen. Eunice was usually the
winner. She beat him at tennis and swimming, and in the
mayor's debating competition. The local paper gave its
junior literary prize to her essay 'On Growing Up', which
she was doing vigorously at the time, in preference to
Felix's sonnet 'On Dunwich Beach' which in a hidden way
touched the same subject. It was above the high-tide mark
on Dunwich beach that he discovered, lying alone with his
fantasies while the Revd Bayne strode on up the Suffolk
coast, that now he could father his own child. As a vicar's
son he was tormented by the Shulamite in the Song of
Songs, who praised her lover for his body like ivory set with

[15]

sapphires, and wondered if his own would ever be much good. The poem's imagery was too obscure for the editor, but Eunice saw through it at once. That should have made Felix suspicious. She was the only girl to share his discovery with, and he assumed that one day they would seduce each other. It would be the proper climax, the final in their long tournament.

Eunice's news, and her laugh as she gave it, that she had swapped virginities with another boy was a knockout. Felix retired to his bedroom for more experiments on the Dunwich theme, practical and poetic. 'How fair and how pleasant art thou, O love, for delights!' the Shulamite's lover sang.

When he got over it, he asked Eunice about the other boy. It was the gravedigger's son, up in the cemetery in a freshly dug grave. The boy liked it because they couldn't be seen. Eunice liked it because it was a kind of death for a girl anyway and the place seemed right. She liked it very much. A coffin was put in the grave next day but for years afterwards, whenever Eunice came home, she laid a bunch of flowers on it.

In 1925 Eunice went to Oxford. Felix was to go to Cambridge, but on a vicar's salary his father said the university must wait. He spoke to his bishop who had a cousin, a retired cavalry officer in Ireland. The Major wanted a tutor to coach his son for an English school, and Felix got the job.

With ten pounds paid by Mr Fancourt for translating a book of erotic Latin verse he bought an old motorbike; and one hot morning at the end of the summer he drove it off a ship and steered through the tremulous Irish countryside towards the Major's home. The sun had melted the tarmac, the tyres sizzled on the road. If the saddle had been softer it would have been the best day of his life. Late in the afternoon he passed through a gateway capped with stone eagles which reduced the brass one on his father's lectern to a sparrow, and flanked by lodges from which countless barefoot children stared. Felix waved at them and almost fell off, but they never moved. There were still two miles of Ireland before the end of the journey. At last he drove over a bridge across the loveliest river he had seen, as big as the Thames, then between white-fenced paddocks full of racehorses and up an avenue of huge, curiously clipped yew trees to the house.

Another young man with experience only of a Surrey suburb and a Suffolk village might have been awed by the house Felix had arrived at. It had once been an ordinary country mansion, grand enough for most people but not for one of the Major's ancestors who had built a castle on top of it. Eighteenth-century elegance, for a nineteenth-century whim, was hidden under a mock twelfth-century shell. Turrets rose above battlemented walls which plunged into a moat spanned by a drawbridge. Above it all, on the highest tower, sailed a heraldic flag. The bishop had said nothing about his cousin's way of life – probably he had never been here – but to the new tutor, innocent and receptive to anything the world could show, it was natural for his patron to live in a castle. And wasn't he himself a kind of modern Merlin coming to bestow wisdom on a prince, and thus could expect no less?

He propped his motorbike at the edge of the moat, freed his trousers which had stuck to him, walked stiffly over the drawbridge and pulled a chain. It was then, looking back at the avenue he had driven up, that he saw what the clipped yews were meant to be. They had been sculptured into huntsmen on horseback, galloping away from the castle in pursuit of hounds that diminished into the distance.

Not a squeak from the portcullis nor creak from the massive doors, nor even the quietest cough or sniff from the butler – it was just Mortimer's sardonic presence, smelling of brandy and soon to be familiar. Felix turned to find himself on the threshold of a vast hall lined with tapestries and animal skins, but peopled only by suits of armour.

[17]

'Mr Bayne it is, I believe,' came from the black-tailed figure, in syllables that curled up at the end like the speaker's eyebrows though they hardly formed a question.

'What – ?' Felix began.

'Mr Bayne it is.' This time the syllables stayed flat. Any doubt had been removed.

'What shall I do with my motorbike?' It looked untidy out there at the end of the drawbridge. Felix wished he had rolled it into the moat.

'One of the chauffeurs will see to that,' Mortimer said, adding 'sir' after the shortest pause that he could be certain would be noticed. 'If you will follow me –'

Travelling through the castle was a bonus to the journey through Ireland, a cadenza to finish off the day. It was hundreds of yards to Felix's bedroom but Mortimer, to impress or confuse him, didn't take him the shortest way. He walked slowly in silence, as if haste or noise would disturb something in the castle understood by him alone, and dispensed brandy fumes like incense behind a priest. They passed out of the great hall into a gallery from which through doorways Felix saw a billiard room, a gun room, a library; then up and down so many stairs and passages that he couldn't tell if he was nearer the battlements or dungeons. Log fires were burning in several places – eternal altars. At a crossroads he heard a scuffle, a muted laugh, a door being closed, but there was no more sign of life before they reached his room. Each time he caught a view from a window it was different: the avenue of galloping horsemen, an inner courtyard, a formal garden with urns and statues round a fountain, a chapel roof, a conservatory. He tried to memorize landmarks in case of retreat. A stuffed wolfhound looked useful till they came to another, then a third. He should have been unravelling a thread of silk.

'I trust you will be satisfied.' Mortimer bowed him, not too deeply, into a room as spacious as his father's vestry. Mortimer was a kind of sacristan.

Below the window, across the moat, was a lawn the size of a suburban sports field, fringed with trees and stretching into fields where cows and sheep were placed in careful patterns. Beyond, drawing the eye as it must draw water from the landscape, a lake lay in the hills, so big it might have been the sea though Felix knew how far they were from the coast. It was the first of the moist, tender Irish afternoons that he came to love.

At the door, before abandoning him, Mortimer intoned, 'Should you need to ring, Francis will attend to you,' and withdrew, shedding another faint 'sir' to evaporate with the brandy.

Already Francis was attending well: a freckled young man in a white coat, one of Mortimer's acolytes with an appealing gentleness, a faint submission in his face, a touch of compliance. He must have unstrapped Felix's panniers from the motorbike and had got here first, beating them on their devious trail through the castle. Now he was unpacking Felix's clothes, putting them into drawers and cupboards. He spread them thinly, but they didn't go far.

'We'll sponge this for dinner,' Francis said, holding up the cheap dinner jacket that Felix had bought but not yet worn. It had been his father's idea, without guessing that it would be wanted every night; without showing Felix how to knot a bow tie. Felix sensed that though old Mortimer was too remote, too superior to be enemy or ally, Francis could be helpful. The castle geography and the daily timetable might be hard without a friend.

5

'Sherry for you, sir,' the Major said that evening when Felix came into the drawing-room.

It was a greeting to the new tutor, also a command to Mortimer. The butler approached with a decanter on a silver tray and poured sherry into a goblet. The Major was drinking brandy and soda. Felix was reminded of a cock pheasant with unusual plumage: blue eyes with yellowish lids, rusty moustache, streaky grey hair, pink and white face, purple smoking jacket. Nothing matched, something had gone wrong in the mixing. Round his feet, wagging and panting, was a small pack of dogs.

Without ceremony the Major introduced his wife: 'Meet Bunty.'

Felix saw a tall woman standing by the fire in a gown like a long black tube, slightly flexible. Gold shoes showed at one end of the tube, the tops of her white breasts at the other. Her face was almost as white, her eyes were green and immense, her hair was pure copper. Felix had never imagined anyone like her, and saw at once that she knew it. She stretched herself a little taller, as if being gently squeezed from the tube, without letting the breasts escape.

'You'll meet the boy tomorrow,' the Major announced. 'Name of Bertram. Idle little runt. Make sure he comes up to scratch, sir. Or I'll have him horse-whipped. His tutor too, I shouldn't wonder. Works like magic. Settles the juice.' He said it again, 'Juice,' pressing it through the gaps in his teeth. 'It's the root of all trouble – juice. You agree, sir? Chief fault of the Irish – too much juice. Know what I mean?'

Felix looked at Bunty for help with an answer, if any was wanted, but she turned to kick a log in the fire with her golden shoe. He thought she smiled. Over the mantelpiece was a large portrait of a racehorse. All the pictures in the room were of horses or hounds.

The Major went on: 'Ever seen a man horse-whipped? Stays with you for life. Stays with him too, I shouldn't wonder. Had to do it once in France, in the war. Nothing like it.' The Major's style of speech came from years of communicating with soldiers and animals. 'Cigarette, sir?' He didn't ask a question out of interest in the answer, it didn't occur to him that there might be one. Even the dogs listened as if they had heard it all before.

Mortimer came up again from behind. Now the tray bore a polished horse's hoof rimmed with silver and filled with cigarettes. A silver plaque on it said that the horse had won the Irish Derby. Perhaps it was the one in the painting over the mantelpiece. Felix took a cigarette from the hoof and Mortimer withdrew.

The Major's voice pattered on like harmless pellets fired at nobody in particular: 'Had a young trooper in my company. All of ten years ago. Must have been 1915. First summer of the war. Never forget him. Name of Robb. By God, the juice in him! Too much by half. We were billeted near Amiens. You know it? The anus of the world. Just the place for Trooper Robb. Caught him in the brothel, time out of mind. Gave him every chance. Plus many more. Only one thing for it in the end. Had the whole company up on the parade ground. Stripped him in front of his fellows. Squeezed him till the pips squeaked. Drums rolling all the time. Took it like a tiger. Looked like one too, by the end. Never forget the defiance in his eyes. Juice – no other word for it.'

Afterwards Felix wrote a ballad about the flogging of Trooper Robb on a parade ground in France during the First World War, and so the name stuck. Otherwise it would have meant nothing when he heard it fifteen years later during the Second World War at the Café de Paris, where the doorman was called Leo Robb.

Mortimer came back with a silver matchbox mounted inside a fox's paw. As the butler lit his cigarette Felix choked at the thought of what Eunice would have said, reading the silver inscription on the paw. The fox had broken cover in the park, taken the hunt across two county boundaries, three rivers and a railway, and been killed after a run of thirty miles – the best day of the century.

'Start on young Bertram in the morning,' the Major announced. 'Draw the first cover after breakfast. Sticky going, I shouldn't wonder. Always is, the first day out. Stiff in the joints. Muscles need oiling. What'll it be – Latin? sums? history? All the same to me. More sherry, sir.' It was a command, like another dozen lashes for Trooper Robb.

'Mr Bayne – may we call you Felix?' Bunty turned from the fireplace and spoke for the first time: 'I've never known a Felix.' Her voice was smooth, creamy like liquid poured from a slender spout. He would put it in a poem one day. She said, 'I don't think you'll have trouble with Bertie – he's very willing, just rather young.'

'If that boy's willing I'm a –' But the Major couldn't think what he might be, other than himself. The explosion which nearly burst inside him turned into a puff of gas, and he went back to something safer: 'Juice – that's what's wrong with our Bertram. Born with a dose too much.'

Bunty said, 'We'll see,' and gave Felix a quick smile that might have been a signal of alliance. She advanced towards him over the carpet, bringing some of the warmth of the log fire; then swerved at the last moment, brushed close past him and glided to the door, trailing the faintest odour of roses, a sigh left on the sterile drawing-room air. The timing was perfect. Someone opened the door from the other side, someone else rang a gong, and Bunty passed out of the room.

The Major said, 'Dinner,' unnecessarily. The dogs had already scampered out.

In the dining-room, with a footman behind each of them, the Major and Bunty sat at opposite ends of a table that could have taken forty people. With an undulating arm Bunty waved Felix to a chair half-way down one side where Francis was standing. A look in her great green eyes, cast the length of the table and back, told Felix that they could talk without the Major hearing. They were helped by a silver fruit basket in the middle, as big as the Revd Bayne's font, loaded with pears and peaches. Round the pedestal, in a frieze, silver racehorses galloped. It was the general theme. Glass finger bowls were cupped in silver horseshoes, toast racks were made of silver stirrups. Ranged across the table at the Major's end, polished till each silver hair glistened, was a pack of silver fox heads staring up from the mahogany. Not an eye blinked, not an ear twitched. For Felix, after the long day and two goblets of sherry, it was too much. Eunice would have begun barking like a dog. He only let out a soft 'Tally ho!' into his napkin and hoped that nobody but Francis noticed.

6

Bertram, whom Felix met next morning, lived most of the day with his pony. He talked of fetlocks and croppers and martingales, he knew the names of all his father's hounds and the ancestry of his horses. Yet something belied the child in breeches and a velvet cap. Felix liked him, partly because he had thought he wasn't going to, partly because he saw the loneliness of another only son. They spent four hours a day at lessons and found an affection, a mutual need unconnected with their own interests. Apart, Bertram groomed his pony or watched it being done by a stableboy and rode in the park all afternoon, while Felix explored the castle library and wrote poetry. Together, they worked and worried towards Bertram's exams next summer, discovering a pleasure beyond the job. In age they were divided – linked – by only six years. They hailed each other from opposite ends of adolescence – from a suburban vicarage and an Irish castle; and often laughed.

'Felix is Latin for happy,' Bertram said with glee, finding it in the dictionary. 'All your days are felix days. Blessed with felixness. Lucky you.'

'Felix-go-lucky.'

'You'll marry a princess and live felixly ever after.'

'Perhaps I'll find her in this castle.'

Bertram thumped the table with his riding crop: 'There's only one and she's someone else's.'

Felix tried to write something every day. If he finished a poem a week he was pleased. By the time he left Ireland the following summer he had fifty copied into a notebook. But the subject of the early ones surprised him. Here he was, in an Irish castle, bombarded by new experiences, the first salvoes of adult life, and he could only write about what he had left. The leafy roads lined with Tudor villas and magnolias, the tennis club and public swimming-pool, the strong legs and stretched blouses of unattainable girls, plimsolls and galoshes, stucco and copperware, macaroons and walnut cake, laughter through the privet and snoring through a sermon – the familiar past was in clearer focus than this exotic present. In the castle library the picture of Eunice Fancourt in gym tunic and school blazer came more easily than the vision of Bunty uncoiling from a sofa to light an Egyptian cigarette. A fleet of herring drifters out to sea off Dunwich appeared sharper than a file of tinker carts winding to an Irish fair.

An entry had to be forced. The castle must be breached to let him into the next stage of a poet's life. It was Bunty, he knew, who would put the key in his hand or turn it for him. But it was Francis, the startling Irish valet with freckles on his nose and wonder in his voice, who revealed the first mysteries.

'Would you be interested at all,' Francis said on a soft autumn morning to match his deference, 'in a visit to the covering shed?'

The place was fit for the purpose: big like a barn, with straw bales piled round the walls and a deep straw mattress spread over the floor. The clock on the stable tower chimed the quarter-hour. Trumpets should have sounded – and did, in the poem Felix wrote – as the doors opened to let the sunshine and two horses in: a stallion and a mare. Momentously, ceremoniously they were led by white-coated grooms to the middle. They hadn't met before, they nuzzled each other over the top of a padded fence. The men hardly spoke: the silence of wonder and excitement. A kind of execution was to be done.

The mare kicked the fence. It was nine days since her last foal, now out in a paddock, was born. Time to start again. In a burst of lust the stallion reared on his hind legs and snorted; tossed his black mane, curled back his lip.

'He won the Derby,' Francis said. 'He won't be kept waiting.'

The grooms folded the fence away; strapped thick felt shoes to the mare's hooves in case she struggled, sponged her with carbolic, bound her tail with a bandage. The stallion, held by the head groom, stood looking at her from behind, frisking and tossing his head. Francis was wrong: he would take his time.

'Come on, come on,' the head groom said, quietly coaxing, and the stallion stamped the straw. Nobody else said anything. The mare stood patiently, she understood. 'Come on, come on.' The stallion walked away, leading the head groom round the shed, then reared and punched the air with his forelegs. 'Come on, come on,' and the groom led the stallion back to the mare. Slowly a ramrod descended, swinging down to the straw, glistening and purple. But he wasn't to be rushed, he stood tossing and pawing; reared again, his tail and forelegs lashing, his teeth bared. At last he acted, as if a signal had reached him from his ancestors: the call to honour a champion's pedigree. He walked straight up to the mare, lifted himself gloriously and lay across her back, fuming through his nostrils and nibbling her ears. One of the men snatched the mare's tail aside and suddenly she groaned, a faint high-pitched sigh from far inside. For a moment the horses heaved, churning on the straw across the shed. Then, as suddenly, they parted.

'Not covered,' the head groom said gently. 'Come on, come on,' and the stallion stood looking at the mare, tossing and rearing. He advanced once more; mounted, failed again.

'Come on, come on.' The quiet voice of the head groom, the silence of the others, the patience of the mare, the nobility of the stallion: the shed was transformed into a theatre for a beautiful performance. The men might have been bawdy, but they were polite.

The stallion came on a third time, hissing and arched and terrific; mounted the mare swiftly and with a scream from one of them they were locked. They staggered together over the floor in great heaves, uttering awful unearthly noises. Then they were still, while a champion's heritage drained away.

'Covered.' The head groom too was satisfied, perhaps moved. The stallion withdrew. The horses stood apart on the straw, at peace for a moment before being led out into the sunshine, the mare back to her foal, the stallion to his stable. He would be doing it again in the afternoon. The stable clock chimed the half-hour.

[26]

'Fifteen minutes,' Francis said. 'And thousands of pounds to the Major. You never know – perhaps we've seen another stupid Derby winner got.'

7

Bunty's enormous bed was quite unlike the covering shed. But lying in it between her long thighs that afternoon, when the Major and Bertram were out riding, Felix couldn't forget the earlier ritual. Some of the movements and noises were the same.

'"On a poet's lips I slept."' Bunty wound her limbs round him with fervour and a touch of greed. 'Shelley, in case you didn't know – *Prometheus Unbound*.'

'I've never read it.'

'Perhaps you think I make a habit of this. But you're the only poet to come my way. A first for me, a first for you.'

He tried to disentangle himself from memories of the stallion and mare, and Bunty made it easier. She was so generous yet exultant. The bed was limitless, like the bed of the ocean. He was twined with a myth, a creature half sea monster and half sea anemone and all goddess. She gave him no time to wonder how he had got there.

'You'll pour this into poetry one day,' she said with delicious accuracy. 'Everything thrown in. Me coming into the library after lunch. Tiptoeing up behind. Trying to read over your shoulder –'

'It was about the sea on the Suffolk coast – a place I know. I was turning the breakers into white lace curtains.'

'Putting up your hand to touch me without looking up.'

'I felt you were there,' Felix said, untruthfully. He had thought with mixed horror that it might be Francis.

'Your fingers climbing up.' Bunty took them now and put

[27]

them to her lips. 'Me coming round the chair and sitting on the table in front of you. Kicking up my legs. Laying myself out across your bits of paper.'

'Like the surf at Dunwich.'

'"I'll be your poem this afternoon," I said. Not very subtle. Not very fair.'

'It worked quite neatly.'

'You played better than I expected.'

'I wasn't sure where to begin, it all looked so –'

'One of nature's lovers. I see a great career ahead, Felix. I'd like to be watching. Think of this, from time to time. Are you taking notes? You should be, like a true professional. Making love in an Irish castle on an autumn afternoon. The ticking of the clock on the mantelpiece.'

'Spoilt sheets and stickiness.'

'The wind coming through the window.'

'Blowing goose pimples on your skin.'

'The clouds outside.'

'Colour of golden tea.'

'Perhaps it'll rain soon, like a purge.'

'Raining tea.'

'Tea for two. Shall I ring for Mortimer and have it sent up? He wouldn't smile. "Will madam be expecting the Major to join her too?"'

'I'd rather not.' Felix kissed her ear, and remembered the stallion this morning.

'You must read *Prometheus*. It's a man's poem. A song of pleasure. You're just the age for it.' Bunty unravelled herself and went to shut the window. 'That's when I read it. On Crewe station – coming back from school in England for the last time. I missed my connection for the Irish Mail and had to sit up all night. Crouched over a little coal fire in the waiting-room.' She got back into bed. 'I was an anarchist by the morning.'

'Or an angel.'

'The trains hooted and whistled on their journeys to

nowhere. And people came in, shivering and fussing over their puny little lives. And the great rhythms of *Prometheus* washed over me. Like your breakers on the shore. We belonged to the elements that night, Shelley and I. I thought how marvellous to miss one's connections. I'd go on missing them all my life – which I suppose I have. We'll read it aloud. I've never done that. Here, one afternoon – shall we? The delights in store!'

Felix was surfeited. He couldn't grasp his luck, his joy. There were too many ingredients. Bunty saved him from his emotions by stabbing gently at the most tender.

'This is a sort of lovely blasphemy for you, isn't it?' she said. 'All those holy commandments you were pumped with.'

'My friends and I sang profane versions of the psalms.' He must justify himself. 'We stuffed potatoes down the organ pipes.'

'But fornication!'

'I wrote parodies of the Lord's Prayer and the Creed.'

'Now the wrath of God will fall.'

'I read the Song of Songs during the sermon. The Shulamite with breasts like two fawns that feed among the lilies – getting so excited in my trousers I could hardly stand up for the next hymn.' It was happening now, without trousers, with Bunty's breasts so close.

'The vicar's son in the arms of a wicked lady.'

'Not quite the scarlet woman.'

'You haven't been struck dead yet. And how can such fun be sin? Were you going to be chaste till your wedding day?'

'I haven't said my prayers since I came to Ireland.'

'Knocking down the old idols – it's all you can do at eighteen, before setting up your own. Wait till you meet Prometheus. He's a modern man. One of your friends. Even yourself.' Cunningly, with talk and love, Bunty wrapped herself and Felix into such a confusion of thoughts and bodies that he couldn't separate them. 'The rebel who wants to live in freedom and fights against convention. At last the painted veil is torn aside and he's free. Classless. Stateless. King of himself. Gentle and just and brave. But not free from pain or guilt. It's great stuff, it goes with the Choral Symphony.'

'I go for Byron myself. He was modern too. Suspicious of heroics. Sceptical and angry. And terribly funny.'

'I hardly know him. Give me a line.'

'"Her stature tall – I hate a dumpy woman."' Felix was pleased, stretched along the naked length of Bunty.

'Shelley idolized Byron. He threw himself at Byron's feet, he called himself the worm beneath the sod.'

'I'll win you over,' Felix said. '"Pleasure's a sin, and sometimes sin's a pleasure." We'll read *Don Juan* too.'

'That's the name of Shelley's boat, that he was drowned in.'

8

'Like a mount tomorrow, sir?' the Major asked at dinner, from beyond the silver pack of foxes.

Behind his chair Felix sensed the servile Francis twinkling to himself. He looked at the Major, then at Bunty at the other end, then back at the Major, uncertain what he was talking about.

'First meet of the season. Show you what hunting's meant to be. Catch a fox and put him in a box for you, I shouldn't wonder. Have you blooded by the end of the day.'

'I don't think Felix has ever been on a horse,' Bunty said. Her voice, like the licking tendril of a vine, reached down the table to touch her husband, circling her lover on the way.

The Major choked on a mouthful of pheasant; spat it out on his plate and put it back: 'Fix you up with something. Soft mouth. Quiet. Not too much juice. Sit up and trust him – that's all there is to it. Grip with the knees, sir. The horse'll do the rest.'

'I could follow on my motorbike,' Felix suggested.

Six days a week he spent the morning tutoring Bertram, the afternoon in the library or Bunty's bed. On Sundays he rode away from the castle on his bike and drove great distances across Ireland. Everything was a new wonder to him: the empty day, the solitude, the road ahead. All went into his notebook, a stockpot of scraps which long afterwards, far away, he would dip into. A child who played with a pig in a cottage door; a fish that leapt from the fermenting water of a river; a thundercloud lying over yellow hills; a sense of expansion, the future rolling to infinity like the road ahead; a sudden bend in an oak wood, wet with leaves where he went into a skid and fell off, twisting a mudguard and a shoulder; a shout from a mad old woman cutting turf in a peat bog, her cackle piercing the engine's drone; a shaken fist and a flying stone from a group of men at a street corner in an empty town; an immense Georgian mansion gutted by Republicans, roofless to the bloodshot sky, its window sockets ringed with fire streaks and staring across the abandoned park; an impression of the country's menace and goodwill; a reminder of his own singularity, belonging to nobody but himself: it was all tipped into the stew, to be skimmed or simmered, kept or thrown away.

'Motorbike!' The Major's pheasant almost came out of his mouth again.

So Felix followed the hunt with Francis in the shooting brake, a big Rolls Royce. After breakfast the hounds, the Major's private pack, were assembled in front of the castle.

[31]

Silver trays with sandwiches and sherry were carried out over the drawbridge to the riders. A dog barked, a whip cracked, a horse raised its tail and dropped a heap of digested oats on the gravel, steaming in the crisp morning. A kitchen boy in apron and shirtsleeves, scrubbed raw like a carrot, ran up with a brass bucket to shovel the offence away. At a word from the Major the huntsman blew his little horn and the crowd trotted off down the avenue of clipped yew trees.

'This was meant to be an ambulance in the war,' Francis said. 'For driving over the Flanders fields, loaded with wounded soldiers. Or the glorious dead. Or stupid poppies. Instead it's got us and the picnic, chasing an idiot fox.'

Beside the chauffeur sat a groom, with Felix and Francis in the back among hampers of cold salmon and turkey, fruit, a Stilton, claret and a flask of brandy for the Major. All morning they pursued the pursuers; waited at the edge of a wood while the hounds sniffed and yelped in the undergrowth; then careered down lanes to keep in sight of the galloping dogs and horses. The Rolls Royce, upright and eager like a thoroughbred, joined the chase. At lunch, as if by arrangement with the fox, the scent was lost by a stream where the hampers were opened and stories of the morning's great adventure told. Afterwards, with a fresh scent and a toot on the horn, the hunt went on.

Fired by the absurdity – the Major's scarlet coat and white breeches, Bunty's magnificent pale animal as unearthly as herself, Bertram's silk cravat pinned with a gold horseshoe, and their friends and neighbours galloping round them – Felix abandoned the Rolls Royce and took to his feet. Francis went with him and they ran over fields, across streams, through woods in the direction of the hunt. Towards the end of the day, from a hill, they could see the mad procession stretched across the landscape: the fox out in front, hardly bothering to escape but proudly ambling to his death; the demon hounds, screaming for meat; the

[32]

motley pack of humans in full cry, hanging on for their lives, driven by some dim instinct, hunting for a glory of their own.

'There she goes!' Francis cried, picking out the same phantom horse as Felix. 'Wasting no time as usual.' Bunty was up with the hounds, lifting her horse easily over the land. 'Gripping with the knees,' Francis said, putting on the Major's voice and digging at Felix with a thumb. 'The horse'll do the rest. No lack of practice, I shouldn't wonder.'

Felix was racing downhill. Seeing the hounds closing on the fox, he judged where they would catch it; jumped two ditches, pushed through a hedge, ran down a lane and reached the corner of a field at the same moment as the fox. It stopped in front of him and for an instant they stood looking at each other, animal and man. A stab of truth – mortality compressed into the last seconds of a life – flashed between them before the hounds burst into the field. The fox turned towards the pack and for another instant it lived: wild and beautiful, master of itself. Then they were on it, ripping and biting till skin and flesh and bones were gone, and only the mangled face and sleek uneatable tail remained on the red grass.

'Well done, sir!' the Major called, riding up with the rest of the hunt, finding that Felix had already got there. 'Put you on a horse next time.'

9

'You've made a great impression on your master,' Bunty told Felix one winter afternoon.

'And my mistress?'

'You need telling? If I were modest I'd put it down to Prometheus. Instead –' She took his cock and stroked it: 'Shall I have it mounted in silver with an inscription?'

'"Drawn from cover after lunch –"'

'"Ran all afternoon. Honoured for sportsmanship, deeply admired for stamina." Mortimer could bring it to me sometimes on a tray.'

They read aloud between bouts of love. The Major spent most afternoons on his horse, visiting the stud and kennels or hacking round the enormous piece of Ireland that he owned. Bertram went with him or was left to play with other boys from the estate. The lovers were safe. During the winter they got through most of Shelley and Byron and in the spring, leaping a century, they began on Eliot. 'The Waste Land' had been published three years before, it was new to them both and they fumbled through it together; jumped at a meaning, laughed at every shaft of clarity in the puzzle.

'Dead trees and dry stones – I don't think that's suitable for this,' Felix said. 'Languishing in bed with you.'

'Aren't we part of the postwar futility? The spirit of the nineteen-twenties? Feckless and uncertain. Adrift –'

'It goes better with the English scene.' Felix's father had written about the General Strike. The suburbs had risen to preserve King and Empire from the revolution. The Bolshies would be beaten. The Revd Bayne had turned his vicarage into a defence headquarters. Eunice Fancourt, who had been expelled from Oxford – caught in bed between two students – had sought out her first lover, the gravedigger's son who was now driving a hearse for an undertaker, and got a job laying out the dead.

'It's too lush here,' Felix said. He wanted something less agreeable. This soft Irish interlude was useful, as the suburban years had been, but he needed a more sordid flavour. He wasn't yet nineteen, he would travel, he would rummage in the dark corners. Factories and offices and stagnant canals, lodging-house bedrooms awash with cigarette ends and condoms, pints of beer in the public bar, baked beans out of a tin, sweet tea in a chipped white cup, cheap eau-de-Cologne in an armpit: raw material, the rawer the better.

Bunty said, 'You'll soon be back in it. All the squalor you want. You'll slip away –' She racked her memory: 'After bestowing one final patronizing kiss and groping down the unlit stairs – how does it go?' She reached for 'The Waste Land' and found the place: ' "She turns and looks a moment in the glass, hardly aware of her departed lover." '

'That woman was a typist.' Felix felt indignant, defensive.

' "Well now that's done, and I'm glad it's over." '

'And the man was a house-agent's clerk.'

' "She smoothes her hair with automatic hand, and puts a record on the gramophone." '

'You haven't got a gramophone.'

'Don't get the idea that I'll be unhappy, pining in my castle. Just because you're a poet –'

'A poet's nothing special. He's an ordinary man – more ordinary than most.' Felix hadn't thought of it before, but as he said it he believed it: 'An extension of the common man. The normal taken to its ultimate.'

'I'll never look at "The Waste Land" after you've gone, I promise.'

[35]

He leant across to lick a nipple, sprouting on the white: 'Let's have that bit about the two men walking up the white road, and the invisible companion who joins them.'

Bunty read it out: '"Who is the third who walks always beside you? When I count, there are only you and I together. But when I look up the white road, there is always another one walking beside you."'

Felix said, 'They were polar explorers – Shackleton and his men. I looked it up in the library. Their ship had been trapped in the ice and broken up. They'd drifted on the floes. Then they took to an open boat and sailed across the Antarctic seas.'

'Through constant gales – don't tell me.'

'They reached land, but had to cross a frozen mountain range.'

'Unexplored, of course.'

'One of the great journeys. At the worst moments Shackleton noticed someone else, a stranger at his elbow. He kept quiet till one of the men said, "Boss, I had a curious feeling there was another person with us." It's not unique. Other travellers have seen the same. Climbers, sailors –'

'Poets.'

'Remember old Slocum, sailing round the world alone. Eating some plums and cheese for supper which went bad inside him. A storm blew up and he was doubled up with pain in his bunk, he couldn't sail the boat. But in his delirium, through the storm, he knew everything was being looked after – the sails reefed, the sheets trimmed, the boat kept on course. When he felt better he got up on deck and there at the helm was a stranger. A tall man –'

'Wrapped in a mantle, hooded –'

'Wrong – a Spaniard in a red hat and whiskers.'

'A stowaway.'

'The man smiled and said he was one of Columbus's crew, and he'd steer the boat till the fever and the storm had passed.'

[36]

'And told him not to eat plums and cheese again.'

'Often after that, Slocum was visited by the Spanish pilot who came on board for the company.'

'And the adventure.'

'They go together.'

'That's what you'll do, Felix. Tag along with people for a time, so long as it suits you. For company, for adventure. For your notebook. Screw them and leave them –'

'That word –' It was too harsh for this refinement.

'You prefer poke? Poking's straight, but screwing's got a twist. I love it with a twist.' She was showing him. '"But who is that on the other side of you?"'

'Nobody at all,' Felix said.

But it wasn't true. He was in love with Bunty but he wouldn't lose his heart, though one day it might happen. And she was right, there was someone else – a shadow beyond her, hazy and elusive. It might be his father, or the mother he had never known, or Eunice, or an unknown stranger, or even his own dim other self. Sometimes it was a dark woman with a foreign accent, faintly admonishing, hardly more than a wraith but desirable and irresistible: the Shulamite with eyes like doves behind her veil and temples like a piece of pomegranate; the woman, if there was one, whom he might marry.

10

There was one more thing to do before leaving Ireland. Felix couldn't explain or justify it, he viewed it without distaste or excitement, he simply knew that to omit it would be a waste. He mustn't go back to England with regrets. On his last Sunday he drove away from the castle, across the

[37]

park and through the lodge gates with Francis on the pillion. The barefoot children stared as usual, as rigid as the eagles.

'You never did this with *her*!' Francis shouted behind Felix's ear, gripping his hips to stay on.

'Have a guess,' he shouted back.

It was a brilliant June day. The wind tore at their trousers, tears blew from their eyes. A fly went up Felix's nose, a bee got into Francis's shirt. Through the smell of hot oil, beyond the engine roar, the summer afternoon waited under the sun.

'Where the hell are we going?'

'Swimming.'

Twenty miles away was a lake that Felix had once seen, bigger than the one near the castle, far from any house. He drove off the road, down a path between brown tussocks and lumps of rock. The motorbike bucked between his legs and Francis gripped harder. The path ended at the edge of a low cliff fringed with vivid turf. Below lay a bay of sand so bright they had to squint, lapped by water stretching a mile to the far shore. They left the motorbike ticking as it cooled, and slithered to the beach.

'First in!' Felix sang, peeling off his clothes and running into the lake; splashed through the shallows, tumbled forward and began to swim. The cold shocked his body, his breath was choked. He kicked and gasped, and turned to shout, 'Come on!' The figure on the beach grew whiter and smaller as its clothes came off.

'You stupid English idiot,' Francis spluttered, swimming up. They swam out to the middle of the lake, laughing, then headed back to the beach; stepped on to the bright dry sand, and ran.

'Come on!' Felix knew that Francis was a step behind him; knew how they would end up. It happened easily, without check or doubt. He ran the length of the beach and there, barred by rocks, turned to meet Francis who caught him round the waist and they fell over, wrestling on the sand: 'Come on!'

'You and your "Come on, come on". Remember?' They were the head groom's words last autumn.

'Well?'

Drops of water trickled off them. Running in the sun had warmed them after the cold bathe. Each knew what the other wanted; gave it gladly – for the sun-white beach, the wide lake, the summer sky. No awkwardness, no questions to answer or consciences to soothe, nothing to spoil their discovery: only stark delight. Suddenly a line from his sonnet 'On Dunwich Beach' came back to Felix. But there wasn't a drowned city under the water here, or waves washing metaphors through his head, to rinse his emotions and upset the scansion. They bathed again, swimming along the shore, and landed in a bay with a stone boathouse at the water's edge. Fishing-rods hung from the rafters under the roof, over a rowing-boat with oars ready. Francis wanted to take it out, but Felix could see some tweedy sportsman arriving for an afternoon's fishing to find his boat out in the lake with two naked men on board. They swam back to their beach and made love again, with more gentleness in the softening day. 'Horseplay' was Francis's word. Felix, mindful of the unknown fisherman, thought of it as sport, though no sport had come to him so simply. He could never take it up for life. Taught by Bunty, he had adopted other joys. But he would remember the pure pleasure of today.

The afternoon tapered into evening, the beach lost its sparkle as the sun, slanting down the sky, threw a milder light off the lake. Shivering, they dressed and clambered up the low cliff. They would drive back to the castle in time to wash and change for dinner. At the long table, eyeing the Major and Bunty far away at each end, Felix would take his place in the middle with Francis behind his chair.

But the motorbike wouldn't start. Felix stood on the

crank pedal and swung it fifty times, then another fifty; tickled the carburettor till it flooded, and cranked; waited till the petrol evaporated, and cranked again; took out the jets to blow them clear; unscrewed the plug to scrape off the carbon. Nothing would make it spark. They pushed it up the path and along the road, running beside it to get up speed. Felix jumped on the saddle, threw in the gear, let out the clutch, but it hiccupped to a halt.

'Idiot bloody thing.' Francis would be in trouble with Mortimer, he might be sacked. They should be back by now.

'Only one thing for it.' Felix started down the road. Pushing the bike they made hardly three miles an hour. And soon it was dark: 'All we need is a good rainstorm.' It never came, but nor did the moon to light the road. They were hungry, they didn't speak, they walked more slowly as the night deepened. Hills appeared where they hadn't noticed any this afternoon riding to the lake, and Francis's shoes were hurting. It would be two in the morning before they reached the castle gates. But they never did.

Passing through a village towards midnight they saw a light in a saloon bar. Voices, just as faint, could be heard behind the curtains. When Felix tried the door the talking stopped. He knocked, but nobody stirred in the pub or elsewhere in the dark village. He tapped the window and the light went out.

'Anybody there?' he called, hoping to sound harmless.

The edge of a curtain moved, but nothing showed behind the glass.

'Can we use the telephone?' Not that anyone in the castle would be awake. 'We've walked twelve miles – another eight to go. Anybody there?'

A chair in the saloon was knocked over. Someone spoke quietly. Then the creak of footsteps behind the door.

'We've broken down, we'd like to telephone.' Felix's words, addressed to the door, fell dead in the village.

[40]

'What's your name?' A man's voice came out, hard and metallic as if speaking down a tube.

'Bayne.' And again, 'Bayne.'

As the door flew open a light was switched on to dazzle anyone outside. A torch was trained on Felix's face. A man stood in the doorway, dark against the light, with others behind him. A breath of whisky crept out.

'Bayne,' Felix said a third time, helplessly.

'Who's that?' The man tossed the question with a jerk of his chin, followed by the torch beam, towards Francis holding the motorbike in the road.

'Ha!' Someone laughed – a younger man. 'To be sure, it's Francie-boy. I know him from the seminary. Francie-boy, the darling of the fathers. Who served at the altar. And sang like a canary bird. And much else besides. Himself indeed – ha! Just fancy that. Traitor to his race, he is. Remember me, Francie? Remember?'

'Have you got a telephone?' Felix asked, alarmed now.

'You get going,' the first man said, advancing half a step. 'Quick now, or else. On the road – get going.'

'A drink? We'd like a drink.'

'On your way – you heard.' The man withdrew.

'Please –'

The door was slammed. Bolted inside. Behind it the younger man laughed again, a single 'Ha!' before the silence came back.

'Mother of God,' Francis whispered in the dark road. 'That's Hogan in there, no doubt at all. The one who laughed. I never thought he might come back. It's a long time –' His voice had lost all tone, it was dry like an empty tin. A rattle was the best he could get from it.

'Come on.' They were the only words Felix could find today. 'Quick, we'll get away – I don't like it.' He might abandon the bike in the village, but it would be surrender. He took it from Francis, gave the crank pedal a useless kick, then set off pushing it into the night again.

[41]

'We were at the seminary together.' Fear rose in Francis's voice. He hobbled on sore feet to keep up and the story came in patches. 'Five years ago – Hogan and I. I heard he went to America afterwards. Now he's back. But I was never told.'

The breeze blowing across the road carried the scents of a summer night – peat and heather and the sour-sweetness of dry grass with the dew on it. A few cars had passed before they reached the village, but there would be no more traffic tonight. A dog barked far away behind them.

'They gave him charge of the pilgrimage money – collecting for the nuns to go to Lourdes. You heard the way he laughed? It was always the same with Hogan. Five years ago he laughed like that.'

They were a mile from the village now, perhaps more. It must be past midnight. In three hours the sky would start growing pale. The dog barked again, closer.

'He laughed like that when I found where the money went. Machine-guns, Mills bombs, detonators, fuses – that's where. To blow up the English, you idiot English who still had a bit of Ireland. What could I do except what I did?'

The soft night, soothing on the cheeks till now, began to rasp; the breeze to bite with the old anger of Ireland. Arson and murder sniped from behind the Celtic crosses. Felix remembered things he had hardly thought of since he came here: the Easter Rising ten years ago, the Republican army, the money from America, the weapons and explosives that came ashore from boats at night or were smuggled past conniving customs men. But the civil war was over, the years of grievance had surely faded. In this gentle countryside it was hard to believe in terror squads, booby traps, a bullet in the heart. Hard at least on a summer afternoon by a lake. Easier at night – pushing a broken motorbike, tired and frightened, with a companion dragging behind with blistered feet and memories.

[42]

'Hogan knew who it was who gave him up. He said he'd settle with me – one day when he got the chance. They gave him six months in Dublin jail, then he emigrated. I wasn't safe even with him in America. I suppose I knew it. I wish I'd never told the fathers. I wish I'd never come with you today – you and your stupid bloody motorbike. They might have warned me he was back. I could have done something. Gone to England – anywhere. That's what I'll do, I'll come with you. When the bike's mended, yes? You'll help me, you'll have to – after that bloody lake of yours. I'll go where Hogan can't get me. Did you hear what he called me? Did you hear the way he laughed? Did you –?'

It came again, the sharp 'Ha!' from the young man in the saloon, not far behind them. Other voices too, urgent and shrill, hunting. And the dog was closer, barking on the road they had come along.

'Mother of God!' Francis was swamped by fear. He started running but tripped and yelled, picked himself up and ran again, whimpering. The dog had been let loose. Snapping at them in the dark.

For Felix the nightmare of the next ten minutes, the next ten hours, was heightened by its outrage. He had never been so affronted. If he hadn't been terrified he would have stopped to argue. This was worse than cowardly and cruel, it was illogical. Nobody should be treated this way. Or nobody who wasn't a fox. Nobody with a trace of courage. But when Francis began to run, Felix pushed the bike into the ditch and ran too. Up the dark road, faster than in his life before – he was amazed how fast. His feet lost weight, springing from the road as they touched it and skittering forward.

Francis was quicker. He vanished into the night ahead, or off the road to find sanctuary in the fields and woods and bogs; to lose himself in the sorrow of an Ireland not big enough to hold both him and Hogan.

Felix kept to the road where he could run faster. Off it, he would get lost. He ran for his life, spurred by the surprise of his own speed. He went on running long after the pursuers had given up, when their shouts and the barking stopped. He slowed to a jog and halted at the top of a hill where he called Francis's name, not loudly, and listened. No answer. No footsteps ahead or behind, no noise anywhere. Francis must have taken to the country. They would find different ways back to the castle. Felix had started again, half walking and half running, when the dry thud of an explosion reached him from behind, muffled by distance. He knew it was the petrol tank of his motorbike blowing up. Turning, he saw a yellow flame lick the darkness, then fall back. Perhaps the dog barked once more, Felix couldn't be sure. Perhaps it was a cry.

For two hours he followed the road, passing occasional dark houses without stopping. He had no friends here. The lodge gates were shut but not locked, he slipped into the park and felt safe. Behind the towers and turrets the sky was bleached with dawn when he arrived at the drawbridge. No lights in the windows, no sign of Francis. The stable clock chimed three and gave Felix an idea. Waking nobody, he found an empty stable and slept on the straw till breakfast time.

The body was found next day, its head cut off and lying at the blistered feet. Fear had gone from the face, which stared up between the legs and showed only surprise at the unfamiliar view. Nearby was a burnt-out motorbike. The news was given to Felix, lying in his room at the castle, by Mortimer who also brought a silver tray with sandwiches and beer.

'Or you may have tea if you prefer,' the butler said, without the 'sir', making clear that it was too good for someone who had escaped a nasty death.

Bunty never appeared during Felix's remaining days. Without saying good-bye she took Bertram for a holiday by the sea. Felix signed a statement for the police and was warned he might be called back to Ireland as a witness if an arrest were made, but he heard no more. The nightmare was already changing, the agony receding to leave a few hard facts of horror.

The Major, who was otherwise speechless at the whole thing, blamed it on the usual cause. 'Juice,' he muttered, till Felix left for England. 'That's the trouble – too much juice.'

11

The eighth of March 1941 has been a bright day, a Saturday of early spring. Londoners can congratulate themselves on getting through the winter's bombing and watch the crocuses coming up round the shelters in the parks.

This morning Felix Bayne walked from his flat off Tottenham Court Road down to Trafalgar Square and along the Strand to the City. Lend to Defend, the posters on Nelson's column commanded. Drink delicious Ovaltine, they said at Charing Cross. Britain was fighting for its life and profits. Don't waste Food. Ask for Haig. Buy a Spitfire. Get it at Harrods. Pick a Piccadilly. Take Bile Beans. Join the RAF. Give her Black Magic. Barrage balloons floated on strings in the sky, and the golden cross on St Paul's shone in the devastation as it had done throughout the raids.

This afternoon Felix wrenched a dozen hexameters from the staring walls of his flat. This evening he went to Eunice Fancourt's party in Bayswater where he met Guy Ronson and they came on to the Café de Paris.

'Have you noticed,' Felix asks Guy at the bar, 'how everything's changed?'

Guy turns to look at him: 'The Blitz is a thing of the past?' Last autumn the bombers came fifty-six nights running. Recently there has been a lull. But there is a rumour that the

Germans are planning something worse. Hitler is boasting of his secret weapon.

'The different flavour, I mean.'

'It's a poet's war, I read.'

'All wars are.' It is a year since Felix's last book was published – a long verse narrative covering the twelve months before the war. Since then he has tried to find a way through the chaos: synthesizing the antitheses, he called it in a poem he scrapped. 'But this one's changed so often. D'you remember at the beginning, the way the danger put an edge on things? The shiny streamlined years were over.' Sometimes Felix catches himself picking words from his own poetry. They were ground in hell, they keep a lingering validity like scars. 'London looked so lovely, those early days. It was crying out – look at me! Take me while you can. Live before you die.'

'And nothing happened.' Guy turns back to his martini. 'The phoney war, the great bore war.'

'Carefree in a way, once you saw it wasn't the end of the world. A sort of adolescence – we'd grow up when the war turned serious. Till then you could enjoy it.' Felix was half quoting, half improvising. 'The blackout. Taking the dog for a walk in the dark for the hell of it. Trekking like boy scouts to a pub. Falling over sandbags, colliding with lamp posts. Flashing torches at strangers. All very jokey.'

'Jumpy.'

'Making friends. Glad to bump into someone else, to compare notes and share your nerves. Like tourists in a foreign country. Working out the currency, struggling with the language. Swapping advice and comfort and hoping you didn't give yourself away. And suddenly the shooting began, coming closer. Not just Poland and Finland – it was Holland, Belgium, France, going down like skittles. Three months' terror.'

'That was my bit,' Guy says. 'I was at Dunkirk, I've done nothing since.'

'Then the Battle of Britain. Holding your breath. Screwing up your eyeballs, clutching your other balls.'

'Our finest hour.' Guy closes his eyes as if in prayer. To mock Churchill is sacrilege and treason.

'Then the Blitz. The horror. But the passion too.' As well as working in the BBC, Felix is an air-raid warden.

Guy says, 'I wasn't in London,' and brushes cigarette ash off his uniform.

'The feeling we were all in love.' Felix wouldn't talk like this if he hadn't drunk a lot at Eunice Fancourt's party. And he is excited at making a new friend. 'Something personal, for yourself. You'd been singled out. Picked for the part.'

'That goes for Churchill. His life was leading to this.'

'For everyone – it was your chance to be yourself. You had to make do, you lived from day to day. And nothing was too improbable. The unlikeliest thing was the most likely. You wondered why you felt so good when it was such hell. Just like love.' Since the first day of the war Felix has been on the brink of love with Violet, the black singer in Snakehips Johnson's band.

'What about that all-in-it-together stuff?' Guy asks. 'The people were in battle, united –'

'But individuals. Public bravery, private superstitions – even the bombs were personal.'

'If your number's on it it'll hit you?'

'Zigzagging down – it seems haphazard, but it's not a fluke, it's coming for you,' Felix says. 'I love the little tricks, the twists of chance. It's why I play cards.'

'D'you believe them?'

'Why not? I'll tell your fortune.' Felix could ask Harry for the pack he keeps behind the bar, but sees that Guy is too rational or sober. He says, 'There's something Priestley said in a broadcast – "It's as if the poets have gone and the politicians are coming back." The defiance is over. Nobody can keep the passion up. Back to normal.'

'You can come to the Café de Paris.'

[47]

'But you're not in the front line any more, in the cut and thrust. It's been turned over to the professionals – let them get on with it. The war machine's in charge now. And it isn't such fun.'

'Or so dangerous.' There hasn't been a bad raid on London for six weeks.

Felix orders two more martinis and looks round the place: the beauty, the effervescence, the colour. He remembers the poem he would have written ten years ago about the Café de Paris. It would take a painter to get it right – Manet, Degas, Renoir. Perhaps, you may think, that is all it is: a brilliant canvas and the people only blobs of paint.

It is filling up, the high spirits rising higher. Half the men are in uniform, some of the women too. Many are foreigners. People throng the foyer waiting for Charles, the head waiter, to give them a table; or find places at the balcony where they can look down on the dance floor. The word has gone round that Douglas Byng, famous as the rudest entertainer in town and usually star of the show, isn't here tonight. He has an engagement at a charity ball in Park Lane: he will rejoice for it tomorrow. But Violet is as ravishing as ever and Snakehips' band is warming up, playing *Run, Rabbit, Run* for the third time. It is set to be a good party. A cousin of the Queen is here and an archduke and a daughter of Stanley Baldwin, last Prime Minister but one, and a maharaja with his fourth wife, a flying ace whose many previous husbands were rich and even semi-royal but never descended, like this one, from God. Names will be dropped tonight, and if blood is to be spilt on the deep carpets and polished parquet much of it will be blue.

Or is it, you may ask, another Duchess of Richmond's ball? The arrogance of people who are going off to fight tomorrow. The false jollity that conceals real terror. The last crazy hours of dancing before the bloodshed.

Felix says, 'Guy, I'll tell you something you didn't know,'

[48]

afraid of sounding drunker than he is. 'The bombs dropped on London in the last six months weigh less than the dog shit dropped on all the pavements.'

Felix's own dog, a German schnauzer that he brought back from Berlin in 1933, became mascot of his air-raid wardens' post and was killed by a bomb last November.

12

In the autumn of 1926 Felix went to Cambridge. He was nineteen, older than most freshmen, which put him apart. After his Irish castle and afternoons in bed with Bunty he was impatient with the boys who filled the college, loud and hearty and unconfident. He might drink with them in pubs or have them to winter tea parties in his room with crumpets and honey for the sake of Rupert Brooke or join them on the river in the summer, punting under the bridges and winding the handle of a gramophone – fifteen years later in the Café de Paris, when Snakehips plays *Tiptoe through the Tulips*, Felix can smell the river water stirred up by a punt pole and see the emerald duckweed under the Cambridge willows – but he made few friends there. And the girls taking notes at a lecture or bicycling in the town, clenched to the handlebars in a fluster of skirt and gown, belonged to another race. In three years he never spoke to one.

He wore bright shirts and butterfly ties and went into a shop to buy a silver-knobbed Malacca cane, but came out with a big ash walking-stick. Wotan, lord of the gods, had carried an ashplant. It was the tree of life. Felix liked the feel of it in his hand and propped it by his fireplace where another student would have a cricket bat. It was fun at first to have his own room with his name on the door and a man to look after him. When he left Cambridge in 1929 his college servant, Nipper, was the only person he was sorry to say good-bye to.

Nipper might have been any age between forty and seventy. He wore a bowler hat on his rattish head, walked crookedly as if he had once been caught in a trap, changed for work into a green baize apron worn shiny by greasy hands, and kept the stub of a Woodbine stuck always to his lip. He wasn't up to the Mortimer level, but attended to Felix's parties with a jaunty deference near to flattery and brought meals from the college kitchen or beer, and more beer, from the buttery.

Drinking was the symbol of freedom. At the vicarage the Revd Bayne kept only an honorary bottle of sherry for the bishop's visits: to get drunk was to lose one's self-respect. For Felix that was the point. Self-respect led to complacency. Churchmen and politicians and industrialists, imperialists, nationalists, the boss class in general, the world's troublemakers, were soused in self-respect. They questioned nothing, they were too busy behaving properly. Being drunk could be unpleasant, but it gave the illusion of clarity – a short cut into innocence and fantasy. Filtered through alcoholic eyes, stripped of reverberations, a new poem could be seen more starkly. Words squeezed out in sober agony now lay like drops of truth. They were unique and perfect and his own: nobody could take them away or spoil them. Though Felix couldn't start a poem when drunk, he could pick at one more boldly, and next morning he liked the changes he had made under last night's freedom.

Nipper encouraged drinking. It was virile, a sign of manliness and bulldog character, and he didn't mind clearing up the mess. He dismissed aesthetes and intellectuals, he admired footballers and rowing men. Though he was suspicious of the fancy shirts and ties, he was pleased with Felix's capacity for beer.

[50]

'You're different to what some of my young gentlemen are,' he told him. 'It's books books books with them.'

'I read books too,' Felix said, though glad to be acquitted by Nipper.

'Ah, now that's another thing, isn't it? What I say is, if a gentleman can't have a good time when he's young he never will.'

Felix tried to guess what sort of time Nipper had had. There was still a boy in the shrivelled old man: there might have been an old man already in the boy.

'Now take the war,' Nipper said one day.

It was something Felix was often asked to do. He knew men whose fathers or elder brothers had been killed; others who felt guilty for having been too young. He himself was thankful, and felt a coward for it; then was thankful for feeling a coward. Hating the holiness of the war he wrote a poem called 'The Great Whore' for a student magazine which roused some indignant patriotism. It was winter and snow lay over Cambridge. Someone went out at night into the college court and trampled in big crisp letters, 'Bayne fuck off'. Next morning it was frozen into the snow, picked out by the winter sun. It lay for a week, printed for the public, and the magazine was sold out. For Felix it was a fine blow to his self-respect, another welcome step down the ladder. A porter was sent with a spade to wipe the words out, but the trampled snow had killed the grass and when the lawn began to grow in the spring they came back, brown against the fresh green.

'Now take the war,' Nipper said, and Felix knew he was in for the old man's favourite treatment: the warriors of an earlier generation. 'In them days the young gentlemen came for a term or two before they was off to France. Tea and toast with Nipper one week, plum and apple in the trenches the next. Not to speak of death and glory. There was fourteen of my gentlemen copped it and a finer lot I'll never hope to see. Heroes, one to fourteen, numbering

[51]

from the right.' Nipper wiped his hands on the green apron, snapped to attention and saluted. 'Talk about the final fling and making hay and that – they had me running from here to the buttery and back till I had blisters on my feet like strawberries, and I'd do it again, call me weak if you like. I knows a privilege when I meets one. It was like twilight for them – see what I mean?' The stub of Woodbine trembled on Nipper's lip. 'Twilight for me too.'

Before the footprints faded from the grass Felix was caught in another jolly incident. Having won its races the rowing club rounded off its annual dinner in the usual way – burning a boat. A box of fireworks was put in it before the flames took hold, to improve the blaze. When it died down the members prowled through the college with hunting horns and rattles in pursuit of more tradition. Their first victim was tackled and had his arms pinioned, his socks and shoes pulled off, then his trousers. But it wasn't enough: he hadn't kicked or pleaded, the pack was unsatisfied.

'Strip him!' one of them bellowed. It was Upton La Touche, known to friends as Up Yours Too, or Up for short. As the clothes came off, Up shouted, 'Look, it's our poet!'

'Bayne!' the cry went up, 'Bayne, Bayne!' till Felix lay naked under twenty oarsmen, wondering what would happen. For an instant he remembered as a child being read to by his father from the lives of the missionaries, and dreaming of being attacked by cannibals. Once more he was waiting to be cooked. But the picture was washed away by a jet of beer in his face. When his eyes cleared he saw a barrel held over him by two men who were shaking out the dregs.

'Duck him!' Up yelled, in charge of the rites.

Felix was hauled to the fountain in the middle of the court, and tossed in. Soon his clothes were hanging from the scallops, stopping the spouts, while he swam round like a fish in Bunty's moat. It was a warm night, he didn't mind at all, though he wished he had thought of it himself. His pleasure was caught by the rowing men: 'Good idea!' In bow tie and dinner jacket Up jumped in, followed by the others with the empty barrel.

Bathing on a summer night in a baroque fountain set off an unlikely friendship between Felix and Upton La Touche. Up envied Felix's coolness under torture, Felix enjoyed the contrast of their personalities. Such extremes could never be united, there was no need to try. It was a loose and easy friendship, in the lazy Cambridge climate where neither felt inclined to work.

Felix, who couldn't afford another motorbike, invited himself for a spin one Sunday in Up's famous machine, a two-seater Bentley painted racing green with a strap over the bonnet to hold the power in and four exhaust pipes that burst like entrails and curled back into a single silver fishtail. The handbrake, the size of a railway signalman's lever, stood outside the door. Hood and windscreen were folded down in whatever weather, leaving driver and passenger protected by two half-moons of glass. Though the body tapered astern like a boat, the effect was more of an aeroplane. Sitting in the fuselage beside Up, goggled and helmeted like an aviator, Felix sometimes saw the spinning disc of a propeller beyond the nose. And in the villages they roared through, people stopped to look up into the empty sky, wondering where the bomber was.

'Feeling all right?' Up shouted above the engine, accelerating out of Newmarket and heading east. At any moment he might pull back the joystick and climb off the ground.

'Terrific! Can she loop the loop?'

'Never tried. We'll have a go – hang on!' Up's eyes glistened and grew bigger behind the goggles, his kid gloves squeezed the mahogany wheel, the car shook in a spasm of excitement. A chicken crossed the road and was left flapping behind, a diminishing pile of blood and feathers.

'Coming up to climax!' Up shouted, biting hard and glancing at his instruments. Felix remembered him describing the convulsions of a Cambridge waitress whom he had treated very like a Bentley. The piston noise rose higher, the bodywork throbbed to the point of uncontrol, the fishtail discharged a mounting song of triumph to match the driver's bliss, till 'Orgasm!' he shouted and settled back in his seat with a smile of peace.

'Where the hell are we going?' he asked when the car had slowed to a cruising speed and the vibrations calmed down. It was the question Francis had asked on the pillion of the motorbike that distant Irish afternoon, before being butchered by Hogan's gang.

The answer was to another beach: 'Place called Dunwich,' Felix shouted. 'On the Suffolk coast.' They drove through Bury St Edmunds and Stowmarket towards the sea.

'Dead straight – might be a Roman road.' And Up might be a charioteer.

Felix hadn't been to Dunwich for years; to the sea that rubbed and scooped the coast day and night, never satisfied. He was afraid it might let him down, but it was the opposite. The two young men walked a mile up the beach, turned round and walked back. It was a perfunctory day. Swinging his ashplant, Felix couldn't talk about the drowned city or look for cornelians among the pebbles. Up only wanted to inhale the ozone as he strode along, or play ducks and drakes with small flat stones, spinning them over the sea and counting their skips. A man was standing with a fishing-rod, his line sucked out under the breakers. Up asked him what he hoped to catch and wished him luck, man to man; then strode on.

Felix enjoyed Up's company less for its own sake than as material for something he would one day write. Long ago –

last year on another shore – he had made love with Francis. Time was playing a trick. He felt younger today. He had reverted with this raw student in a Bentley to a more childish age: this was the place he had come to every summer as a boy, the place of the pubescent sonnet. Yet also he felt older, grown muscular with his poetry. It lay ahead as well as behind – a line that continued beyond visibility like the shore, vanishing in both directions but stopping nowhere. Straining his eyes he had a vision of himself with a wife here one day, but like sunlight in a burst of spray it flickered out. He felt himself two people, distinctly separate: one, stretched in time, leaning back to a half-invented past and forward to a half-imagined future; the other, ashplant in hand today, swiping at a dead starfish stranded by the tide, listening to talk of cylinders and barmaids, thirsting for a pint of beer. One self spanned a life, the other stood at a single moment.

They returned to the car; found a pub and ate a huge Sunday lunch; buttoned themselves into goggles and helmets and drove back to Cambridge, borne across the flat land in Up's great machine.

The Cambridge years passed like the acts of an unsurprising play. Felix hadn't gone there to study, he stopped attending lectures, he wasn't lured by academic life. The dons at the high table in the dining hall seemed as lifeless as the ones in portraits along the walls: their brains too prodigious for anything on a normal scale beyond trivialities. They often discussed railway timetables, though few were seen to travel as far as Cambridge station. After dinner, a brotherhood of clever eunuchs, they crept into their common room and got carefully drunk, cracking walnuts and passing the port and snuff. Their wit, if any, was genteel or stale. One who lived at the top of Felix's staircase had been dead for days before anyone noticed. Under the bedclothes in an old suit he was obscured by the mildew of sixty years' scholarship: curtains and cushions exuding tobacco, empty bottles, heaps of unfinished lecture notes given up to earwigs, copies of a mammoth book he had written which had been superseded by a rival, a maggotty fruitcake and two kippers on a plate.

For Felix the one reality, the only serious thing, was poetry. He saw the passing days as a gift to be drawn like metal into the finest, clearest tension. But it was he who passed; who would live and die and leave the days still passing. He would drink the wind, breathe the rain, ravish the night, clasp the morning. He believed in everything that was life and in the stuttering truth inside him and in the future of his youth. He loved the world, the smell of the earth, the taste of the sky; loved the people – their strength and weakness, their infinite behaviour and misbehaviour. He wrote it down and crossed it out and threw it away and wrote it again. He worked at nothing else till the month before his final exams; then read a dozen books, more in contempt than fright, and got an excellent degree.

'What will you do with it, dear boy?' It was an odd question from the don who had read fifty of Felix's essays without the least concern for Felix's life. Famous for the immensity of his mind, he was better known for his deification of Sherlock Holmes. He recited the stories from memory, and after years of research and analysis could make his idol's career more boring and futile, less relevant than the original. But it was his one link with the world outside the college: suitable for a man who, in some ways so wise or so silly, was in other ways not a man at all.

'I was thinking,' Felix said, though he hadn't thought of it before, 'of going to Berlin.'

13

'Here comes Eunice,' Guy says.

Eunice Fancourt, her fur coat thrown back off her shoulders to show a sumptuous red dress, steers towards them at the bar, ignoring other people and calling 'Happy birthday!' loudly as she comes.

'Like a fire engine through the traffic.' Felix pulls up a stool for her. 'Ringing your bell and making for the hot spot.'

'Happy happy – mm –' She envelops Felix and herself in a gigantic hug, smothered by the fur coat and containing, deep inside, an extravagantly long kiss: 'birthday!' she ends, when they come apart. 'I remembered it after you'd left the party, so I had to come on here. Thirty-four today! Soon it's my turn. Thirty years since John the Baptist and Cleopatra –'

'You're not going to start another spitting match.'

Eunice's beauty is a matter of energy, voraciousness, ardour. A dynamo spins inside, fuelled by love and hope, impelling her through a life of surprises. If you feel you have seen her before, it is only that you recognize a figure from the mythology of the times. She is adored by almost everyone who knows her, feared by a few and widely rumoured about by many who have never met her. Usually the stories are less sensational than the truth. On being expelled from Oxford she was married for six weeks to an opaque suburban estate agent, an aspiring politician in a mock Tudor mansion. After slipping away at breakfast while her husband was crushing toast between his yellow teeth she pursued her capricious line of happiness: a child of the 'twenties, a woman of the 'thirties, an adventuress caught in the bizarre limbo of wartime London where reality and unreality are hard to tell apart.

'I've brought Lionel and Celia,' she says. 'The party fizzled out after you two had gone – you traitors. Call yourselves friends! Only the dregs were left and no gin at all. Isn't it the total bottom when a girl can't buy a bottle of gin for love or –' She laughs at herself: she will call herself a girl till she is ninety, if she gets through the next few hours.

Lionel and Celia, holding each other's fingers, reach the bar in the swathe cut by Eunice. Lionel is about twenty-two: the shallow, callow man-about-town you might have seen in the Café de Paris before the war. Now he is a fighter pilot and the Battle of Britain has put ten years on him. He killed four Germans before baling out over the Thames estuary when his Hurricane caught fire in a dog fight, leaving a cobweb of vapour trails above him as he swung on his parachute through the bright August afternoon. On his uniform is a medal ribbon for bravery, but he hardly knows what to do with Celia.

Celia is the same age, also in the air force: a WAAF corporal in Fighter Command all day, raking coloured discs across a map of England like a croupier in a casino. Each chip is a squadron, and the odds are with the Germans. Her boss, an air commodore who flew aeroplanes against the Turks in the last war, likes to stand behind her and watch her legs: the best he has seen since being kicked out of bed in Baghdad by a memorable pair, muscular yet refined, owned by a Russian ballerina who wouldn't let him have more than he paid for. Tonight Celia isn't in uniform. She wears a turquoise dress and a soldier's tin hat over her red hair, and looks delicious. She is giving Lionel all the help he needs.

'We were diverted by Goering,' Eunice says. 'There's a raid on – did you know?'

[58]

'We were waiting for a taxi. Standing in the street.' Celia talks in little gasps, the words coming out like bubbles from a goldfish, and flaps her big blue eyes at Lionel between each gasp. 'Outside Eunice's flat. And the siren went. It's early tonight. That awful howl. A dinosaur with a tummy ache. Then a taxi came.' You can't believe she is as silly as she pretends. Under the doll, under the tin hat, must be a fiery young woman. 'Things are hotting up outside.'

'Nothing to what was going on inside the taxi,' Eunice says. 'Pawing each other all over, practically copulating on the seat from Bayswater to Piccadilly.'

'We saw a car lying on its back. At Oxford Circus. Like a beetle. Wheels in the air. Still kicking. Blown over by the blast.'

'How she saw anything!' Eunice turns to Felix and Guy: 'Lionel was in a state of lechery and she wasn't objecting. She knew how to bring him on, not a foot wrong. But with me there . . . The darlings – aren't they adorable?'

Celia says, 'The taxi driver said we'd be all right with him. He had a charmed life. His wife and kids were killed in Stepney. He always escapes. His passengers are lucky too. But it's going to be a dodgy night. He said so. Because of the long lull. There's a whopping barrage going up. It's a gorgeous sight.' So is Celia.

No sound of bombs or gunfire reaches down here, just as nothing of this music and laughter can be heard up in the street. But Felix, who has been an air-raid warden since the beginning of the Blitz, knows what it is like outside: the criss-cross searchlight beams waving over the roofs, converging and separating in the sky like the stalks of a giant weed; the sharp flashes of anti-aircraft shells; the increasing glow of fire over the city, folded in smoke and igniting the clouds with a false and evil dawn.

'The driver wanted to take us to Quaglino's,' Celia says. 'He nearly refused to come here. A dangerous place, he said. But it's the safest in London. It said so in the evening

[59]

paper. Down all these stairs. And Quag's has gone right off. Only fit for the old and crusty. Nothing less than a colonel.' She particularly doesn't want to risk meeting the air commodore. He once took her to Quaglino's as prelude to a lively night in his flat where he showed her some of the joys forbidden by the ballerina, while incendiary bombs crackled in the mews outside. 'Anyway Regent Street was blocked. Must have been an incident. What a silly word! Sounds better than bomb, I suppose. Not so panicky. Nobody could be frightened of an incident. So we had to come round the back. Through Soho. Past all the tarts. I had to cover Lionel's eyes. We do have fun.'

The band downstairs is playing *Little Sir Echo*. Lionel squeezes Celia's fingers to stop her talking: 'Let's go and dance.'

But she won't be hustled. She likes to tease him, she knows it will pay off: 'I shouldn't be here at all. Not if Mummy had her way. She's very psychic. Mostly about me. I'm in the front line. Being a hero. She's in Wales. Living in a fishing hotel. Off the fat of the land. Gorging on salmon. Fresh mutton off the mountain. Black market butter. Eggs galore. They don't know about rationing there. A funk hole, I told her. She ought to come back. Hold the fort etcetera. Set an example to the plebs. Or there'll be a revolution. Look what the East End's been through. Now it's the West End's turn, thank God. About time too. That lovely bomb on Buckingham Palace. The best thing yet. If the King and Queen can take it, so can we. And those sweet Princesses. But if you knew Mummy. She sent a telegram this morning. Begging me not to go out tonight. On bended knee. She's terribly good at that. The bleeding-hearted parent. She had a dream last night. I was lying on a table wrapped in a sheet. Typical. But you mustn't stretch your luck. Hence the tin hat.' Celia tips it over her eyes.

Lionel tips it up again and kisses her on the nose: 'Let's dance,' and leads her from the bar to the top of the staircase.

[60]

From the balcony you can see them go down, their fingers locked and Celia still bubbling. They go down the gold and crimson stairs to dance, pressed tight to each other on the crowded floor below. They go down – or one of them does – to be stabbed while dancing by a dagger of flying glass and fall limply dying in the perplexed, helpless, yearning, unscratched arms of a lover who never was.

14

From the balcony you can look down and watch Charles, the courteous but never obsequious head waiter, assigning people to their tables. Sometimes he comes up to the foyer with a sheaf of menus to tell his clients that he has nothing except on the balcony, or to suggest another drink while waiting, or to announce that at last he has a place downstairs. He conducts the lucky ones down the lovely staircase, curving into the noisy, smoky pit and round the crowded little dance floor to the table he has chosen. It may be near the front, unexpectedly vacant, or further into the murk or back against the wall. Nobody complains if it isn't what they hoped for. It is enough to be favoured at all by Charles.

He is incorruptible, they say. Bribery will get you nowhere. And nothing, as far as anyone knows, will procure more than one of the gentle smiles he grants to everyone. He bestows them, like his tables, according to a code which nobody has cracked. But Charles causes no rancour, only disappointment. You can see, watching him, that there is no choice but to submit.

Among the chief servants of the Café de Paris – Leo Robb at the street door, Harry at the bar, Snakehips Johnson on the platform – Charles in the most elusive. Leo is a splendid, hearty doorman; a sergeant of a dubious kind; a ready friend for anyone stepping from a taxi or stumbling through the blackout into the welcome of London's brightest restaurant; an ally against the long wartime winter. Harry is the cosmopolitan barman, polished by his Paris reputation, masterly at shaking up a cocktail of liquors unknown in these days of siege. Snakehips is the famous showman, maestro of the latest hit and telling mood and tonal modulation, whose name would be in lights from here to Leicester Square if it wouldn't bring the whole Luftwaffe to a bull's eye target.

But Charles is an enigma, the odd man out. He speaks little, his accent is indefinable. He is neither English nor obviously anything else. His past is unknown – you almost believe he never had one – and tonight his future too is dark. He is the ideal man of the moment. You can't imagine him playing another part, in another costume. His appearance – his disguise – is perfect. His face is ivory, with pouches under the eyes that could mean dissipation, but on Charles suggest sadness or fatigue. His hair is greased back from a widow's peak, flaring in a pair of glossy wings over his ears and finishing precisely above his high stiff collar. His tailcoat is longer than any other waiter's.

He is showing people to their tables; allocating them – some of them – to their death. Charles has extraordinary powers tonight. You may suspect he knows it, and being compassionate and not quite humourless he would like to apologize to the ˌlosers and congratulate the rest, but it would give the game away. There will be surprises among the fatalities as well as among the escapes. The blast of high explosive works in strange ways. A glass splinter can be hurled far, striking at random in an otherwise undamaged zone. A table by the dance floor, with the best view of the cabaret, may be as lethal as death row. A seat behind one of the pillars holding up the balcony, where nobody wants to be, may mean certain survival. A place at the back and safe enough, you would guess, may be a place along an execution wall. The job will vary, depending on the victim. For some it will be crude butchery, for others neat assassination.

Like a guide, a nurse with a soothing word, Charles ushers them to the brink of peril and leaves them there. They trust him, they take what he gives, they know there is no comfort here except from him.

What of his own fate? Having seen to the filling of the lifeboats, does he go down with his remaining passengers? You can't tell, looking at Charles, whether he is a hero or a coward any more than you can be sure, if you had his job, what you would do. You may wonder where he will put himself when the show begins. You only know that he will complete his role, in character to the end.

15

Felix left Cambridge in 1929, aged twenty-two. He shed his fancy shirts and ties and gave the ashplant to his college servant. Nipper whipped off his bowler hat and twirled it on the end of the stick, saying he would keep it in memory of a real gentleman – which Felix, in his mood of renunciation, could have done without.

He got drunk once more with Upton La Touche and persuaded him to start up the great Bentley. Out on the open road, with Up's blood throbbing to the engine, it was easy to set him towards Harwich. There Felix bought a ticket to Berlin, asked Up to telephone his father and stepped on to the boat. It was an impulsive move, not the obvious first step in a career – not something to please the vicar – but there were others who felt the pull of a country that had been in ruins since its defeat in 1918. Blowing through those ruins were ideas more lively to a restless young Englishman than the stale exhausted ones at home. Felix was to stay four years in Germany and bring back a wife.

He earned money from English lessons and translations. He lived in dim boarding-houses, moving on when he could no longer stand the landlady or the lodgers or the smell. He enjoyed his independence and even his poverty, which for the only time in his life made him feel heroic. He found friends among other foreigners, German students, Jews, Communists, anarchists, atheists. He ate terrible meals of offal soup and stewed horse, but sometimes treated himself to ham and eggs or a Wiener schnitzel and ordered wine rather than proletarian beer, as he might sleep with a cabaret dancer instead of one of the girls he knew, migrants in his bed, sunburnt and eager with their bodies. He made love with an indifference that astonished and amused him, and left him breathless for more. And all the time – writing, writing, writing – he taught himself to be a poet.

As a boy alone in the vicarage he had played with words, arranging them like soldiers, giving victory to the good ones, wiping out the rest. In Ireland and at Cambridge, though liking other people and enjoying being liked, he had kept the aloofness of the poet he wanted to be: not a propagandist, still less a prophet, but a mixture of entertainer and sly observer, an informer who told tales about his enemies while flattering his friends. Now in Berlin, cut loose from old influences, he felt released to live the poetry he wrote; to use the bewildering material of life – his own life and the touchable world around him.

'Don't you think it's time you told the world what you think?' one of his pupils asked – a passionate young man called Peter who came once a week to exercise his English.

'What I think before I've thought it? D'you suppose the world is interested?'

'You have an opinion, don't you?' Peter suggested.

'On the classless society? On inflation? Expressionist painting? Twelve-tone music?'

'Or nudism if you prefer. Sodomy, suicide, anything –'

Most of Felix's friends weren't so earnest. They were the children of the sun who spread their oiled, baked brown bodies through the woods and beside the lakes. They lived for the moment, spending what money they could find and sharing a simple yet sophisticated freedom which intoxicated him. To be free was to be modern. Modern was the watchword. A startling piece of architecture, all glass and naked concrete, rose among the drab old buildings. A theatre opened for obscure, elliptical plays. Paintings, novels, compositions appeared, stark and innocent. Experiment and novelty and the latest gimcrack fashion flashed and bounced like little balls on a pin table, ringing bells, promising fortunes, disappearing into holes. And if art was to be modern, why not behaviour? Parties went on all night, party-goers found themselves in unexpected places. Blurred by new attitudes boys often looked girlish, girls boyish. Life was sensual and sunlit, mostly sinless too.

For Felix it was a time of defiance as well as repletion; of irritation with the complacency of his father's suburb as much as the pleasures of Bunty's castle and the futility of Cambridge. On recent visits to the vicarage he had found it duller than ever. How could a man measure his life by the number of Sundays after Trinity? How could he be nourished by the thin promise of another world when there was so much to adore in this? Yet he loved his father and almost envied him his faith – the breath of glory which the vicar called the Resurrection and which inspired his days. What it exactly was, behind the besotting ritual, Felix wondered if his father knew. But it made him as brave

[65]

and true and generous as a poet, which was Felix's best compliment.

But a poet, as he had once told Bunty, was nothing abnormal. He was merely spokesman for the public, using the language that everyone used. At moments he might hope to be their conscience, asking their questions and voicing their instinct for truth and charity: man, conscious of himself as common man.

Felix read his poetry to anyone who would listen – in a beer cellar, across a café table, through the smoke of a night club, over a rumpled pillow. Sometimes he sold a poem, but that wasn't the point. The excitement was to tackle a problem, of form or subject, which he hadn't tried before. The beginning was the purest joy, the completion only a new beginning.

'That one doesn't work,' a lover told him – an American girl who made a living by sending stories of Bohemian life, invented by Felix, to her home town newspaper. He read his latest work to her while they were eating ices in a fairground before riding on the roller-coaster, which would probably make Felix sick; and he remembered little Eunice Fancourt dressed as Marie Antoinette, sicking up her pudding all those years ago. This girl had something of Eunice's voraciousness, without her perception of his poems.

'Why can't you understand,' he asked her, 'that it's not important if a poem fails any more than if today is rainy? Tomorrow might be better.'

The day was fresh each morning and he was reborn each time he sat down to write. No wonder – no matter – that he didn't always succeed. The vital thing was to find strength to be himself, a poet. It was easy to join the cult of happiness in Berlin; easy to see how pointless, precarious, empty it could be. People's lives were turned inside out and sometimes it was funny, sometimes macabre. But Felix felt a difference in himself. He was isolated in his imagination: the single responsibility, the nugget of his existence.

He wrote about what pleased him: the Berlin streets and squares, the trams, the zoo, the winter trees, the summer bathers, the joy and agony of a city with its people's glancing lives and sharp collisions and brief relationships. He saw that life was a monster but on balance it was worthwhile, and his duty – his delight – was to celebrate the news. He must offer something in return for life, for the people who shared its vast conspiracy. He would do it in words, chosen for their tone and rhythm and the patterns in which he could make them dance. His poetry was haunted by a whiff of melancholy, a whisper of elegy, a suspicion of loss.

It was the texture of life that attracted him: not the rigid, fixed veneer of things but the sheen and flicker that came and went; the flux, the wind-blown hint, the shifting moment, the burst of laughter and tears that cracked the stillness underneath. There was plenty to engage him in Berlin, and if he found more pleasure in the play of light on a typist's scarlet fingernails than in the problems of slump and unemployment, or in the strains of jazz through a hotel window than in the dark politics of those years, it wasn't because he only liked the superficial, but because through the surface he could reach the heart.

Nobody could have lived in Berlin between 1929 and 1933 without being sucked into the tumult, and he surrendered happily. The gay-grim city was at the edge of civil war. From their extremes the Nazis and Communists tore at the republic and at each other. Poverty turned to anger, despair to agitation, hope to bathos. An air of doom settled on the people. Hatred, like the plague, trod the streets. Violence burst from nowhere. A scuffle in a doorway, a riot in a cinema, a brawl in a swimming-bath, a police whistle, an ambulance racing through the traffic – and nothing was left but a pool of blood waiting for someone to bring a bag of sawdust. Bullets cracked, razors flicked. Felix saw a man pick up a beer mug by the handle, smash it on the table and grind the broken glass into his companion's face.

Peter took him to his first Communist meeting. They were checked at the door by hefty youths with hammer-and-sickle armbands, and returned the salute with clenched fists. Inside the hall Felix was stirred by such eagerness and passion. There were students like Peter and teachers, journalists, artists, but the solid bulk was workers: a pale, intent mass of faces fixed on the platform as if up there, in speech and gesture, the future was being declared. It was their own thoughts put into words, soon to be put into action. Eyes shone with recognition, applause throbbed with purpose. Peter whispered that these men – not the police or the army or the politicians – were the masters of Berlin. Felix loved them, knowing he could never be one of them even if he wanted. He would march and cheer, drink to the Red Front, go out at night with a paint pot and leave slogans on the walls, but he could never enrol in the working class. His job was to be an outsider, a free agent, a spy.

'My soul?' he said, when Peter enquired. 'My soul's quite well, thank you.'

'Does it approve? Of your politics, your friends, your poetry –'

'It tries its best. It aims for a better world in its fashion. But sometimes it says things that don't work.'

'The way you spend your life –'

'There's more to me than soul, thank God.'

'Your snobbery.'

'Call it that, I don't care,' Felix said. 'I like a man because of the things he likes.'

'His prejudices.'

'His books, meals, clothes – everything that goes with him. Or her.'

'So when you take a girl to the cinema,' Peter said, 'you're

[68]

taking her silk stockings? Her new handbag? Her shade of lipstick?'

'Remove them, peel off the clothes – what have you got?'

'Ah.' Peter smiled.

'A mere body. Butcher's meat. No garnish, no sauce, nothing but raw body. You can buy one anywhere – cafés, clubs, street corners, public parks. Without paying extra for the cinema.'

'Bodies don't behave the same. Different habits, different manners –'

'Mannerisms, you mean. Affectations, gestures – picked up and dropped like the rest. Behaviour comes off with the silk stockings. All that's left is body.'

'There's still a mind.'

'Strip the mind too. Tear away the glib ideas. Chuck out the box of tricks. Forget all the fashions it's full of – the latest cult and phoney philosophies and second-hand thoughts –'

'And what have you got?'

Felix said, 'Raw body can have its uses. Raw mind is totally boring. It needs a context – the trimmings. You must season it with education. Marinate it, spice it with society –'

'With snobbery.'

'If you like.'

The first Nazis appeared in the streets, stiff and self-conscious, their uniform no longer banned. They were important, they knew where they were going. People stopped to smile and let them pass. These young men, so blond and promising, would clean up the mess. Old Berliners stood up in the cafés and saluted when any Nazis came in. Others, devout or cautious, put photos of Hitler in their windows which they lit at night with candles. He would redeem the fatherland; save it from the shame of defeat and chaos, inflation and depression.

The city was assaulted by strikes, demonstrations, elections, scandals, rumours. Trams were overturned. Proclamations were made. People were marched away into the

[69]

darkness. Torturers, like pimps and abortionists, were never out of work. The war cries were slung back and forth – Marxist scum, Fascist swine, murderer, lackey, toad – till they lost all force and fell clattering like spent bullets on the pavement. Stalin's portrait frowned over the aspiring, exploited masses. Goering's voice shouted from the street corners that Germany was waking up. The social democrats danced the same old foxtrots of the last ten years. Beethoven, Goethe, Bismarck watched from their stern pedestals.

Felix was given a schnauzer puppy for his twenty-fifth birthday by friends who thought every Englishman should have a dog. He didn't want it and was glad when it escaped one day in the park. But it was caught and brought back by a black-haired girl with large eyes full of amazement in a china-white face, delicate as a teacup.

He wasn't sure he wanted her either, but in time she became his wife, mother of his son.

16

Miriam's father had a shoe factory and a polished brown face like fine leather, with two bright eyelets, which might have come out of one of his own boxes, wrapped in tissue paper. He boasted that his shoes were bought only in the most fashionable shops, walked the smartest streets, stepped out of the biggest cars into the grandest houses, trod the deepest carpets and were kicked off by the most extravagant lovers. By the end of 1933, after his only child had got out of Germany with her English husband, he was making jackboots for Hitler's officers. But he didn't boast about it. And it didn't save him in the end – as he knew it wouldn't – from the midnight arrest that began his journey

[70]

to a concentration camp. Under interrogation he soothed his terror with the thought that no boots of his were used for the strutting and stamping of a stormtrooper's feet: only for the sharp click of an officer's heels.

Miriam's mother was a shrunken, faded woman who puffed in and out of the rooms of their apartment like a shunting engine. She carried plates, poured tea, watered the flowers, rubbed the tables, fanned her cheeks, tidied and folded, blew and sighed and puffed. Felix never saw her without a feather duster or a fly swat or a lace handkerchief to flick at anything that needed it. He wondered how she could have a daughter like Miriam.

'My father is rich, he will do anything for me,' Miriam told Felix the first time they went out together. In a short pleated kilt and tartan socks, leaving her knees bare, she looked like a boy. They took a train far from the city and walked through pinewoods by a lake where they held hands. And Felix, whose life was suddenly emptied of everything except the moment, thought how Bunty would laugh if she could see him from her castle, brushing his tongue across a Jewish virgin's lips when nobody was watching. Miriam laughed too, a schoolgirl's laugh that rang like a little gong from her serious face, and soon she wasn't a virgin any more.

'I give you my body, you see, quite easily,' she said, undressing in his boarding-house when so far they had only shared some ice-creams, two films and one ride on the roller-coaster. 'But you will have to work harder for my heart.'

A luxuriant black plume grew from the gully between her thighs like an oasis in the desert. Her breasts, small and smooth and white, smelled of something that must be frankincense or myrrh. They were the breasts of the Shulamite in the Song of Songs – the rose of Sharon, the lily of the valleys who had tormented the vicar's son long ago, promising to give him love as the mandrakes give forth

[71]

fragrance. But Miriam's eyes had lost the first amazement that Felix saw in them when they met in the park. Under the bed, as usual, his schnauzer puppy was asleep.

It was Miriam who taught Felix to play cards. She took the low numbers from a pack, told him to choose from the rest, shuffled, asked him to cut with his left hand, then dealt the cards, picking and discarding till she had a semi-circle on the table. Spread before her she saw good news, a meeting with a friend, something lucrative and something naughty, a dark figure, a prison, a touch of obstinacy or foolishness, an early old age. It was all vivid and believable, and infinitely fertile. Miriam could sow a future with her fingers, casting luck like seeds and reading them as they grew.

Felix asked himself why he had fallen in love with her and went on asking till he fell out of it one autumn morning in a London pub six years later. Once, shortly before they got married, he asked Miriam.

'Because I am quite new,' she said. Her English syllables were precise and fragile – glass beads strung on a silver wire. Without doubt she was the Shulamite, black but fairest among women, comely as Jerusalem, sleeping under an apple tree. He had woken her and she had ravished his heart. 'I am as exotic for you as an oriental. I fascinate you, I mesmerize you. I open the window of your stuffy room.'

'A lot less stuffy than yours – you and your tight little family knot, your cousins and friends and your profits and your holy confidence.'

'Confidence, you think? Shall I tell you what my father got on his desk this morning? A note to say – beware, we will pay you off, you lousy Jew. We give you one week to get out or else you are dead. We have warned you.'

'They're ridiculous, you can't believe them.'

'That is why they are dangerous. We laugh at them now and we shall go on laughing till the end.'

'You believe them?'

'Perhaps it will be more than a week. Perhaps a month. Perhaps a year.' Perhaps Miriam had read it in the cards.

'What will your father do?'

'Nothing – just wait.'

'He could get away.'

'Never, never. He will stay. He has the factory, he will never leave.'

Miriam was half right. The Shulamite was a garden of spices who had called him in to eat the precious fruit and drink the wine. Felix loved her because she was so alien, so far from his suburban childhood, from Ireland and Cambridge, even from the cafés and nightclubs of Berlin which he had come to enjoy so much. He loved her for her rarity as well as her sharpness and vitality. Part of him was appalled how much the other part loved her. It was an exquisite betrayal. When he went to her home he felt he should leave half of himself outside the door, just as he had once propped his motorbike at the drawbridge of Bunty's castle. The heavy carved furniture in the apartment, the clutter of what-nots and gewgaws, the cloying scent of ancient Jewish veneration and modern German materialism were more than he could have suffered alone. After ten minutes he would look for a chance to bolt out of the door, grab his precious other half and flee to the nearest bar.

But Miriam held him. She was a bird that had flown to him from a world he could never inhabit. She sang, she fluttered and twittered, she tilted her head on her long neck and said bright, surprising things. She would come to perch on the arm of his chair, cooing and preening, and at once the need to escape was gone. Then her mother would wheel in a trolley, of tubular steel and false marble, with pumpernickel, wurst, cheese, cucumber, bottles of beer and a samovar of tea. Her father would bring up his favourite standard lamp – a plaster model of a woman's leg rising from a silver high-heeled shoe – and put his hand up the thigh, feeling under the lampshade-skirt to switch it on.

[73]

And they would discuss Heine and Shakespeare or put Mozart on the gramophone. It was very different from the vicarage. All the time Miriam would dart and dazzle, attentive to each blink and breath of the *goyisch* English lover who was soon to be her husband and save her from the dark. But one day, he knew – it was in the cards, he had seen it for himself – she would fly away.

'What will your mother do?' he asked, when their plans to get married and leave for England were ready. 'She could come with us, I suppose' – though he hoped she wouldn't.

'She will never leave my father. And you must have seen – she is studying Hebrew, to read the Bible in it and the old texts. She is going back to the beginning, thousands of years ago. She wants to forget the Nazis. Forget Germany, forget even Europe. Just pretend they never existed and return to where we started.'

'She could go to Palestine, to the settlements.'

'Not without him. And there is no shoe factory for him in Palestine. And they want young people there. So she goes only in her mind, turning back the centuries. It is the dream she lives in, even when she is dusting the tables and cooking cabbages and listening to us talking. She will live in it till they take her away, till they –' Miriam shuddered at the unsaid fate. 'Perhaps it is the best way for the older ones.'

Felix went with the family to a concert in a baroque hall weighed down with imperial pillars and dusty statuary. The audience, weighed down too by a fierce devotion to string quartets, scowled at the floodlit players on the platform – the priests at the altar – as if challenging them to perform a miracle: spin the notes into gold, perhaps, and turn it into good hard currency.

Felix cared nothing for music. He believed it could have been a substitute for poetry and was still a threat. He hadn't got room for both. He shivered and shifted, the only person aware of the cold hall and hard seats, trying to remember the exact flavour of Miriam's nipples, wondering how long before he would taste it again – honey and milk lie under the Shulamite's tongue and the smell of her garments is like the smell of Lebanon – and guessing what Peter would think of this way to spend an evening.

In the interval the Jews, shunned by people whom they thought were friends, spoke among themselves in wary frightened voices; sinking old quarrels, politely asking after each other's families, laughing quietly in the knowledge that for many of them there were no concerts left. They would be arrested in time – this week, next month, in the spring – if they didn't get away.

Back at the apartment Felix and Miriam fed each other with sausages and fruit, while her mother opened her Hebrew grammar. Her father drew back the curtains to stand for an hour looking through the glass at the street and the houses opposite and the people going home: a condemned man, fixing them in his mind.

17

Felix's last winter in Berlin trickled away through the tired grey city, seeping into his memory. Peter vanished into the police headquarters, some people said for ever. Miriam's father opened a bank account for her in London. Martial law was expected and three new varieties of treason were announced.

Peter reappeared, having been shown the body of a Communist leader with his ear torn off and been made to spit on a picture of Lenin. Miriam said that in Russia he would have been put against a wall and shot. The news-papers said that good times were on the way. The travel agents said there was sun and fun for everyone in Naples,

Tangier, Honolulu. In the cinemas a flickering world of cocktails and chocolates and beautiful women was offered. Shopkeepers bit coins in their teeth or rang them on the counter for fear of forgeries.

Peter vanished again, perhaps liquidated – a word often in people's dreams but seldom on their lips, unless they were very brave. A crowd began singing *The Internationale*, but stopped when an armoured car turned its machine-gun on them. Berlin was to be cleaned up and the homosexual bars were raided. Two girls in a cabaret, in nothing but little black waistcoats and long black boots, were arrested while lashing each other with whips, but their admirers suddenly lost their admiration and didn't object when the girls were taken away to the barracks and fresh whippings. The Jews, according to some people, had nothing to worry about because they had money salted away abroad. According to others, they were grubs who were indestructible and would come crawling out of the ruins when Berlin was bombed by the Russians. According to the grubs, Hitler didn't believe anyone was indestructible.

Peter turned up once more, after the police had tried to arrest him and he had kicked one of them in the balls, been shot at and wounded but had escaped by jumping between two moving trams, and then he disappeared again. A photographer famous for his studies of nude boys was stripped and beaten and dumped in a crowded street, naked except for his Leica round his neck. Hitler was made Chancellor of the Reich, the Reichstag was burnt down, swastikas were waved, throats were slit, operas were performed, tangos were danced, roses were kissed and pressed into ample Teutonic bosoms. Felix and Miriam, floating in a heated swimming-pool with a machine for making waves, argued about the Jewish crime of killing the Christian god. Jewish businessmen were boycotted and Miriam's father's factory was plastered with abusive posters. Makers of electric slimming-machines did good trade; so did astrologers, psychoanalysts and peepshow owners, but banks went bankrupt. Beggars hoped for snow, to sweep away for a few pennies, but the winter was nearly over.

Felix and Miriam, riding on the big wheel at a fairground, had reached the top when they saw Peter in the crowd below, but when they reached the bottom he had gone. Stories went round of new camps being built where Jews were to wear yellow stars and homosexuals pink triangles, and both were to be worked harder and fed less till they could neither work nor eat, when they would be allowed to die. The fashion for experiment, perverted from architecture or film or drama, found new practitioners. Miriam's mother stopped puffing in and out, and sat down at last and shut her eyes and recited a psalm in Hebrew. People began stepping into the gutter when Nazis walked down the pavement. Nobody was allowed to leave Germany without a permit. Singers crooned of moonlight, Goebbels screamed of treachery. Felix decided there could be no sight so horrible as the goose-step – the ritual crash of a jackboot into someone's face.

Peter appeared for the last time, having been on the run for a month. He had found shelter with friends, sleeping by day and moving on at night, but though nobody refused to take him in, he saw the terror in their eyes and knew how dangerous to them he was. Now he would try to get to the frontier – Denmark or Poland or France. Miriam made him some sandwiches and Felix went to a bookshop and tore a map of Europe out of an atlas for him. He kissed them gaily, sang a bit of a Schubert song – 'the spring will come' – and slipped away down the stairs. They knew, and so did he, that he would never get away.

18

'Little Sir Echo, how do you do?' Violet sings: this succulent Jamaican, sick to death of a Saturday night that has many hours to run and of a war that is none of her business and thinking, you may guess, of the lizard-green sugar fields and purple mountains and opal beaches of her childhood, or of the emptiness of the words she is paid to kiss into the microphone, or yet of the strange and gentle English poet who has lain in her bed every Sunday morning since the war began, but won't be doing so tomorrow – though neither of them knows it now.

'Hello!' Violet croons across the little vortex of dancers – but nobody in Jamaica would call this dancing and there isn't a black among them – and is answered an octave lower by a wistful *'Hello!'* from her brother on the alto saxophone.

Lionel and Celia have gone down to dance. Eunice too goes to the balcony and looks into the pit. She is a little drunk, on many things: the din and dazzle of this lovely place, the spectacle of such pleasure, the promise of good food and friends and love. And the youth! Youth is precious to Eunice these days, she is surrendering her own too quickly: not without hope of more fun in life – she knows herself too well for that – but still with sorrow. Everyone down there looks so young, the men all handsome, the women beautiful; Lionel with his lust and foolish innocence, Celia with her tin hat and breathlessness. Eunice feels an urgent desperation, a need. She must try to take it in, absorb it all, to ponder over when she gets home tonight and to weep over in bed, a little, in the last moments before sleep – if she does get home tonight. There is an unpredictability in her life that she cherishes.

'Charles!' she calls suddenly to the head waiter. 'My table – you've given it to someone else.' There is a favourite place Charles usually keeps for Eunice near the band. She too has a special interest in the musicians.

Years ago, before the war, she crossed the Atlantic with a runaway baronet. She met him by appointment one evening in a bedroom of the Savoy Hotel, round the corner from the divorce lawyer in the Strand who employed her as a professional co-respondent. It was her first assignment, also her last. Never a woman to miss the best things in a job, she saw what they were in this. Though told that her duty need be only nominal, she turned it into delight and by next morning the baronet's adultery was fully proved: 'To the hilt,' he said, showing what he meant. After giving Eunice the most energetic breakfast of her life, as if no patch of bed was to be left without evidence of crumbs and coffee stains, he took her off to Germany. His tastes were simple. Airships were his present passion. From Berlin they sailed as baronet and baronette on board the *Hindenburg* to America, floating for days over the ocean in a trance of luxury and rapture.

In New York the baronet was caught by another woman, the much-married daughter of a rubber tyre millionaire, who wheedled him out of airships into fast cars and drove him away to Niagara with Eunice in pursuit by train. Trying to keep up, she found her desolation was lost in the increasing farce. Once, in the years since her brief marriage, she had worked as a courier for Thomas Cook, but no seven-day circuit of the sights of Europe could match this lightning flip across a continent. She trailed the couple to the Grand Canyon, the Rockies, Yellowstone Park and on through California to Mexico. At Acapulco they vanished, their tracks covered by clues laid by the heiress: the baronet could never have invented anything so neat. And though it didn't happen often, Eunice knew when she was beaten.

She went back to New York, sore but not sorry, and penniless. Somehow she must raise the ticket money home to England. Her last job there, before the night as co-respondent at the Savoy, had been as model in an art school, which didn't qualify her for much. She went to an employment agent who listened to her story and warned her that as an alien with a record of near-immorality she could be deported. She chose to go in comfort. With a technique of shock and charm and laughter – to the amazement of a secretary who was told to count out the dollars – Eunice persuaded the agent to lend her the tourist fare to Europe, to be paid back with ten per cent added every week. She bought a ticket on the next liner, the *Queen Mary*.

Other women had worked their passage washing dishes or minding children. Eunice's way meant more money, more fun – earning her berth, many decks down in the third class, as a prostitute up in the first. She was amused that the colossal ship which admitted her, for four days and five nights, to the ancient and absurd profession should bear the name of the dowager Queen, widow of George V, collector of antiques and patroness of doll's houses. Most of her lovers, drunk or seasick, were beyond anything but paying her outrageous price, and by the time she got to England she had made enough to return the loan by cable, with a profit left.

In the ship's orchestra was a luminous Jamaican boy on the alto saxophone: a lovely contrast to the passengers who hired her for a few flabby sweat-sticky hours in their cabins and as different from the baronet as another man could be. His name was Baxter, he knew at once the game Eunice was playing, and slid her an unambiguous smile each time they met on board. Kept busy at her trade she couldn't offer him the chance that she knew would bring pleasure to them both. Disembarking at Southampton she passed him her address in London. Baxter took it in silence; did two more Atlantic crossings in the *Queen Mary* and turned up at the Bayswater flat with his saxophone and stunning smile.

She had never heard him speak before, and hardly heard him during the week he stayed with her – a week lost among the most intricate thrills she had ever felt. Baxter was relentless, Eunice was inspired. Together they fell into a pattern where day and night, food and drink, bed and bath, toe and tongue, black and white, were mixed in luscious dissolution. But she was glad when he went away: demand and surrender were too exhausting. On the slenderest acquaintance she wrote to Snakehips Johnson, who gave Baxter an audition and signed him on. Later the sister Violet was brought over from Jamaica. So Eunice can claim a hand in bringing them to the Café de Paris.

This evening especially, after her party and the crazy taxi ride through the beginnings of an air raid – and with a suspicion that the night may end more surprisingly than usual – she would like to be sitting with her friends at her favourite table near Snakehips' band; to catch Baxter's smile and remember with appalling joy the dreamy week they shared.

'Who are those monsters at my table, Charles?' she demands.

Charles may have his reasons for giving it away, but keeps them to himself. He only apologizes. If he had known Miss Fancourt was coming, if she had telephoned first, if it were any night but Saturday, if she could see how hard it is to fit everyone in, with the Free French thinking the Café de Paris belongs to them, and troops pouring into London from occupied Europe and the Empire, clamouring to come to the brightest smartest safest place in town . . .

Eunice can't rant for long. She looks down over the rail to inspect the usurpers at her table: two Canadian Scottish officers in kilts, with two Canadian nurses.

'Colonials!' She scowls and shakes her fist. In return they

[81]

lift their champagne glasses to her and cheer. Perhaps the figure on the balcony up there embodies the famous British spirit which they have come from Canada to defend – like the girl in a tin hat dancing with a fighter pilot. One of the officers holds up a champagne bottle and points it towards her with his thumbs on the cork; mimes an invitation to come down and join them, then lets off the cork. She tries to catch it, but it flies into the foyer behind. Through the noise she calls down 'Later!' and sees the froth spilling over the man's hand. She is quickly mollified. Surveying the glittering view she remembers the furnace of a blazing building she once saw in an air raid – tonight? yesterday? weeks ago? There is warmth and light down here too, of a miraculous kind.

She goes back to the bar, to Felix and Guy: 'Happy days!' and takes the martini they have bought her. 'Especially birthdays.' As she drinks she sees on the floor the champagne cork fired at her by the Canadian officer. She goes to pick it up; lifts her red dress and slides the cork into the top of her stocking, against her thigh: 'It's lucky, someone told me' – but she can't remember who.

'I was asking Felix', Guy tells her, 'if they've got a place like this in Berlin.'

'I've only been there once.' Eunice tries to focus on her hectic trip with the baronet, dashing to catch the *Hindenburg*. 'Felix knows – he lived there, he brought back a wife.'

But Felix is thinking of the night ahead: the hours he will have to sit here before Violet can be taken home. She isn't singing at the moment. The band is playing *In the Mood*, one of their best numbers with some clever key changes by Snakehips. Violet must be sitting on the little gold chair beside her brother.

19

Four years after being seen off by Upton La Touche from the Harwich dockside Felix landed there with Miriam, two days after they were married in Berlin. It was 1933, a bright summer morning and the first thing was to have a honeymoon. By midday they had sold a silver tea set, a present from Miriam's parents, and bought an old Morris Minor. On Miriam's bank account which her father promised to keep topped up, and ten pounds advance for Felix's first book which was all it ever earned, they would tour England before visiting Felix's father at the vicarage. By the end of the summer they would know where to settle down.

Settle down: till now Felix had considered marriage as something not to be considered. For others it meant becoming duller than before, flattened by salary, mortgage, life insurance, pension – not just bleak but ridiculous. It could never happen to him. People married because they were lonely, and found that two of them were twice as lonely. People married to be together, and were never together again. Though he adored Miriam he couldn't think of them as a couple, yoked by love and muzzled by its cares. She was bright, she understood, she must feel the same. Now, within hours of landing, she went to arrange the schnauzer's quarantine – she owed her escape from Germany to a lucky meeting with a dog – while Felix had a pint of English beer and sketched a poem about the exile's return.

The Morris Minor hadn't got the style of Up's green Bentley, but with the sunshine roof pulled back and the wheel bucking in his hands, with Miriam beside him laughing at her first sight of England and pushing up her skirt to air her thighs – jewelled like the Shulamite's – Felix's future was full of promise. They drove into Suffolk and up the coast to the pub at Dunwich where he and his father used to stay. He felt a boost, like a jab at the throttle of the little car he had been driving all afternoon, on signing in. There hadn't been a Mrs Bayne since his mother died at his birth. He knew this one better – well enough to expect surprises. Fair as the moon, clear as the sun, is the Shulamite. And she was his wife.

'I do not like the sea,' Miriam said after supper as they sat on the cooling shingle and watched the night fall on the water. Her syllables, hard and round like the pebbles she was filtering through her fingers, sounded more foreign than ever on this English shore.

'I love it,' Felix said, wondering how he had married a woman who didn't love it too. The cry of an oyster-catcher came piping through the dusk.

'It is a desert out there. It is not even blue, it is dirty brown and wet and cold.' Miriam didn't feel safe on this patch of land surrounded by water. 'It is waiting to kill me because I cannot swim.'

'There's a town out there under the sea – a port like Harwich.' Felix tried to remember what he had seen that morning: 'Ships along the quay. And cranes, warehouses full of boxes, bales, sacks –'

'You can see all that?'

'Three thousand people live down there.'

'They are dead, they are no use to me. They have been eaten by the crabs.'

'Shops, pubs, windmills –'

'Only pieces of them, fallen down, and the fishes swimming through the windows.'

'Streets and a famous market.' But Felix couldn't hope to touch Miriam with the magic of this place. She had her own

[84]

enchantment – the Shulamite's, spiced with cinnamon and saffron. 'And tall black sheds near the waterfront where they cure the herrings – the Dunwich herrings packed in barrels for the monasteries of England. Or loaded into ships and sent to Germany. What would your mother do without her Dunwich herrings?'

'My mother hates herrings.'

'Luckily she is unique. The profits here have come from the sea, in fish or cargoes. The sea and the wind –'

'I also do not like the wind.' Miriam's legs were turning to gooseflesh in the breeze off the land behind them.

'The sea and wind, and the people's cunning.'

'That is better.'

'They have a sheltered harbour, one of the best in England, with a hundred ships. Masts and rigging, spars, sails drying –'

'You are just romantic, Felix.'

'Listen! – you can hear someone shout that a ship is coming in. With French wine, Spanish swords, blubber from Iceland. Or corn or wool or hides. The merchants get richer with every ship and build bigger houses or another church. And more ships. They send a fleet to help the king –'

'There are Jews in this place of yours?'

'Of course.' Felix was watching a flock of sandpipers on the wet sand at the water's edge.

'Moneylenders, you will tell me.'

'But a law was passed.'

'So you are the same, like everyone else – you good kind people of this island. You are not as perfect as you think.'

'The Jews were banished unless they chose to be baptized.'

'Your gentle English blackmail.' Miriam made it sound like the gentle English rain – something she had heard about and would have to get used to.

'It's a boom town. Shipbuilders, sailmakers, chandlers,

tanners, shoemakers like your father. All praying and swindling and whoring –'

'How long ago?'

'Seven hundred years.'

'That is no good to me.'

'But it's still there. You can smell the tar and leather.'

'And kippers and drains.'

'The roses in the little gardens.'

'And the corruption.'

'I love corruption,' Felix said. 'You can't have a city without it, you must have a flaw. Riches are too good alone. Dunwich can't go on for ever.'

'So what happens?'

'The sea and the wind.'

'I hate them, I tell you.' Miriam pulled her skirt round her legs and moved closer.

'The sea out there, and the wind blowing up and down the coast, to the ports of Europe, Scandinavia –'

'But that is how the riches are brought, you say.'

'And taken away. The spring tide reaches the houses. Sometimes the people are flooded out. They sink posts along the shore and build a wall of sand and stones. Pack it with clay, sticks, anything – but it's washed away, they can't repair it fast enough. One winter a gale comes from the east, the night of the highest tide. The sea piles up and spills through the streets. The shingle drifts and next morning the harbour is blocked. They dig it out and keep it open for another generation, two generations, but Dunwich is slipping into the sea. Sinking like a ship. They don't believe it. They've lived here for centuries, their houses are built on land that belongs to them, it's their property, it's proved in deeds and documents. They go on making money –'

'And love.' Impatiently Miriam picked up a pebble and threw it at the sea.

'They fight the French, the Dutch, but the true enemy is

[86]

the sea – the tides washing up and down and the shingle grinding at the town. It takes a hundred years, so slow that nobody worries. Or nobody who counts. The first houses to go are down by the beach. The poorest. Wooden frames, lath and plaster walls, thatched roofs – they can't stand up to it, they're built on sand. A few big waves on a stormy night and a dozen houses are just wreckage in the sea. Nobody cares. Nobody bothers to make room at the top of the town for people who've lost everything. They drift away like flotsam. Years can pass with no damage, then there's a bad winter and a street is taken in a single night. Or a whole parish. The people watch their town being worn away. Their spirit too. They lose heart. They get into debt, they turn to piracy –'

'They are sinners and this is God's anger.'

Felix watched Miriam – his wife, unbelievably: this Shulamite with lips a thread of scarlet. 'The decay is terrible. Or wonderful. One evening the alarm goes up – the sea is into the town and still rising. By midnight it's lapping the guildhall. It'll fill the market place unless the wind drops. Families bundle themselves up – babies, blankets, food, any treasures they can save. And trudge through the streets looking for shelter. The churches are full of refugees. They're camping up here on the common land behind us. Usually it's left to the rabbits. Or sometimes a boy and girl on a summer evening – they say they've come to pick blackberries, though they're not ripe yet. And it's a thing we might do ourselves, you and I, my Miriam – shall we?'

'But not among the rabbits. Let us go back and do it where it is not so windy, in the bed.'

'Anyway I've finished.' With his eyes shut Felix could hear the sea roaring like a wild animal, snarling and eating at the timbers and tearing up the cobbles in the streets, and the people wailing as they packed up their things and carted them inland, and in the distance a laughing merchant who had got away to Ipswich or Yarmouth before it

[87]

was too late, and always the relentless sea. 'The sea has undone all it did,' he said. 'City, harbour, people –'

'Destroyed by brimstone and fire, like Sodom.' So Miriam had been listening, she might even hear the Dunwich church bells ringing out there.

'There's only a shingle bank under the surface,' Felix said, 'which is good for cod.'

'But you must not eat them because they are poisoned by the wickedness of the city where they live.'

'Nothing is left of the fleet. Only a couple of boats pulled up on the beach. And that man with his rod at the edge of the water – he's always here, he was here when I came with a friend, years ago. And some cottages up at the back –'

'And our pub.' Miriam was on her feet, shivering and stamping on the shingle. She took Felix's hand and pulled him up: 'It is time to pick blackberries – quick!'

Next day they took the road again in the Morris Minor, up through East Anglia to Norwich, the engine singing for the sulphur mustard fields, the mudguards snatching at the cow parsley; across the fens to Peterborough, down to Ely and Cambridge, over to Oxford and Stratford, on into Wales, before driving back to stay with Felix's father in the Surrey suburb: a month of cathedrals and castles and mansions, summer walks and country pubs, a tourist's honeymoon. Most of the places were as new to Felix as to Miriam: he could share her wonder at what they saw. She chattered beside him as he drove the car and curled her fingers in his hair or slipped them into his trouser pocket.

'Miriam!' the Revd Bayne cried, his arms spread to embrace his daughter-in-law on the vicarage steps where John the Baptist and Cleopatra had once had a spitting match. After four years, with only a telegram as warning that he was on his way home with a Jewish wife, Felix couldn't be sure of his father's welcome. But he had forgotten the Old Testament. Miriam wasn't an English saint, she wasn't even the Shulamite of the Song of Songs, she was something better – the sister of Aaron, a prophetess who took a timbrel in her hand and sang to the glory of God in ecstasy at the drowning of the Egyptians. 'Sing ye to the Lord,' and the vicar sang for all he was worth, 'for he hath triumphed gloriously.' Miriam was an old friend, a girl struck with leprosy and banished from the camp of the Israelites for seven days for having stood up and challenged Moses.

Felix felt excluded, though he didn't mind. He was glad of this intrigue between his wife and father, and of her independent biblical self which he hadn't met before.

'He is too good for that job,' Miriam said as they drove away a few days later. 'He ought to be a rabbi.'

20

They found a flat in London at the top of a tall house in Belsize Park and fell into a tidy pattern of life. Miriam arranged herself in the kitchen, Felix sat at a table in the window, trying to write. The schnauzer came out of quarantine to join them. Miriam's father sent money every month – enough for them to live on, which pleased her: it gave her substance in this foreign city. She knew nobody in London and didn't seem to want friends. Having never kept house she set herself to learn and soon was expert, not with the fuss and puff of her mother but in her own efficient, thrifty way. The frying pan was spotless, the furniture gleaming, the lavatory so bright that Felix felt uncomfortable using it. But generally he felt too comfortable under the numbing happiness of their love. It pleased him to shell peas into a bowl, or chop parsley to sprinkle over new potatoes, or slice a lemon for a drink, or light a fire with sticks and coal to make toast for tea – to make love in

[89]

front of, later. They went shopping together, to choose a cut of meat or a vegetable they hadn't had before. They went for walks on Hampstead Heath, shuffling through the leaves, whistling for the schnauzer and discussing it with strangers who had their own dogs for comparison. Twice a week they went to the cinema, squeezing each other's hands in the dark and drifting into the silver-screen Hollywood heaven.

Sometimes, not often at first, Felix stopped and wondered what had happened. Was this what he wanted? Was it enough? When would it end? When would it begin?

'Where the hell are we going?' he asked one morning aloud, but quietly to himself and not expecting an answer. It was Francis's question eight years ago in Ireland and Up's later in Cambridge. The sun was pouring over the coffee cups and Miriam was plugging in the vacuum cleaner.

'To the fishmonger for a piece of turbot,' she said. 'And this afternoon to the Heath if the sun still shines. And this evening to the Empire at Golders Green.'

They never went to the serious, clever films that had been fashionable in Berlin, but to big romances from America so that Miriam could swoon at the heat of passion, the palm beach sighs and moonlit heartthrobs and close-up kisses, and wipe her cheeks in the interval when the electric organ came up through the floor in a stream of rainbow light to fill the cinema with its trembling purple sound. Or they watched gangsters, comedians, cowboys, Mickey Mouse – anything to save them from real life. During the newsreel Miriam slipped peppermints into Felix's mouth and hers. No scenes of unemployed workers or blathering politicians, still less of goose-stepping Nazis, were allowed to spoil sweet dreams.

Though Miriam no longer lived in Berlin she never began to live in London either. She enclosed herself and Felix and the dog in a lovely glistening bubble that floated through the weeks and months and years with no purpose. Felix was amazed how she could fill her time with trivialities and still provoke his fascination. She was both primitive and sophisticated. Half of her was a dark-eyed odalisque who sipped jasmine tea, tossed off her sandals, chattered like a mechanical puppet in a toyshop. The other half was the careful housekeeper tinkling in and out of the kitchen, working out a menu, folding their lives into the pastry. She could chop herbs and vegetables all day to make two bowls of soup, but between chopping and stirring she would gossip and make coffee and put records on the gramophone – symphonies, opera, jazz, film music, whatever suited her mood or put her in another one. Sometimes dancing alone to a tango, taking off her clothes and dropping them around the room – how beautiful are the Shulamite's feet in sandals, O prince's daughter! – she would dance naked till Felix couldn't bear it and undressed too, though he had been trying to write, and they made love on the floor or the table or the sofa while the gramophone needle clipped to a halt as the spring ran down. How could he protest? This was the essence of Miriam. Her whole body, not just her prattling tongue, must be kept busy. Often it was in the bath: the taps trickling hot and cold on their skin, and feet or thighs breaking through the froth of love and lather.

But Felix couldn't write poetry inside a bubble. He wanted to prick a pinhole through the wall and listen to the world, but it wouldn't be a bubble any longer with a hole. His first book was published and he collected poems for the next, knowing they weren't getting better. He wanted to write about solitude, melancholy, hope, doubt, nostalgia for a freedom that he thought was lost, which were the things beating in his mind, but it would be treacherous to Miriam. So he was treacherous to himself and wrote about the little domestic rites, the erotic details, the waste of time, the tantalizing afternoons on Hampstead Heath which was the only place in London where the bubble expanded a little, though it never burst. Every month they drove away to the country in the Morris Minor. Because Miriam wouldn't go back to the sea – it made her uneasy on this precarious island that might sink and drown her – they headed for the Chiltern hills, the Cotswolds, the Welsh border, where the bubble could grow into a promising balloon, liable to be buffeted by the wind and punctured on trees or hilltops. But always it stayed intact and they got back safely to the flat in Belsize Park.

In 1936, three years after they were married, when Miriam began to pine and refuse food like an animal taken from the forest – the Shulamite who came out of the wilderness, perfumed with myrrh and frankincense – she lay down on the sofa, clasped her hands across her stomach and said, 'In October I shall have a baby.'

For an annunciation it was neither joyous nor solemn – more of a calculation – and pregnancy hardly disturbed her life. As her body swelled she weighed it and watched it in the bathroom mirror and got Felix to take measurements which she wrote in a notebook. He kept another for sudden ideas and words and flashes that might come in useful for a poem: a child on its way, climbing the long stairs to this top floor flat. He felt thrilled and threatened and appalled and elated and frightened and overwhelmed with love for Miriam and himself and what they had done. When the child arrived it was a boy. They called him Peter after their friend in Berlin who had disappeared.

Miriam left the flat rarely now, tending her motherhood as obsessively as she nursed the baby, not trusting Felix with his son. Probably she was right, he thought, and tramped down to the street with the dog and shopping basket. At first he hated the loneliness of these expeditions, seeing how much the decisions had been made by Miriam – whether to buy kidneys or liver, how many onions to get, which walk to take – but soon he began to relish them. Alone, it was easier to get on with shopkeepers. They gave him better service, feeling sorry for him or hinting that he was a more favoured customer than his sharp decisive German wife. And London had a new colour without Miriam. He began looking at it through his own eyes, not hers. He had never lived here before, he had come as a stranger with a foreigner. Now he felt a Londoner.

The expeditions grew longer, taking up most of the day. Miriam didn't mind even if she noticed, absorbed in her own rapture. Felix adored her no less intensely but more distantly, more as a worshipper than a lover. He wasn't important in the holy family. He could slip away for a while to ponder how his life was being cleft down the middle, the two halves falling hopelessly apart.

He telephoned old friends from the callbox at Belsize Park underground station: 'A voice from the past,' he announced and was glad not to have been forgotten. They arranged to meet, and talked about books, travel, politics, love, never mentioning Greta Garbo or Gary Cooper or the price of veal escalopes or the way to bring up a baby's wind. He made new friends, through his publisher or the staff of magazines and papers that took his poems or employed him as a critic: sitting in their offices, watching them at work with colleagues and secretaries to defend them. Felix could join in, play the game, make money as well as any of them; beat them on their own ground. Writing didn't have to be done in an ivory tower with an ivory wife and child. This was real life, he told himself, being lived by real men in a real world; and wondered if it was; and decided it wasn't, later, as he came out of the underground and walked home. Up there at the top of the house, with Miriam and their son Peter, with nursery rhymes on the gramophone or 'Children's Hour' on the radio, with a casserole simmering for supper and the double bed afterwards, the flat was at that moment the one real thing to be sure of.

Sometimes they went out together with Peter in the pram, the old invisible bubble floating round them and people smiling at the sight: such a charming, contented couple with their dog and baby. At the top of Hampstead Heath one day Felix grabbed the pram and ran headlong with it to the bottom, whooping down the grass while the dog barked at the wheels and Peter clung for his life and laughed, then shrieked at the imminent lake ahead. They stopped at the brink, out of breath and choking with fun and looked back at Miriam, a small rigid figure of fury on the skyline.

'Never never never will you do that again,' she said when she came raging down the hill and plucked Peter into her arms, squeezing out the laughs till they turned to sobs. 'You see how you have terrified him, you stupid man, you might have killed him.'

Mother and son melted into a bundle of fright and indignation which they kept up all the way home, while Felix pushed the empty pram. He felt no remorse, he couldn't remember being happier. He glimpsed the old collusion between father and son, and prayed for Peter in his irreligious way; prayed for him to see the blessedness of things, the music in the trees, the beauty of the hour yet the ambush in the clock, the danger of the little grey men everywhere, the bane of caution and blight of repetition, the prison of a hankering and cluttered life, the need only for a cheap compass and a map of sorts – the simple baggage that the older, German Peter had carried with him.

And Miriam that night, when little Peter was asleep, piled her hair into a turban and slipped into a muslin dress that showed every stitch of her lavender underclothes; brought out the cards and dealt them on the carpet at Felix's feet. She was still the Shulamite, her navel like a rounded goblet, her belly like a heap of wheat set about with lilies. Drink, yea drink abundantly, O beloved, her lover sang.

His poetry too was beginning to go the way he wanted.

21

'What happened to the other two?' Eunice asks, at the bar with Felix and Guy.

'Lionel and Celia? – they're dancing downstairs.'

'I mean Betty and Humphrey. They were at my party, they promised to follow on. Took another taxi, got lost in the raid – oh God.'

'Perhaps they went to Quaglino's.'

'Harry, be an angel –' Eunice speaks to the barman. 'Ring up and ask if Betty and Humphrey are there. Get them sent on.'

'Through an air raid?' Guy says. 'Better stay put.'

'This is the safest. Under ground, cosy as bunnies. Besides –' Eunice has another reason: 'I like my friends round me, as many as I can. And Lionel and Celia are so young, they make me feel ancient. Betty and Humphrey are my age – our age, Felix.' She nudges his thigh with her own, feeling the champagne cork in her stocking. 'What I like about us is we've never been lovers, thank God.'

'So we can tell the truth?'

'Some of it.'

'Eunice, you've told the truth to everyone.'

'Hope so – I've tried.'

'More than I can claim. Honest to myself, that's all.'

Harry comes back to say he can't get through to Quaglino's, the telephone is cut.

'When the siren goes they clear the lines.' Felix is a part-time air-raid warden.

'Tell you what,' Guy says. 'I'll go and see what's

[95]

cooking.' He slips off his stool and crosses the foyer to the stairs up to the street.

Felix says, 'I like that man,' watching Guy disappear. 'Where did you get him?'

Eunice looks at him: 'I know what you're asking. The answer's no.'

'Be gentle. He's tender for his age.'

'I'm not a mincing-machine.'

'You've got a record.'

'He's rather lovely, though.'

'He's breakable.'

'It's time I had a man. All this damn winter without. Now it's spring.'

'He'll melt.'

'He'll love it.'

'He's soluble.'

'Nobody is these days,' Eunice says. 'There's a war on. Guy's been in it. He fought in France last summer. Got out at Dunkirk. There's blood on his hands.'

'Soft centre.'

'You don't go through that and stay soft.'

'Brittle.'

'We'll see. How's it going with Violet?' They can hear her at the microphone downstairs, breaking into *A Nightingale Sang in Berkeley Square*.'

Felix smiles: 'She gives me Saturday nights.'

'Nice of her.'

'I find it plenty.'

'Any more and you'd be in tatters?'

'The permanent thing – I remember what it was like, day after day. Expecting too much, asking the impossible. No privacy, no purity –'

'So no poetry?'

'No time to be nothing but myself.'

'Side-tracking the human genius.' Eunice loves to tease him.

'Always a husband, father, lover, cuckold –'

'You did them beautifully, I'm sure.'

'Even alone I was shadowed by the anxiety, like a private detective she'd hired.'

'Poor Felix – married five long years, was it?'

'Six. They fizzled in the sky like a rocket and a wet stick fell down.' It is a line from his notebook, never used.

'Six weeks were enough for me,' Eunice says.

'I persist, I must finish a thing even when I know it's crap. I'm glad I tried. Glad I stopped.'

'How pleased can you get?'

Felix ignores her: 'These things – we make them too important. Fun, but a dead end. Tell yourself a woman is all you want and you destroy yourself.'

'Destroy the woman.'

'Whosoever will save his life shall lose it.'

'Felix! – always the vicar's son.'

'The analysts, therapists – they're no better. Their job's to patch things up. Make your marriage work. Save your life for you.'

'Did you try?'

'I settled for poetry.'

'Opting out?'

'Out of the cocktail, yes.' Felix picks up his drink. 'Gin and vermouth, lemon peel, a tot of cointreau, a dash of bitters, throw in a couple of marriages and a few affairs, shake well, serve cold – with Freud the great swizzlestick and a terrible hangover afterwards. But poetry isn't running away. It's to grab something.'

'Grab life – I'm with you.'

'Grab death too. The one certainty, the mainspring –'

'Inspiration from the grave?' Eunice remembers her virginity. 'I'm surprised it lasted six years.'

'It was a big charade, but I had to find out – like the novel I tried to write once.'

'What was it about?'

'Mostly you.'

Eunice drops a little sigh, dropping the subject and picking another: 'At least your son was born in wedlock, unlike my small bastard.'

'How is he?' Felix asks.

'Hugo? All the wonderful things you can think of. An English peach, a Bach fugue —'

'For God's sake! A thunderstorm, a laugh when you don't expect it —' Felix can add to the list for ever: the thrill of bringing off a difficult line, Violet's palm-oil skin as she undresses, his son Peter's belief in an infallible father . . .

Eunice says, 'Mix them up, you've got my son. How's yours?'

'Going to school in America, last I heard.'

'She took him there? I didn't know.'

'Saluting the flag and singing *America the Beautiful*. If the war goes on another ten years he'll be coming over to win it for us.'

'It'd better not.'

'It'll be worse when it stops.'

'How so? Even if we lose there won't be the killing.'

'Don't imagine it'll go back to what it was before — the piping days of peace.'

'They piped happily for me.' Eunice's voice softens at the memory.

'For most people the war's the biggest thing in their lives.'

'Being bombed is a big thing? Shot down? Sunk? I can wait.'

'People will look back with nostalgia.'

'*Nostalgie de la boue.*'

Felix laughs: 'It's a comforting thought — what we're living through now is the good old days, and there's worse to come.'

'Bloody pessimist.'

'Not so. It's the future that keeps me going.'

'It's death that keeps you alive?' Eunice likes the paradox.

'The poems to be written. Meanwile I enjoy today more than people who think tomorrow will be better.'

'We're very similar, Felix darling. We're happier than we deserve.'

22

A month after the war began, one October day in 1939, Felix got drunk for the first time since bringing Miriam to England six years before. He had delivered his third book to the publisher; passed it to a girl who took it blindly, keeping one hand on her typewriter, and in a moment he was back in the street. The thin package sat on a pile of biographies, novels, histories, guides, children's books, cookery books. It was itself a bit of each, a narrative of the past year, month by month; a calendar of twelve poems in different metres and rhyme patterns; a diary of seasons, memories, jottings from September 1938 to September 1939.

Now he was light-headed and bereft, an empty man in an empty street. The intensity of invention, the delight of trimming and tidying, were over. There was no purpose left. He walked down the street, crossed over, walked back along the other side; watched the publisher's office for a sign that someone had found his book. A shout, a cheer, a bang and a puff of smoke would do. Nothing came. He went into a pub and began on beer, and soon changed to whisky.

The poem was a summary of those twelve months; also a farewell to Miriam and his son Peter, and to youth. It began with that mad September day in 1938 when the old umbrella man, the goat-faced Chamberlain, flew away in an aeroplane to crave peace from Hitler. War was in the wind, trenches were being dug on Hampstead Heath, gas masks were issued to the people – a death's head for everyone, with a smell of rubber inside and a misty view of Armageddon. People listened to the bulletins, pounced on the evening papers, chattered like animals in a forest fire. The newsreels were coming true, London was to be bombed into dust like a Chinese city. But Felix hadn't joined the Communists or marched with hunger strikers or fought in Spain or signed the manifestos. He stood for nothing but himself, whatever that was. The Munich crisis was his own private crisis, almost lyrical. The leaves on the planes were turning yellow and soon would drop off. What would London be like when they grew next spring? The umbrella man flew back from the precipice, dizzy but dignified, waving his piece of paper for the cameras, to say he had had tea with Hitler: it meant peace for our time. Whose time? Felix knew the war was coming, and the end of his marriage. It was a month of impotence and lies. Miriam bought a new shade of lipstick, Felix wondered why; also a blue winter coat and a bottle of cooking wine and three pigeons for a stew. 'Yesterday they were flying in Trafalgar Square,' Felix said, which put little Peter off and he wouldn't eat, but went to the window to count the balloons sailing over London. It was a city of fear and shame.

In October they went to Wales, the rickety little family spinning away in the Morris Minor. On the back seat Peter played 'I spy with my little eye', but he had forgotten his alphabet and lost his temper before falling asleep. At the wheel Felix, spying with his own little eye, watched the road in front and planned his poem; waved at a man on a motorbike in the mirror, remembering himself in Ireland once. Beside him Miriam clutched herself inside the new blue coat, saving her soul for a future that wasn't far ahead, round the next corner or the one beyond. Felix loved her – the Shulamite whose love is better than wine – and would never stop.

[100]

In November, filling the back garden in Belsize Park, an air-raid shelter appeared – a corrugated iron shed sunk into the soil and covered with sandbags. Soon the floor was awash and Miriam said she would rather be bombed than live in that. Plans to evacuate London were published, and if the people panicked the troops would be called in. An Indian army officer was appointed to handle unruly crowds: the hand of Empire was to grip the capital, the voice of Poona was to be obeyed. Another voice, madly screaming, came through the radio to confound the umbrella man. In Germany a new campaign began against the Jews. Miriam's parents sent a hundred pounds, the last she heard of them. Someone telephoned, a refugee who wouldn't give his name, to say they were missing from their Berlin apartment which was boarded up and painted with Nazi slogans. Miriam had always known they would be taken in time, swallowed by the camps. She didn't cry but lost a little of her gloss, her fragrance, and went into the back garden to plant daffodils round the shelter.

In December, with the last of the petrol ration, they piled once more into the Morris Minor to spend Christmas with Felix's father. Miriam, with no parents now, resented being married to the son of a Christian clergyman and lost her warmth for the Revd Bayne. But she decorated the tree and cooked the turkey, safe heathen symbols, while Felix took Peter to sing carols in church. Eunice Fancourt was there – her father was still churchwarden – and as they trailed out to shake the vicar's hand they arranged to meet on Boxing Day. Peter laughed when Felix gave him a devil's mask with a long nose and horns, better than a gas mask, and stuck a lollipop in the mouth. The vicar got out the bishop's sherry and they drank to the man of peace, not the one with the umbrella. Next day Felix slipped away to see Eunice. The pubs were shut, they walked through the jerrybuilt winter suburbs, across the recreation ground, past the empty tennis courts and swimming pool, the shopping centre with its electrical gifts and beauty parlours, down the laburnum groves and acacia avenues of their past. They were thankful to have got away.

In January 1939 the umbrella man, worrying that Hitler wasn't keeping the bargains made at Munich, flew to Italy to persuade Mussolini to have a word with his German friend. In February he announced that General Franco, another friend of theirs, was the rightful ruler of Spain which saddened the people who had fought against him in the civil war. In March, when Nazi troops took Czechoslovakia, the umbrella man saw that Hitler had turned Munich upside down and couldn't be trusted. He promised that if Poland were attacked he would come to the rescue; shook his umbrella and was photographed with a frown, the nearest he could get to a roar. By the end of the month Miriam's daffodils were blooming round the shelter.

In April, in the flat in Belsize Park, the doorbell rang and Reuben was standing outside.

'Reuben!' Felix called loudly, to warn Miriam.

'I found your address, I just . . . I thought I'd look you up . . . I heard –' Reuben shuffled from foot to foot, uncertain where to put his weight. He was immense: a champion boxer, son of a Whitechapel tailor, grandson of refugees from an earlier pogrom. Felix had met him in a newspaper office where a journalist, incited by Mosley's fascists, was collecting material on the fate of Jewish immigrants.

'Come in, come in,' Felix said, wondering what greeting the visitor would get.

'I'm sorry . . . I hope I'm not –' This big bear of a man, rolling his shoulders, grinning with apologies as he must grin when entering the ring to massacre another victim, stalked into the flat. 'You said . . . I think . . . I . . . you –' Reuben couldn't finish a sentence, as if this was a practice bout and a few soft sparring words would do. In a fight he would keep hitting longer, harder.

'This is Miriam,' Felix said, and saw the same amazement

he had seen in her eyes once before. Trying to remember when it was, he looked through them again for the last time; looked at the harmless giant, his great kindly mouth and massive dimpled chin and curly ox's hair and broken boxer's nose; and saw for a brilliant instant that this man had come to take away his wife. And why, oh why, Felix asked, do I do nothing about it?

'Miriam,' Reuben said, loping the few paces across the room and wrapping her hand in one of his, careful not to crush it. He could mince her body in a moment, though it seemed unlikely he would break out of slow motion. 'Miriam,' he said again and a third time, 'Miriam,' more gently so as not to damage the name, only testing it as he might try out a new punch to see if it was worth adopting. Felix saw it would be a killer.

They ate biscuits, drank coffee, talked diffidently. A shadow had entered the room with Reuben and stood beside him like a trainer, noting his moves, giving advice between each round. Reuben never dropped his guard but listened, judged, took his time. Felix and Miriam could only wait. Suddenly he would stir himself and strike, and in a few blows someone would be pulped. Till then they watched him nibble the corners of a biscuit and toy with a coffee spoon in his huge fingers, teasing them, playing with the future.

At the beginning of May Reuben moved into their spare room with a kitbag of possessions and a punching-ball; with his muscles, his hesitation and innocuousness. He had nowhere to live. The war was gathering, people felt a need for solace and companionship. There was nothing Felix could do about the ancient covenant joining Miriam and Reuben, the ancestry they shared, except cling to anything that kept him in the conspiracy. Perhaps he could make his own pact with Reuben, so let himself be dragged into the boxing world. It wasn't painful, he might profit from it; get what fun there was, before the drastic end. For love is as strong as death, the Shulamite sang, and jealousy as cruel as the grave. Felix spent hours in the gymnasium where Reuben was training, crouched in a corner and taking notes. He went to a fight and saw Reuben, gleaming and relaxed, dance for half an hour like a man of rubber, then tauten into steel and smash his opponent into the ropes; and wipe the ferocity off his face on the back of his gloves, to let the pity and gentleness return.

'You see . . . I only tried . . . there was nothing else,' Reuben said, back in the flat. 'He was a nice boy . . . I didn't mean –' Like a tamed animal he wanted approval.

'What will you do with it?' Felix asked. The summer was passing too quickly. He wanted to rationalize the experience, knowing he couldn't control it. There must be a symmetry in it, if only he could take a proper look, but he was too helplessly deep in it and there was no time.

'I thought that in America . . . you can always find something –'

'As an instructor, you mean – teaching boxing?'

'New York, Chicago . . . my mum's got cousins . . . maybe Boston –'

In June a beautiful new flush grew into Miriam's face. She sat alone and played cards, without showing Felix what they told. He held his breath, watching to see what would happen; knowing and dreading it, though far inside him something inaudible rejoiced. Reuben began giving little Peter boxing lessons and they marked out a ring between the furniture. Felix had taught his son the names of the trees and the stars and planets, and how to tell a haddock by St Peter's fingerprints on it and the way to pour a bottle of beer without frothing and when to pull the string to stop a kite falling down and why some boys have a foreskin, but never how to box. He felt a surge of misery when he saw Peter so happy. It couldn't last much longer. All he hated was about to be destroyed; and all he loved, except his imagination.

In July the first British conscripts were marched away into uniform: something that hadn't been seen for twenty years, though this time they were given pyjamas as well as battledress. Felix had the sensation of an old nightmare: falling down a shaft into darkness, clutching at the walls, dropping into an infinite pit. He shut his eyes, hunched his knees to his chest, clenched his mind. Falling for ever into the dark, rolling as he fell. When he opened his eyes he was alone in the flat, giddy and frightened. It was afternoon, he must have come in from the street, he remembered nothing. Had he been taking the schnauzer for a walk? The flat was empty. All three had gone – Miriam, Peter, Reuben. For a moment he thought there should be boards over the windows, swastikas on the walls. It was the suddenness that hurt, a stunning blow. Return, return, O Shulamite, that I may look upon thee! He reeled, put out his hand for balance, blinked at the pain. No concussion could be like this. Miriam had left a note which his eyes were too full to read: something about being lonely in her heart. She didn't have to tell him, he understood it all. She had saved Felix from the loneliness he needed by adopting it for herself. Now Reuben had taken it from her and given it back to Felix. There was a rightness, a kind of perfect agony. The dog looked up and shook its foolish stump of tail.

In August, the holiday month, London was quiet. People had gone away, some wouldn't be coming back. Felix found a flat for himself and the dog in a dark gothic block off Tottenham Court Road. Like a prisoner thrown into a cell, tapping the walls to find a loose brick, he searched every possibility of escape from the certainty of divorce and war. He missed his son, it made him numb to think of him. Peter was his immortality. But not Peter alone, thank God. He would be a better poet now, he knew; and somehow found the force to live, to work all day and most of the night, as the narrative hardened into shape. Events, moods of the past

[105]

year filled the pages. Thoughts, summoned by the poem, slid into the pattern. At the end of the month Hitler and Stalin, sworn enemies, signed their friendship pact. A trial of the London blackout was spoilt by the sightseers who came to watch.

In September, at dawn, German troops crossed into Poland. By breakfast Hitler's bombers were over Warsaw. A Member of Parliament shouted, 'Speak for England, Arthur,' and Arthur spoke. The umbrella man spoke too: the thin dry voice of the old stick himself, on the radio, telling the people they were at war. 'God bless you all,' he said, over the corpse of his plan for peace. The old men's war was being repeated for the young men. It was Sunday morning and many people were in church, praying too late for something that had gone. Others were tinkering with their cars, planning a jaunt to Southend or Tunbridge Wells in the afternoon. Felix never went to church except his father's and had sold the Morris Minor, the little honeymoon car that died in the little family crash. That morning he was in bed in Pimlico with a Jamaican singer he had met the night before. Making love to Violet was another fantasy, a mad phenomenon in a mad world, to finish the extraordinary year: her tropical vigour, their bicoloured passion and the news as they lay together that war had broken out. It seemed suitable, it started a habit. The next Sunday morning, and most Sundays till a random bomb fell on the Café de Paris a year and a half later, Felix woke up in bed with Violet.

The last pages of his epic, in a variety of rhythms, echoed the counterpoint of September 1939. Everything had come to an end and it was high time. The chromium plate was wearing thin, the gin-and-lime was finished. The language of the psalms throbbed from the stained-glass windows of Felix's childhood: the London sky was filled with the sound of trembling mountains and smitten enemies and terrible revenge. In fact the weather was glorious, to make up for the lack of glory or sacrifice in the public mood. On that first Sunday, while the King was committing his country and empire to God, a liner sailing to America was sunk by a German submarine: kings and gods counted for nothing to drowning passengers. When an aircraft carrier was torpedoed the captain said, 'That was a damn good shot,' and went down with his ship. The Russians crossed into Poland, and by the end of the month Hitler and Stalin had divided it between them. In London the blackout was the harshest sign of war. Darkness fell on the streets like an Olympian curse. The number of accidents doubled. Tottenham Court Road became an abyss of total black, a theatre with the lights out, waiting for the play. Violet and her brother Baxter could smile at jokes about bumping into niggers in the dark, now that everyone was the same. Felix made cardboard shutters and stuck tape on his window-panes against flying glass. The first sirens gave him an exquisite fright, though they were false alarms. Sorting out his books he found scraps of forgotten happiness between the pages: a snapshot of Miriam shivering by a Welsh stream, another of them both in a Berlin beer garden, a ticket to the string quartet in a baroque hall with painful seats – nothing to the pain that stabbed his memory. But it was nostalgia for the future that he felt most sharply, an impatience for his unwritten poetry. The leaves falling in the London squares lay like shredded litter, the parting kisses of twenty summers of peace. The season was over, it was closing time in the playgrounds and pleasure palaces. Theatres, cinemas, football grounds were shut to avoid mass slaughter. Felix remembered each year fearing the same loss – the diminishing autumn days, the evenings drawing in – and this time it was coming true. He picked up Peter from Belsize Park, filched him from Miriam for the afternoon and took him to the zoo, too late to see the elephants: they were nervous, they had been evacuated. Poisonous snakes and spiders had been put to death, and

[107]

the keepers given rifles and told to shoot any animals that escaped during a raid. Many people had their pets destroyed. Half a million dogs and cats were gassed in the first four days, to the tune of *There'll Always be an England*, but Felix's schnauzer wasn't stoned in the street like dachshunds in 1914. There was no flood of patriotism or flag-waving, no public hatred of the Germans. The silver blimps, puffing in the sky, gave heart to the people underneath. In a wind the wires that held them sang like violins; in the sun, reflected in the water tanks that appeared at street corners for the fire brigade, they swam like magic fish. Millions of children were shepherded into the country to escape the bombs that never fell. People began hoarding sugar and petrol, and happiness too – there was a rush of marriages, beating all records. Reuben, with Miriam and Peter, got a passage to America. If you find my beloved, the Shulamite sang, tell him I am sick of love. They were at sea when Felix heard. The bubble had burst, there was nothing left, not even a space where it had been. He set about getting a divorce.

He finished the poem, sixty pages wrung from the tormented year, and delivered it to his publisher. The bereavement couldn't be cured, though it might be drowned. Drinking in a pub he felt purged. He had spent all he had. The world had become only his own and he was alone in it. In spite of war – because of it – he had a wonderful sense of being alive. He had emerged from the dark chrysalis, cast off the flimsy shell. A new purpose, or a rebirth of the old, would come tomorrow. It was vivifying, it gave him a gladness that he hadn't felt for years.

23

Guy – Lieutenant Guy Ronson, a dashing figure in uniform
– runs up the stairs two at a time and opens the doors on to
the street, careful not to let the light out into the blackout.
Though the moon is up it is a few seconds before he can see.

'Sir!'

Someone switches on a torch masked with cardboard over
the lens. It is Leo Robb, the doorman, who clicks his heels
and salutes. A tall man of fifty, also dressed for the part:
maroon overcoat trimmed with braid and buttons, clipped
at the neck and reaching below his knees; peaked cap with
Café de Paris in gold letters; the ribbons of the last war –
Pip, Squeak and Wilfred – on his chest; three gold stripes
on his sleeve, though he was never a real sergeant in the
army. He was once promoted to lance corporal, but stripped
within a week on being found in a brothel in Amiens and
reduced to Trooper Robb again. It wasn't enough for the
manager of the Café de Paris, who was never a soldier at all
and elevated all titles out of habit. So Leo Robb was made a
sergeant. Having lived on his wits he knew he deserved
it, and began rubbing vaseline into his moustache and
twisting it into points.

Guy salutes back: 'What's going on?' and looks up and
down Coventry Street. A line of white paint marks the kerb.
In one direction he can make out the entrance to Piccadilly
underground station; in the other, the dim lights of a
late-night milk bar in Leicester Square.

'Things are warming up nicely, sir.' Leo has never seen
Guy before tonight, but knows him as the man who arrived
with Felix Bayne. 'Jerry's come over in force. Quite like old

[109]

times. There was a bomb fell in Shaftesbury Avenue. They
got Garland's Hotel, I heard.'

'I was going to Quaglino's to look for friends.'

'On foot, sir? Not if I was you.'

The drone of bombers, thrumming in waves, is cracked by
anti-aircraft fire – the angry London guns. Explosions peck
the sky, searchlights flick and sweep around the moon.

'There and back in ten minutes.'

'There's shrapnel, sir, don't forget. You'd want a tin hat
and even then . . . Wait and see if a taxi comes, is my
advice.'

The two men, smart lieutenant and phoney sergeant,
stand under the entrance canopy. Leo's torch lights a faint
oblong at their feet, glinting on their polished toecaps.

'Full down there tonight, sir?'

'Crowded out.'

'Beats me how they keep it up in war.' Leo is testing the
ground. 'Friend of Mr Bayne's, sir?'

'Only recently.' Only tonight, in fact.

'Very fine gentleman – Mr Bayne. Comes regular as
clockwork. Never misses a Saturday. Friendly with the
band, I take it.'

'So I believe.'

'First time he spoke, he asked me was I Leo Robb. He'd
heard the name before, like I was famous. Asked if I was in
the last war, in the cavalry in France. My belief is, he knew
more than he was letting on.' Leo can have no idea that
fifteen years ago in an Irish castle Felix wrote a ballad about
the flogging of Trooper Robb. 'Always stops to have a
word, on his way in or out. Stays to the end. Though I says
it as shouldn't, he goes home with two of those darkies
from the band. A mite peculiar, sir, to my thinking.'

'What isn't, these days? This war's different from the
last.' Guy too is reconnoitring.

'All war's the same, sir, if you look at it. You're out to win
and you don't mind how.'

[110]

'Were you in the trenches?'

'I was and I wasn't.' Leo Robb isn't giving much away. 'We was lucky in the cavalry. They had us in reserve behind the lines. Might have been Salisbury Plain except you don't get the French women there.' He doesn't say that after his flogging in 1915 he was dismissed from his cavalry regiment and sent up to the front line to join the infantry. For three years, with only a few days' leave, he lived up to his knees in mud while everybody round got killed. 'How about you, sir – they kept you busy?'

'I was in France last year.'

'Saw a bit of fun there, if I know anything.' Give or take a couple of years Lieutenant Ronson is now the age of Trooper Robb in the last war, and Leo found any fun there was.

'Fun!' Guy tries to remember. Perhaps some of it was fun: 'We had a football match against the French – is that what you mean?' It was on the Maginot Line in the quiet winter before the fighting. Hitler was busy with Poland, he hadn't turned to the west yet. The football pitch lay between two concrete forts as big as battleships, half under ground and manned by special French crews. No enemy could get past. Across the frontier was another barricade of forts, the Siegfried Line. British soldiers had a song, *We're Gonna Hang out the Washing on the Siegfried Line*, which they stopped singing at Dunkirk. The enemy had come round the other way, the forts were useless.

'You win the match?'

'The French massacred us.' The British team went to the match in a lorry with 'Berlin or Bust' on it, to be beaten by French soldiers who soon surrendered to the Germans. Now Guy is standing in the heart of London with German bombers overhead: 'But yes, we had some fun.'

'*Mademoiselle from Armentières* and all that?'

'Funny – at first there was more to be seen of your war than ours.'

[111]

'That's what I mean. Singing the old songs.' Softly Leo begins: *'It's a long way to Tipperary –* '

'The relics everywhere. Shelled buildings in the fields after twenty-five years. Rolls of barbed wire in the woods. Old tin hats hanging up in the cafés. You couldn't go into a house without seeing a German bayonet. Or a French ammunition belt. Or a British shellcase being used as a flowerpot. And the cemeteries – '

'Opened up for the next lot, were they?'

'Wooden crosses in battalions, battalions –'

'Four million killed last time. About a million of them were my pals. Some of them were never found. Some were buried in pits, all thrown together.' Leo blows through his lips, hissing at the thought: 'But they never put an officer in with the men – never.' He hisses again, with more contempt: 'I call that fucking unforgivable – pardon the French, sir.'

The two soldiers, standing side by side in Coventry Street, lob their memories across the generations. Above them the air raid is developing in the familiar way: a tide of bombers, then an ebb, then another tide. When a bomb drops in the distance you feel the sudden pressure in your ears before the noise reaches you. When it falls close and you hear the whistle you know you are safe: you never hear the one that hits you, they say. Across the street the full moon, a bomber's moon, lifts over the Prince of Wales' Theatre.

'Good-bye Piccadilly, farewell Leicester Square –' Leo has a good voice, light but true. He stamps his shoes on the pavement, marking time.

'Did you get a visit from the King?' Guy asks him.

'Old George V, beaver and all.'

'We had his son.'

'Came through in a Rolls Royce staff car.'

'Ours was a fleet of Humbers, full of brass.'

'We was lined up for him, and he stood up in the car and

[112]

made a speech at us. George V was a cousin of the Kaiser's and you could hear the German accent.'

'George VI had a stammer.'

'Then he got down and inspected us. Up and down the lines with the band playing. *Pack up your troubles in your old kit bag.* Up and down the King went, up and down. *And smile, smile, smile —*'

'You might have been those wooden crosses already.'

'At the end we gave him three cheers.'

'Lifting your hats and shouting.' Guy watched the same thing twenty-five years later. Soldiers love to shout.

'He went to lunch in the officers' mess. Brought his own food with him – salmon from Balmoral.'

'George VI was taken to lunch in a château.' Guy can see it still: a tall iron gate and a straight avenue leading through the winter noon to a bridge over a river, and a fairy white château taken from a child's picture book and dropped on the lawn. The idyll was broken by the bark of officers and the crunch of soldiers marching up the gravel. While the King was being given lunch by a lot of generals the band mustered on the lawn and played Gilbert and Sullivan. In the afternoon the King came out and was introduced to the mayor, a veteran from the last war who hadn't been invited to lunch. The old man stood bare-headed with his wife and daughters, all in black, and made a speech in French thanking the King for sending his brave English army to fight with the brave French army in the noble cause they shared – the defence of France, which was no less than the defence of humanity. The King didn't understand. A string of geese came waddling from behind the château and trailed through the ceremony. At the end the mayor said, *'Vive le roi!'* and the King understood at last and smiled dimly at the thought that for a moment he was king of France too, or because he knew that 'Long live the goose!' sounded much the same in French. *'Vive l'Angleterre, vive la France!'* The band struck up the national anthems, the

[113]

officers began to bark again, the geese waddled off behind the château.

'I don't suppose, sir,' Leo says, 'that as an officer you get the same fun as in the ranks.'

'It was very peaceful till the Germans broke through.'

'Then it wasn't?'

'Not so bad as for you in the last war.' But now it is hard to remember the danger and fear. Guy spent six weeks before Dunkirk in a state of muddle rather than battle. To a young officer in command of a platoon, trying to explain things to his soldiers when nothing was clear to himself, the retreat followed none of the patterns he had been taught.

'If you ask me, sir – pardon the liberty – the officers was in the dark the same as one and all.'

Guy laughs: 'That's about it.'

'And the regulars wasn't any better than the rest. Worse, I'd say. Because they'd been brought up to it and when it came they didn't know how to handle it. Like it was too hot to touch.' In the middle of an air raid Leo feels brave enough for confidences. 'We had a major in our lot, a man from Ireland. A millionaire, they said. With an estate and a castle full of flunkeys and a fox hunt to himself. A leader of men – that's what an officer's meant to be.' But he has to be careful. He mustn't let on about the flogging. Few people know about it, though under his shirt the marks still show: not battle scars, but a truer record of his service than the sergeant's stripes on his doorman's uniform. 'That major – he couldn't lead a lady up the garden path, never mind lead his dogs to catch a fox. But he had hundreds of us in his power, our health and happiness and lives and all. And he knew as much about men as – as that letterbox over there.' Leo nods across Coventry Street. The top of the letterbox has been painted yellow to give warning of a gas attack, though nobody knows how. And nobody knows what the gas will smell of. Pear drops, geraniums, mustard, horse-

[114]

radish, bleaching powder, floor polish, musty hay – they are told it might be any of them.

'It's not so simple,' Guy says. 'You can be trained –'

'I know what you're going to tell me, if you don't mind my saying. Trained up to the eyeballs, is that it? Till there's nothing left for them to teach, and still you don't know it all. Men aren't machines, is that it? It's not like learning to saddle a horse. Or strip a Vickers gun and assemble it again.' Leo lets the thought sink in. 'So they put you through it, did they – before you went to war?'

'I joined the territorials. By 1939 I was in command of thirty men in France. Football matches, concert parties, royal visits – all that stuff. Even the Prime Minister came to look – Chamberlain, poor sod.'

'Umbrella and all?'

'Dressed like a tourist.' The figure stands in Guy's memory, in knickerbockers, check stockings, tweed hat: the shabby old angel of peace who once had tea with Hitler. 'A country gentleman going off for a day's fishing.'

'Fishing!' Leo says wistfully. 'Give me Littlehampton every time.' He went there with his daughter the month before the war began.

Guy says, 'The Germans came and we ran away like rabbits.'

No training could have prepared Guy for those bruised and battered weeks of marching towards the English Channel. There was a mad gaiety that overlaid the grief, like champagne at a funeral. The light-headedness and desperation doubled the confusion. Anyone who wasn't killed or didn't get to England would be taken prisoner and spend unknown years behind German wire. Marching and fighting and marching, they were absurd figures in a landscape that was irrelevant; acting their parts against a backcloth meant for another play. It was the wrong scenery. Immense farm horses pulled haycarts over the fields, windmills turned in the May sunshine, village children played

[115]

their oblivious games, women scrubbed the café tables and men sipped *pastis*, not looking up to watch the retreating soldiers go by. The lines of poplars laid strips of shadow across the road: a salute from France for the defeated British today, for the conquering Germans tomorrow. They passed a place where fourteen men, being driven to the coast in a lorry the day before, had been blown to bits, but the hole in the ground was mended now and the incident swept away: yesterday was long ago. At night they found billets or camped in the open. Once they had a feast – Guy never learnt who provided it or stole it – of lambs and young pigs stewed with vegetables. The soldiers sang *Roll out the Barrel* and the colonel was caught in tears – from pride or shame or wine, nobody knew. Guy's corporal said it was thinking about his girl that made him feel so lonely, and stole a tulip for his buttonhole. Planes roared over to drown the larks, bombs fell among the dandelions, gunfire bellowed like the cows. But the sun was no less the sun for shining on a war, or a battle less frightening for being fought among flowers.

'You never know when your number's coming up,' Leo says. 'So there's no sense worrying.'

In the sky, like the ribs of a giant cobweb, a dozen searchlights converge on the pale belly of a bomber. It struggles to dodge them but is caught, waiting to be picked off when the anti-aircraft guns get the range.

'Swatting flies,' Guy says.

'Hornets, more like.' A fire engine, bell ringing, comes along Coventry Street and turns down the Haymarket. 'The West End's copping it tonight.'

'I'll forget Quaglino's.' If Eunice's friends, Betty and Humphrey, went there it is best to leave them.

'Not without a tin hat, sir.'

Guy remembers the beautiful Celia arriving this evening in a tin hat; and for a moment he sees another one lying in a puddle on Dunkirk beach, with grass and cornflowers stuck in it for camouflage. Some German officer, Guy thought, would get a souvenir of the defeated army. But his corporal laughed and said it was the top of a British soldier taking cover, who had dug himself into the sand. He wasn't far wrong. When they kicked the hat over they saw a severed head attached, smiling from the puddle. It was Guy's last memory of France before taking his men aboard the torpedo boat that delivered them two hours later on the dockside at Dover.

Flashes of fire explode round the entangled bomber, teasing it. It stoops and swerves, but the searchlights hold it and the shots close in, getting more accurate. For the two men at the Café de Paris door it is a fascinating, disgusting performance. They want the German shot down, but are chilled at the thought of death up there.

'He'll make towards the moon.'

'Or head down river.'

'Too clumsy to get away.'

'He'll drop his bombs anywhere to lighten the load.'

'Shitting himself.'

'Some shit.'

A shell bursts close beside the bomber. It stops for an instant, frozen over Trafalgar Square. Something drops off.

'Stalled.'

'Winged.'

'Feathers.'

Then suddenly it has gone: fallen out of the sky into the dark, leaving the searchlights waving in triumph, sweeping for another victim, fingering the night like giant tentacles. Down the street a cheer goes up from a group outside Lyons Corner House.

'It takes two thousand shells for each one down,' Guy says.

'They're not wasted,' Leo says. 'They make a lovely noise. It does you good even when they miss.'

There are a hundred and twenty-five bombers over London tonight, the most for many weeks.

[117]

24

'Just watched a Jerry brought down,' Guy tells Felix and Eunice, returning to the bar.

You can hear nothing down here of bombs or gunfire above the boom and clatter of people talking, dining, dancing. For all the noise that reaches you, the raid might be over Berlin. Any explosion comes from the percussion, or drone from Baxter on his saxophone, or crackle from Violet's microphone as she strokes it over her silver fish-scale breasts and croons sultrily about *Two Sleepy People*.

'Poor sods in the plane.' Felix keeps half an ear on Violet.

'Poor sods underneath,' Eunice says. 'Fifteen thousand killed so far.'

'Nothing to what they expected – two million in the first two months, they thought.'

'Bonanza for the undertakers.' Eunice had a job, fifteen years ago in the General Strike, laying out the dead. She knows the sour-sweet smell of a corpse, its cold resistance to her fingers, its terrifying helplessness.

'There wasn't enough wood for coffins, so they stocked up with cardboard ones – warehouses full of them. And they'd dig mass graves. Burn the bodies with lime. Or dump them out to sea. They got it wrong.'

Eunice laughs: 'They? Who?' But she knows the men that Felix means, she was once married to one: that fatuous dim-grey husband who went on crunching toast as she walked out of the house. She saw him not long ago in the Piccadilly blackout with another woman, her successor.

'They expected epidemics. And mass neurosis, worst of all. A mental plague, wholesale hysteria –'

[118]

'Suicides are down,' Eunice says. 'Less drunks too. Less everything. Less caviare.'

Felix won't be diverted: 'They thought everyone would panic. They couldn't believe ordinary people wouldn't crack and run, or go mad.'

'They don't know any ordinary people,' Guy says, smoothing his uniform.

'D'you remember Churchill prophesying that millions of refugees would flee from London? Packs of wild animals roaming the country – imagine! Hungry, diseased, looting, rioting in the soup kitchens –'

'He believed it,' Guy says.

'He doesn't know anything about us, he doesn't want to. It's what makes him Churchill – not having people's feelings to bother him.'

'Remember those posters?' Eunice says. ' "YOUR courage, YOUR cheerfulness, YOUR resolution, will bring US victory." '

Felix says, 'Courage is their monopoly, they're born with it. In their bones they distrust everyone else.'

'They look at Russia,' Guy says. 'They're frightened of the people.'

'And privately despise them. It's one of their oldest beliefs. The people are weak, contemptible, wouldn't stand up to the bombs –'

Eunice laughs again: 'So the people have let them down, by not letting them down.'

'Unforgivable.' Guy laughs with her; and remembers Leo Robb saying that officers and their men were buried apart.

'In a twisted way,' Felix goes on, 'some of them wouldn't mind defeat. They saw what happened to France – it's still there.'

'They'd be the collaborators,' Eunice says. 'I know one or two.'

'They see a sort of purgatory to be gone through. But not by themselves. They're let off – by their responsibilities, their lofty destiny. It's only for the people, for the good of their souls. Put them in their place. Serve them right.'

'I saw some brave soldiers.' Guy is younger than the other two, he keeps a trace of loyalty even after the rout in France.

'Soldiers are safe, they do what they're told.' Felix is enjoying himself, while Violet's voice whispers from downstairs – from a Caribbean veranda or a bed in Pimlico. 'It's the civilians who'd be the traitors, buckling under the bombs. Stabbing the army in the back. But in the end it was the army who ran away.'

'Dunkirk was a victory, they say.' Guy was there.

'What does that make the Blitz?' Eunice stayed to face the bombs with her child.

'Dunkirk will be written on the memorials with the other disasters. Passchendaele, Gallipoli –'

'You're doing well, Felix,' she says. 'Have another drink.'

'The most famous battle poem in the language is about a cavalry brigade charging the wrong way.'

Guy asks, 'D'you think anything's changed?'

'Not for us. Only the Germans are fighting for change. Their war is revolutionary, but we want to keep things as they were. We saved ourselves by the skin of our teeth.'

'That's not what Priestley said on the radio,' Eunice says. 'The war's a chapter in a changing world. The breakdown of the vile old order. Privilege, property, greed for power – now's our chance to abolish them. The liberation of man, he calls it.'

'I wish he was right.' Felix shifts on his stool and almost yawns, though he isn't tired. On Saturdays he can stay awake all night. *Two Sleepy People*: some time tomorrow morning he will fall asleep with Violet.

'He thinks we can work the miracle.'

'We're obsessed with the war, we've caught it from

[120]

Churchill. Life's a pageant – a grand opera, quite absurd, and he's dressed us up and made us sing. When it's over we'll be back in a flash to our famous decency and humanity, the silver sugar tongs and social gravy, and who's-your-father? and don't-you-know? and kiss-my-arse and grace-and-favouritism and double-barrelled birthday honours – it's my birthday today, I'll take a peerage, Lord St Felix of the British Empire –.'

Eunice stops him: 'How did we get on to this?'

'I came back to say I'd seen a bomber shot down.'

'I saw two German prisoners at Waterloo station,' Eunice tells them. 'Handcuffed together, marched along by soldiers with bayonets. Boys of about sixteen. One was pathetic, with no boots and his socks trailing on the platform. The other was all pride and defiance – "I'm not beaten, Hitler will rescue me." Nobody took much notice, you'd think they'd stare.'

'Better than in Oscar Wilde's day,' Felix says. 'He had to wait at Clapham Junction on his way to Reading jail. People collected round and jeered, even before they were told who he was – then they jeered more. In prison clothes, manacled –'

'The King and Queen were booed when they went down to the East End. It was hushed up in the papers. You only saw pictures of them shaking hands with the mayor, goggling at the damage.'

'Just what Celia said.' Celia and Lionel are dancing downstairs: rocking together in the crush, lulled by Violet's words at the thought of sleep at last. 'There'd have been a revolution if the Germans hadn't come up to the West End. The one who flew through the balloons, up the Mall and dropped a bomb on Buckingham Palace – the King should give him a medal.'

'The Queen said, "Now I can look the East End in the face."'

'Worthy of Marie Antoinette.' For a moment Eunice sees

[121]

a small girl in fancy dress, thirty years ago, being turned from Marie Antoinette into Cleopatra.

'They're ploughing up Windsor Park to grow potatoes,' Guy sings, to the tune of *They're Digging up Father's Grave to Build a Sewer.*

The telephone behind the bar rings, the line has been reconnected. Harry answers it, and comes to tell Eunice that her friends Betty and Humphrey are on their way from Quaglino's.

She looks at her watch: 'Ten minutes to the show – they'll make it.'

'What's it like for people who've been bombed out', Felix asks vaguely, 'to hear about a load of plutocrats sitting down here in safety, waiting for a row of girls to wave their fannies at us? A leg show for the élite, a pick-me-up –' He swallows his martini.

Eunice says, 'I was in the Savoy the night they had a demonstration. I hadn't been inside for years.' Not since clinching the baronet's adultery for him. 'They've made the restaurant into a shelter. Dinner among the beds, and stay to breakfast. And the siren went and a mob came trooping in.'

'The working class – how terrible.'

'They'd been waiting in the street, they demanded to be let in. Blocking the place, worrying the staff – tricky moment for the manager. But he couldn't turn them out into an air raid and they were very polite. Passed a hat round and collected pennies for the chambermaids. Highly organized.'

'By the Communists, naturally.'

'Is this a hammer and sickle which I see before me?'

'The all clear went, so the manager was saved.'

'It hasn't gone tonight.'

'Time to get a table downstairs,' Eunice says. 'Charles, the sod – he's given my usual to a gang of Canadians. You coming down?' She looks at the two men. 'Felix? – but

[122]

you'll be soaking here till dawn. Guy – come and join me.'
She slips him her wonderful smile; slips off her stool, a
hand brushing his thigh for the softest squeeze; leaves
them together at the bar and goes to the balcony, to the top
of the gold and crimson staircase.

25

Leaning over the balcony Eunice catches Charles's eye. He
is coming up the stairs, he stops and raises his eyebrows a
fraction like an auctioneer. What will she bid? She holds up
two fingers. She can't count on Betty and Humphrey, but
Guy will join her. Charles gives an almost invisible nod: the
deal is on. She goes to meet him on the stairs and lets him
lead her down. It is always an excitement: going down to
dinner at the Café de Paris just before the show. On the
lower floor they pass the four Canadians.

'Hi!' The officer who fired a champagne cork at her holds
out a hand: 'I'm James. Glad to know you.'

'Eunice Fancourt.' She catches the friendliness. They
have long ago been forgiven for taking her table. She likes
the men's kilts, and can feel the cork in the top of her
stocking, pressing into her thigh.

'Meet Cathy and Liz.' James introduces the two nurses.

'Hi, Eunice.'

'And this is another James.'

'James the Second,' the other says.

James the First says, 'He and Liz got engaged on the way
across.'

'Troopship romance.'

'Love on the ocean wave.'

'Now we're celebrating – the boat was dry.'

'When did you land?'

'Came over in a convoy.'

'Took twenty days.'

'Hunted by U-boats all the way.'

'Dodging torpedoes up and down the Atlantic.'

'We touched Liverpool this morning.'

'Say, this is all secret, we're not supposed –'

'*Careless talk costs lives* – I saw it in the ladies' room.'

'Charles is a spy,' Eunice tells them, darkly. He stands beside her, waiting to show her to a table. Politely satanic, coldly gracious, he makes a convincing secret agent. His sheaf of menus could be orders from the powers of darkness.

'Well, we made it here. Our first night in London –'

'You picked the best place.'

'It's still rolling with the boat.'

'That's the champagne.'

'You call this war?' James the First waves his hand round the radiant scene.

'Don't you like it?' Eunice asks. 'We laid it on, to take your minds off the Blitz.'

'Danger's what we came over for.'

'Wait till your first bomb.'

'I'm waiting, Eunice.' James the First catches sight of Celia in her tin hat, revolving slowly round the crowded floor with Lionel glued to her: 'You British, you're just lovely.' When Celia sees Eunice with the Canadians she releases the hand that is massaging the back of Lionel's neck and gives a vigorous wave. James the First says, 'See what I mean?'

Charles is impatient to show Eunice to her table. She excuses herself.

'Be seeing you, Eunice.' In unison, like bit-part actors, the Canadians hold up their champagne glasses once more: 'Be seeing you!'

The table is half-way back, with a view of the dance floor between two pillars. Eunice can just see Baxter from here.

She asks Charles for champagne and two glasses and he leaves her with a menu, but she won't order before Guy comes down. Champagne is enough for the moment. Till it arrives she can look round at her neighbours.

At the next table is a young naval officer with a much older woman – his mother, obviously. They have finished dinner, they will have coffee while waiting for the show. Eunice has never seen them before, though they look familiar. Strangers, but not unknown. Characters in a story that she hardly has to guess, she can read it clearly.

The son is about twenty-five, his mother nearly fifty: widowed in the last war, Eunice is sure. Her husband was a young naval officer too, no doubt. Drowned when his battleship was sunk at the Battle of Jutland before the son was born. The pieces fit, the picture forms. Eunice watches the woman watching every painful, precious movement of her son's, so like his father's: the way his thumbs tap the table, his cheeks dimple, his hair falls across his brow. A middle-aged mother's eye looks through a young wife's lens again, seeing the familiar details. She knows too well the curling rim of his ear, the softness of his throat, the drop of spit on that enchantingly misplaced front tooth. The face rings true, singing the same bright message as twenty-five years ago. Each spot and crease has been put there like marks on a canvas, proving the genuine thing. The son's portrait is signed all over by the father's hand. The mother watches jealously, proud but fearful of his good looks, his manners, his uniform. She has reared him, her only child, in the image of her husband, to follow him precisely.

All the way to the end, you may wonder? To another sea battle with the Germans and a hopeless struggle in the water? Or to a different, less heroic sailor's death?

The son's eyes – sharp and blue for fixing on the horizon – are not on his mother but on the cigarette girl who wanders between the tables with a tray held on a silver chain round her neck: a wanton pussycat in a dancer's purple tutu. Her

[125]

own eyes signal all the impatience of her body. Her gorgeous but uneasy breasts, trapped in a skimpy bodice, support the last ripples of her tumbling hair. One of them also bears a big brown mole, perhaps artificial, that hints at the treasure further down. Her legs, from impudent tutu to perilous shoes, are netted in tights that strain audibly to their work. The effect is of imminent revelation: a tiny jerk, a snapped hook, a burst stitch and the girl is naked.

The young man beckons her and she comes tripping to stand close by him, the tutu brushing his elbow. From her tray he chooses a cigar; puts it to his nostrils for the aroma, presses it lightly to hear the crackle. The best cigars, he would tell anyone but his mother, are rolled on the thighs of Cuban negresses. This one will do. The girl takes it in her agile, reverent fingers and snips it for him; gives it back and lights it, stroking the match across the blunt end of tobacco while the young man puffs. Eunice, forgetting for a moment that Guy will soon be dining with her and may sleep with her tonight, would like to be that cigarette girl. And she sees how the young man's hand, the one that isn't holding the cigar, would like to run up the girl's leg, climbing the network and feeling for the skin. But he doesn't let it. Not in front of his mother. The same idea strikes the girl, and she and Eunice exchange a private laugh.

A loving, wistful smile grows on the mother's face as the cigar smoke reaches her over the table. It takes her back. She came to the Café de Paris once before and they danced, she and that other officer. He might be an admiral now, perhaps with his son for flag lieutenant, and she wouldn't be a widow on a wretched pension. She could have married again, as many did, but it would have been a sort of treason. The simple progression would have been broken by a step-father. It is as perfect as can be, she wants nothing more than this faithful repeat from one generation to the next. There is something holy about it, like those tribal lists

[126]

in the Bible, father to son down the years. The wife – the mother – is a mere priestess, guardian of the seed.

Wife or mother, father or son? The woman opens her purse and looks at the old photo she always carries. They had it taken in a studio before he went to join his battleship, the last day she saw him. The leather frame is frayed, the cellophane is scratched and yellow, but it doesn't matter any more. She has the real thing again across the table, enjoying his cigar and blushing a little at some secret pleasure. Like his father, he would never share it. They are a stubborn lot, these men of the silent service. They must be handled with love and care. She has learnt a thing or two about them, from one or other. And tonight they will dance once more. After the show. It should be starting very soon. She is sorry Douglas Byng won't be performing, she likes dirty jokes, without being sure how much of the new ones she understands. She isn't sure either how much will be visible from here, there is a pillar in the way. She shifts her chair an inch, leans to one side, tilts her head to see the dance floor better.

Her son stands up: 'Mother! I won't have it. We'll change places. At once – I insist. It's a command. Come on, mother, you'll do as I tell you for a change, if it's the one time in your life.'

Without protest, rather enjoying her obedience, the woman is on her feet, then sitting in her son's place on the other side of the table. He sits down triumphantly in hers, taking the ashtray and blushing more. It is a fateful move. One seat is safe, the other murderous. Gallantry will be paid for, bitterly.

A waiter comes with Eunice's champagne in a bucket of ice. He shows her the label, wraps the bottle in a napkin, pulls the cork with a muffled pop; pours a little wine into a glass for her to try.

[127]

26

Felix and Guy up at the bar are on to their fourth martinis.

'Isn't it time –?' Guy begins.

'To eat? I'll go without.' Watching Violet and Baxter eat bacon and eggs will be enough for Felix, after all this gin. 'You go ahead. Join Eunice – she's waiting down there, ravenous for you.'

'I meant, time you published something new. That long poem at the beginning of the war – it kept me going. I want more.'

'They're piling up. Six months and I'll have a book.'

'The same again? A journal?'

'Nothing's ever the same,' Felix tells his new friend. 'You move on, and it shows, or it ought to. Wrinkles, and bags under the eyes. Verbal crowsfeet. Less glitter – the glitter's finished anyway, it went out with the war, like bananas.'

'Plenty of it down here.' Guy looks around.

'I love it, I wish I didn't. But I'm not nostalgic. Ten years ago I'd have written about the local colour – the highlights, the dabs of paint, a touch of lipstick, eye shadow –'

'Verbal cosmetics.'

'Acrobatics. The daring young man on the trapeze, playing tricks, making you gasp. Let go with your hands, hang on with your feet – anyone can do it. Now I know about the big drop. The void with a question mark at the bottom. It's what you do with the empty space –'

'The effect of war, isn't it?' Guy suggests. 'The circus has closed down.'

'It's knowledge. What you know, and knowing how

much you don't. And never escaping. It's easy to find sanctuary. Join the Communists, join the Catholics, commit suicide. It takes guts to make the first move, but once you're in you're one of the boys.'

'That's what I liked – you keep out of the grooves.'

'I don't believe in cures,' Felix says. 'Or trust the creeds. Sign your name and you surrender. Adopt an ideal and you've got a boss. Watch out for the priests. They want us parcelled up and labelled, stacked out of the way, A to Z, so they can keep an eye on the job – getting to the top, becoming bishop, prime minister, chairman of the board –'

'Don't you need a confessor? A colleague – to take the load?'

'I had a dog once. We understood each other. Looked into each other's eyes and smiled. I tried a wife but it needs a knack, a compromise. Besides –' Felix looks askew at Guy: 'I love a single bed.'

'You said you had a friend in the band.'

'Listen –' From downstairs Violet's voice comes through the clink and babble, singing *When You Wish upon a Star*.

'Is that the friend?' Guy gets off his stool and goes to the balcony to look down. The couples on the little dance patch are jammed so thickly they can move only in unison: a pack of people swaying with Snakehips Johnson's rhythm. Celia's tin hat is conspicuous in the middle, but Eunice is out of sight under the balcony. At the edge of the platform in a dazzling spotlight, Violet lifts her face and strains her sad brown eyes beyond the mirrors and gilt to catch a star to wish upon. Far above the ceiling of this lovely place, up in the moon-washed London sky, a man is lying on the floor of a bomber, waiting for an order from his captain. You can't be sure, from Violet's promise of a hopeless dream, that she isn't aware of the nightmare it will be. But Guy has no suspicion, on the balcony, that he is staking his luck on the chance of being killed. Anyway there will be some astonishing escapes. More people will survive than die.

[129]

He goes back to the bar and picks up his glass: 'I've never slept with a black woman.'

'The supreme pleasure – I never guessed,' Felix says. 'A new dimension, a twist to the old tangle. And much simpler. There's an ocean between us, between a London suburb and a West Indian island. We can't blend, so we don't try.'

'I've never been married either.'

'In a coma, half awake, doped, drifting through time. Time, time – most of the time passed happily, except when I thought that most of the time was a waste of time. And there was someone outside the coma – a poet with my name. I'd go and join him and we'd write a poem, if we had time before I had to go back inside.'

'Double agent, two-faced.'

'Fun at first – the deceptions I learnt, slipping from one to the other.'

'No fun for your wife, was it?' Guy asks.

'The split got harder to cross. The poet tried to grow, the husband tried to stay the same. They got angry with each other, though they were good at covering up.'

'It's what we all want – living two lives at once.'

'One of them had to crack.'

'The husband.'

'He wasn't a fraud,' Felix says. 'He didn't get drunk or have other women. He genuinely loved his wife. It was innocent, but a game – keeping house, playing families, make-believe with grown-up children. If he looked out and saw the poet laughing at him through the window, he got restless and away he went.'

'The poetry got better?'

'The husband faded.'

'It'll be a lovely book.' Guy raises his glass to it.

'More consistent, I hope. But I'm not reliable, I like the contradictions. Down with the pompous and bogus, down with diehards and puritans, building societies, insurance companies. Up with people who love food and drink and talk and clothes and each other. But it'll be better, yes. I'm more myself, more a whole man – the man in me I most approve of.' Felix smiles at another thought: 'I don't slink away to lick my wounds any more, before I can write a poem.'

'Peace of mind –'

'More than that – it's integrity of mind.'

From downstairs a new tune breaks out, cutting through the din: *'Happy birthday to you.'* Violet's voice, an inch from the microphone, soars above the band. Dozens of others join in.

'Lucky man, Felix,' Guy says.

'I never told her, I wonder how she found out.'

'Happy birthday,' Violet sings, *'dear Jennifer –'*

'Thank God, it's someone else.'

27

The first bad raid was in September 1940, a year after the war began. Felix was on duty five nights a week, in blue overalls with a belt, helmet, torch, message pad and bandages in his gas-mask bag. His post was in a basement near the British Museum. In command was a Brigadier, a compassionate old man who owned the house and made his daughter Diana adjutant: four-square and ginger-headed in check skirt and strong shoes, with her father's straight back and steady eye and a sporting jargon of her own.

Diana put up a notice giving a warden's duties after a bomb fell. Summon the fire brigade or ambulance or heavy rescue squad. Identify poison gas, give first aid, direct homeless people to a shelter or rest centre. Quell any panic. 'First and foremost,' she ordered, 'a warden should regard himself as a citizen chosen by his fellows to be their leader and do the right thing in an emergency.' Her father directed the patrols, but Diana manned the telephone and controlled the supply of tea and torch batteries; and played poker dice with any wardens not out in the streets. She had no need of sleep or fear of danger and liked to slip upstairs into the empty house, with Felix if she could persuade him, to look at the fun from one of the windows.

'Shooting behind the birds,' she said with scorn when shells were bursting astern of a flight of bombers. 'Always the same at the start of the season – they'll improve.' Another time when the guns couldn't find the range, she said, 'Birds flying high tonight – must be the frost, or they're getting wise.' One dawn, as gunfire went up round the last of the raiders flying home, she said, 'Ah – shooting off the old cocks.'

Affected by a poet's company, the deserted house, the whiff of battle, Diana lost her adjutant's manner as she led Felix into room after room to get a better view. She spoke of the days before the war, before her mother died and her brothers and sisters got married, when they had maids in the attic and a cook in the basement – now the wardens' post. Coming off duty in the morning she would ask him to breakfast in the dining-room, and he and the Brigadier sat at the family table while she stood over a gas ring, trying to get the lumps out of a pan of dried egg powder. She pressed him to stay for another cup of tea, another piece of toast; every week she gave him her bacon ration. He knew she wanted to make love in one of the empty bedrooms, and was glad of the excuse to get home and feed the dog before going to his job at the BBC.

'But I'll look after your dog, I'd adore to,' Diana said and hardly flinched when told it was a schnauzer, a German. 'We'll have him naturalized. He's another refugee and some of them are very nice – they hate Hitler as much as we do.' So the dog, the old Berlin puppy, went to live with her

[132]

and her father, and became the post's mascot. 'We must do something about that accent,' she said when it barked at the sirens. But she loved it for its own sake, as well as for being Felix's.

Felix would have liked to be kinder, more honest to Diana. He never told her about Violet, who was singing in the Boogie Woogie Club – the Café de Paris had closed at the beginning of the Blitz – or how he spent Saturday nights and Sundays. She might have been jealous of his mistress and shocked that she was black. The Brigadier, though, would have been fascinated. In admiration or shame Felix wrote a poem about women under fire – their courage, their cool sharing of the work with men. Women's degradation was part of the Nazi creed, but here they were in battle. Felix remembered seeing in a woman's face – after she had driven an ambulance over tangled wires and fire hoses, between craters, through falling bricks to a ruined shelter – her sense of discovery: she was as capable of this as any man. And a woman standing in a caravan in Russell Square, powder and perm immaculate, making tea and spreading margarine while strong men lay on the ground to avoid the blast and shrapnel. And two nurses in cloaks and starched caps running through a hail of incendiaries into a burning house. And a housewife kneeling by her husband who was crucified by a girder, speaking comfort and hope till he died. A coloured scarf, a bright skirt, a bit of rouge or lipstick – a woman would emphasize her vitality, her being alive in the face of death.

So with Diana. More clearly than the wardens, she saw what they were fighting for and the nature of the fight. To her the job was the same for everyone. To the men she couldn't have it both ways: living was no more precious for her than for them, and being killed no worse. Felix called his poem 'For Diana' and sent it to a paper that she would never see. But someone cut it out for her. She said, 'It's the most beautiful thing anyone has done to me,' and quickly,

[133]

so that nobody could watch her crying, went to pin it on her noticeboard.

'Where are the war poets?' the Brigadier asked.

'Under your nose,' Felix said. But he knew what the Brigadier meant: the patriots who wrote some stirring sonnets, then got killed in action.

In the streets and squares of Bloomsbury fresh gaps appeared every night, as September turned to October and the war began its second year. Felix got used to the hiss of a falling bomb rising to a whistle, then the sharp crack and cloud of dust that burst from the explosion, settling to show another hole in a row of houses – another tomb. It was frightening and mad, but sometimes he felt a wild gladness. Knock it all down! Blow it up! Clear it away, forget it, make room, start again. Like tearing out the old pages of his notebooks; burning the books on his shelves; ridding himself of the clutter of dead poets, the burden of knowledge, the massive constipation of the past. Possessions, property, libraries, warehouses, offices, the top-heavy load of architecture – smash the lot! Ring in the Dark Ages again, to be lived through with the bright pin-head belief in survival. The mind had got solidified with masonry, choked with cardboard, clogged with plaster and the accumulated paper of too long.

'What I'll never forget', the old Brigadier said one night, 'is the feeling of Germans all the time. Next thing, they'll be out there in the street. Then inside the house.'

'It's the kindness that I shall remember,' Diana said. 'The unselfishness.'

'The exhaustion,' Felix said.

'The gallons of tea we've drunk,' the Brigadier said.

'And how humans', Diana added, 'can endure such violence from other humans.'

'And how they surprise themselves.'

'How each incident is different. You can't predict – each bomb, each escape –'

'Each death.'

'And how small a body is.'

'And how heavy.'

'The things people believe –'

'That a second bomb never falls in the same place.'

'That one of the searchlights is manned by spies who signal to the bombers and sign the sky with swastikas.'

'The first near miss – d'you remember?' Felix said. 'You felt so proud. You were a veteran now.'

'Day by day the feeling of being humbled,' the Brigadier said. 'And exalted.'

A warden from the post, when his steel helmet touched an electric cable, fell dead. Felix saw a fireman take out his teeth to wash them in the hose, and they went spinning into the flames. At night the water jets were filled with a deep mauve, which faded in the morning. After a raid the first cheerful note was the tinkle of glass being swept up. 'It's nothing,' a bus conductor said, 'it isn't half what they tell you.' Two schoolboys, thrilled with their first bombing, rushed into a rest centre: 'We were in it!' Looking at the damage, a woman said, 'Mr Hitler's taken a fancy to our street.' A new twist of war was the way it touched domestic life, in the kitchen, the bathroom, the back yard. On a church in Bloomsbury a poster urged people to turn to God and a few did, for a while.

'This talk about taking it', Diana said, 'makes me sick. London can take it! If Madrid could take it and Barcelona and Chungking –'

'The people can take the bombs,' her father said, 'but not the neglect. When they're bombed out they get a cup of tea and a sandwich. That's no way to treat the troops.'

'Incompetence –'

'They won't stand for it after the war – why should they?'

A plague of Molotov cocktails exploded in the sky, scattering incendiaries that came plop-plopping over the roofs. A sizzling kilogram of magnesium fell at Felix's feet; with a sandbag grabbed from somewhere he smothered it. Water mains were broken, flooding the street; and gas mains: 'Nobody strike a light.' A sweet smell became familiar, tinged with sulphur, though nobody could tell what it was; nobody wanted to know. Ruins could settle into the scene with the dignity of an ancient monument, or the inconsequence of a rubbish tip. A big Rolls Royce appeared in the street and Felix wondered whose it was – war profiteer? property tycoon? ambassador? – but as it passed he saw it was a hearse: the only person to afford such luxury was travelling in a coffin.

'Suppose you were in a bombed house with nothing left but a Grecian urn and a filthy old tramp,' Diana said, 'and you could save one.'

'Every time,' Felix said, 'the Grecian urn.'

'I don't believe you,' the Brigadier said.

Nor did Felix, but he persisted: 'Immortal art or mortal flesh –' But if the flesh was Violet's . . .

A lamp post was buckled by heat, another snapped off by blast. The street could become a muddy lane, the pavement a path of stepping stones. A ghastly, shameless, useless crowd of sightseers – all intact, not a scratch among them – collected to hinder the rescuers, to strip with curiosity a home already stripped by bombs; to stare like a flock of thankful crows. A cold herring eaten like a cat's dinner under the kitchen table could be a Eucharist for deliverance.

'The thing about Winston', the Brigadier said, 'is not that he's descended from the Duke of Marlborough, but he's a schoolboy with a sense of fun.'

'A sense of language,' Diana said, her eye on Felix. 'Those Elizabethan phrases.'

'Like the Old Testament.'

'The power behind the words – he's a one-man fortress.'

From inside the rubble, safely out of sight, a cry grew fainter, ending in a laugh: a laugh was rare those days. A dead girl was found with her cat asleep in her arms.

[136]

Sticking from the rubbish, a leg twitched in a solo dance. A boy in pyjamas, buried twenty-four hours, was brought out alive; also his father with the head off. Blown against the British Museum railings, a corpse was petrified in a gesture Felix had seen inside – a skeleton beckoning from a period of archaeology. A baby was pressed into the London clay; when it was lifted out, the mould was perfect. An Indian woman in a sari, undamaged and talkative, drank a cup of tea on the doorstep of her demolished home, then fell over in mid-sentence and had died before anyone could stop her. A stranger's death – till the belittling effects of fear and duty wore off – was something to be dug out, covered with a blanket, put on a stretcher, taken away. If somebody could find a Union Jack, it added a useful touch of unreality.

The Brigadier said, 'The thing about Winston', hitching up his twill trousers, 'is his view of the fitness of things.'

'Of history,' Diana agreed. 'Destiny.'

'The fitness of himself,' her father said. 'He's incapable of meanness. He can love and forgive, not just hate and fight. Walking through the bombed streets with tears dripping down his face – the most extraordinary sight of the war.'

A rope was lowered into a restaurant and thirteen laughing Cypriots, from baby to grandfather, were pulled out, ace to king like a suit of cards. Buried in her tobacco kiosk, a nice little woman was heard chanting the foulest language while the rescuers, tunnelling to reach her, wondered where she had learnt it. Unaware that he was blind, a man climbed upstairs to soothe his wife – unaware that the stairs ended in mid-air and his wife had gone. In Gower Street a spinster who dreamed that Hitler was getting into her bed, clinking with his medals, woke to find her window blown in and glass all over her. Escaping from a shower of slates, Felix dashed into a doorway that contained a prostitute: 'Take me home, *chéri*, we'll make love *chez moi toujours* for ever,' she whined in cockney French and burrowed into his overcoat; he gave her a cigarette and dashed on. A nun,

[137]

far from any convent, was arrested as a suspected spy with a machine-gun up her skirt. Every night a tall grey lady, said to be a Russian princess, came down Kingsway from nobody knew where, pushing a pram full of corned-beef sandwiches and a samovar of cocoa for the people sheltering in Holborn underground.

The Brigadier said, 'The thing about Winston is that he knows the tragic truth – the fact of life is war, and peace is only a pause to recover. It's his greatness – seeing the drama.'

Diana added, 'And being big enough to share the stage.'

A night in October brought four hundred bombers over London. White flames shot like a fountain from a crater in Percy Street till someone turned off the gas. In Great Russell Street a pub got a direct hit that smashed every barrel and bottle; people scooped beer out of the gutter with teacups, but a week later the odour from inside was of rotting flesh. Crunching over broken glass, a postman pushed letters into any house where people might still live, and took the rest away. All day a young man, the only survivor of a family, sat in an armchair in the street gazing at the roofless shell of his home: the bedroom wallpaper exposed to public view, the bath capsized and hanging by its taps, the furniture tossed downstairs, the secrets given away. A house without eyes or hair or teeth or stomach had never looked so like a house before.

The Brigadier said, 'The thing about Winston –'

'Is his courage,' Diana interrupted.

'His fantasy,' Felix said. 'He's mad. Irrational. A prophet.'

'His feeling of adventure,' the Brigadier said. 'War is bloody hell but it exhilarates him, he loves the battle and he's told us we love it too.'

Felix said, 'It helps to ease the fear.'

'For a time,' the Brigadier said.

A team of looters – with policemen, firemen, wardens

among them, it was said – went through the empty houses. In Museum Street a jeweller's, wrecked by a land mine, had been cleaned out by thieves before the owner got there. A burning house sent up a poplar tree of smoke, or a huge mushroom, or delicate fronds waving like seaweed from the windows. The moon looked clean and bland above the murk. Three friends in a Bloomsbury drawing-room went on playing trios through the bombs: Beethoven, who stood on a Berlin pedestal in Felix's memory, could unroll his relentless order across the chaos.

'Whatever next?' Diana announced, reading the evening paper. 'They're opening some of the night spots that closed at the beginning. The Café de Paris is starting up again.'

'Really?' Felix said, knowing that Violet was engaged to sing there.

'I went there once – a hundred years ago, with a boy in a Bentley, a thing like a motorboat. And we danced till the cows came home. And got swept out with the empties. And drove round and round Hyde Park, I don't know how many times with the boy trying to seduce me, shouting above the engine. But he couldn't take his hands off the wheel and I couldn't stop laughing – he was a big baby. I suppose he thought he'd have me then and there at the crack of dawn, with the grass deep in dew. And the sun came up and the horses appeared in Rotten Row and we went for breakfast in the taximen's hut at Hyde Park Corner – sausages and egg before he brought me home.'

'Glad you held out, my dear,' the Brigadier said. 'Or I should be alone in this barn of a house. No fun without a daughter.'

'No fun for anyone with him. He joined the air force and rose to dizzy heights.'

'Was his name Upton La Touche?' Felix asked, remembering it from another life.

'Good God! – he was a friend of yours.'

'He threw me in a fountain once.'

'He had a squadron of Spitfires and they shot down about twenty Jerries. Bagged several brace himself before they got him – you heard?'

'Killed?'

'Three months ago. Poor Up. Typical.'

Everything was typical if it was unexpected. The shocking became the usual, the ordinary became peculiar. The war turned the days upside down. After a night on duty Felix went back to the flat for a bath, then walked to the BBC, spent the day with colleagues in an office or studio, ate in the canteen, discussed programmes and made business calls – the proper business of life, not the trivial one of death. Other people had had a rough night too: bomb stories became boring and were better untold.

Sometimes after work he walked in Regent's Park. The light faded in the gold-green planes as it had last year and the year before: strange, that they were unconscious of the damage round them. On the lake two swans sailed in the peace they had preserved from before the war, just as the Brigadier had kept a bottle of whisky and Diana a box of marrons glacés. They were shadows of the past, teasing the brain of a man whose memory had gone. It was wonderful, but somehow shameful, that swans could be indifferent to the war.

Early in November, after fifty-six nights, London had its first without a raid. 'Quiet in the butts all down the line,' Diana said, when Felix rang for orders. 'Birds must be nervous.'

Felix was nervous too, waiting for the siren in the half-empty honeycomb of his block of flats, and went out into the stillness of Tottenham Court Road: the vacuum filled in every crack with darkness and a hush. He could touch the mystery, the enveloping contact with London's most fundamental sense. People couldn't believe their luck and scurried along the edge of the street, expecting to be pounced on. It was a trap, this stolen peace. Whispers came

[140]

out of the dark, muffled for fear of bringing down the whole Luftwaffe. The masked beam of a torch marked someone's route and a sudden glow lit up a man's face, cupping his hands to a cigarette – his cheeks sucked in, his eyes bright in the flame. Someone yelled at him for breaking the blackout. London was on edge.

The bombers turned on Coventry, Plymouth, Liverpool, but didn't forget London. On a rainy Sunday afternoon Felix walked home from Violet's and Baxter's flat in Pimlico. Taxis hissed in the wet streets, the winter had declared itself. Felix was tired but happy. Casually, not thinking that it wasn't the quickest way, he turned down the street of the Brigadier's house.

It was gone. A direct hit. Brigadier, Diana, their home, the wardens' post – demolished. Nobody could have survived.

A pile of rubble lay in the space between the neighbours. Inside the shell some bits of habitation clung: a fireplace hanging in the rain, a bathroom mirror where Diana must have stood naked and steaming, and the track of a vanished staircase which she had climbed to watch the raids. Perhaps she had watched this last one: 'Good shot, sir!' she might have called, sporting to the end. Felix could see the pink thighs, strenuous breasts, triangle of ginger hair that he had never seen. There was an extra quietness in the street, as if everyone was ashamed of what had been done – this blasphemy on a Sunday – and had gone away. A rope had been put across the front of the incident: the usual gesture, like closing a dead man's eyes. And a dead woman's. And Felix's dog too was under that heap of lava.

Anger was the first thing. Sorrow would come after the rage that seared his bones, cauterized his heart. Death was only trivial because there were no words big enough for it except in the language of God. Dust to dust, Diana to dust, the gentle Brigadier and the Berlin dog to ashes, bones, blood, hair, the mangled rubbish of an ended life.

[141]

28

Violet and Baxter, sister and brother, inhabited a flat in Pimlico on the first floor of a house that had once been grand. From stucco cornice to pavement balustrade it offered a face of resignation: flaking cream paintwork, wrinkled mouldings and plate-glass windows covered with netting to stop splinters.

But the flat, like the fruit inside a gnarled unpromising nut, was full of delight. The first time Felix went there with Violet from the Boogie Woogie Club, the night before the war began, he felt he was entering the tropics. He had once been told that the water for the sea lions at the London zoo was brought in tanks from the Bay of Biscay; he could believe that the air in this Pimlico flat was piped from the Caribbean. The moment that Violet unlocked the door and pushed through a curtain of beads and shark's teeth he was enclosed in moisture, warmth, abundance. The atmosphere parted as he walked into the room and softly closed behind him; soothed and stroked him, and blessed him with sultriness and innocence. It was heavy with spices – a climate in itself, like a perpetual monsoon. He never learnt how it was achieved. The few electric fires couldn't have done it, it must have been exuded by native Jamaican sensuality.

Green walls, purple ceiling, floor striped blue and orange and spread with rush mats – everything was cheap though luscious. The tall windows were never opened, but draped with brilliant cottons. In the middle a palm tree, planted in an oil drum, touched the ceiling. Slung between its trunk and a window handle was a hammock filled with rainbow cushions. A bunch of bananas hung from the mantelpiece; it was replaced when they were eaten, till early in 1940 when no more could be bought and the last stalk was left to dangle as a memory. There was sparse furniture – a low table, a few chairs and lamps, a yellow couch where Baxter slept – but vegetation was rife: rubber plants and vines growing in tins, and ivy ramping over a model of the *Queen Mary*, bought to remind Baxter of his days at sea. Two of his saxophones lay like big gold flowers in the foliage, among paper butterflies, advertisements and travel posters, magazines, sheets of music, photos of film stars, shells and sea urchins and lumps of coral.

Felix might be in a tropical garden where humming-birds flew freely round him, darting through the plants and sucking at the nectar. In Violet's bed that first night he could hear the ringing of cicadas and rattle of bullfrogs. He expected fireflies to come winking through the dark. There should have been mosquitoes.

But the only animal was a cat, white with jade eyes, called Windsor after the duke who had visited Jamaica as Prince of Wales on an Empire tour. Nothing in Felix's life gave him the same jolt of excitement as the sight of Violet – that Sunday after Chamberlain had launched the war – sitting naked like a carving on a bamboo chair, with a necklace of cowries kissing her ebony breasts and the snow-white Windsor purring on her polished lap.

From the kitchen came the smell of continuous cooking. At any hour there was an oily stew simmering, a chicken boiling, a haunch of meat roasting or some strange vegetable steaming. The place burst with yams, capsicums, pineapples, bags of beans. Felix never knew who ate it all. After his Sunday visits he found it hanging on the breath, seeping from the pores. Monday at the BBC was a day of echoes.

The only other room had space for nothing but Violet's huge brass bed, with a narrow gap all round. She kept some

[143]

of her clothes in a suitcase underneath, but most of them hung from pegs on the walls – masses of costumes that formed a padded lining to the room: 'To protect me from the bombs,' she said, lying with Felix in the middle. With the war, clothes became drabber and scarcer, but Violet had a source of startling garments that never failed. Usually she wore very little, always something different. New clothes were added till they became so deep on the bedroom walls, the front layers threatening to fall inwards on the bed, that she had to unhook the ones at the back and give them away. From week to week Felix watched the collection, like a torture, advancing round him to the point of suffocation before suddenly retreating.

From hints on Sundays he got a picture of what went on in the flat during the week. Working every evening and half the night, with rehearsals and sometimes broadcasts, Violet and Baxter were too busy for much else. They spoke of people whom Felix didn't know: West Indians, musicians, neighbours – he could only guess. He didn't want to upset them, he wouldn't risk spoiling the easy, lazy pleasure they enjoyed together. They were strangers, which was how he liked them: strangers were often preferable to friends. The Pimlico flat was a torpid pool which shouldn't be disturbed. What happened when he wasn't there didn't matter. If he asked too much, Violet got as indignant as she could.

'Questions!' she said, her black flesh shaking with her rising temperature. 'You English want everything, not just the bloody Empire. Always asking, never telling.'

'You should be flattered,' Felix said. 'I wouldn't want to know if I wasn't interested.'

'It's the slave trader in you,' Violet said, hotly. 'You're trying to kill him out of guilt. But the habits won't die. Cracking the whip, clapping your hands for the boy to bring another drink –'

'The girl to strip her clothes off,' Baxter added.

'The white man's dividends.'

'You're studying the natives, you can't leave us alone, you must be making notes and sending back reports.'

'To show how superior you are.'

Felix protested: 'You know it isn't true.'

They never got closer to a quarrel, they avoided anything to dent their triple friendship. It was a good arrangement for them all, as far as Felix could see. On Sunday afternoons they walked along the Thames embankment, Violet between her black brother and white lover, three wayward laughing Londoners.

'Write a poem for me to sing,' Violet asked Felix. 'I'm sick of the crap they give me. *Boomps-a-daisy*! *Give a little whistle*! It's for morons, kids. *Three little fishes*! Nobody writes about the big fishes any more.'

'What are the big fishes, Violet?'

She laughed and squeezed his arm: 'You're a poet and you don't know?'

'Well?'

'The meaning of it.'

'Of what?'

'The truth. The answers.'

'You'll be in deep water. Stick to the little fishes.'

'How d'you know I don't like deep water?'

'You like floundering? Being mystified?'

'I like to sing about things I can't understand. Because nobody else can either. But they listen and if I puzzle hard about what it's about, they believe I know. And it comforts them, so I feel good.'

'It must be nice.'

'She's right,' Baxter said. 'It's best to be in the dark. If you know where you're going it's easy – it sounds easy, which nobody wants. The great ones – they've been struggling to reach something. They don't know what it is, so they never get there. They just keep struggling on. You hear it in the music.'

[145]

Violet had no other lovers, Felix was sure: otherwise she couldn't have been so open. She was too generous, too frank to cheat. He would have been astonished to find one Sunday that someone else had slept with her that week. There was one possibility, a thought that struck him once and never vanished: that Violet and Baxter were lovers to each other. Baxter would spend a week or two of total passion with a woman, as he had with Eunice Fancourt, then keep away for months. It might suit them to share their sensuality in secret mutual pleasures. Brother and sister, the one as beautiful as the other, lovers together – it was something for Felix to cherish.

He did discover who owned the flat: Herbert Robinson – a rodent of a man like a more prosperous but less endearing version of Nipper, Felix's old college servant. Nipper had worn a bowler hat, Herbert Robinson had a green pork pie. Nipper kept the stub of a Woodbine on his lip, Herbert's was a Gold Flake. Nipper's voice was a squeak, Herbert's came in rasping grunts. Nipper's raincoat was stained and frayed, Herbert's had padded shoulders, epaulettes, little belts round the cuffs and mock leather buttons. A mild peevishness in Nipper was a shifty evasion in Herbert. He was some kind of businessman as well as petty landlord, but didn't care to be specific. He tended to turn the talk away from himself. On Sundays he came by bicycle to collect the rent and was given a glass of rum, but never took off his raincoat or trouser clips. He wouldn't stay long, before pedalling away to another appointment.

'What's your line of country, Mr Bayne?' he asked, screwing up his eyes for a narrower view.

'I'm a poet.' Felix wondered what it meant to Herbert Robinson: a blurred character, Wordsworth-Keats-Tennyson made up of names overheard long ago at school, or a row of waxworks at Madame Tussaud's, or a wraith in a velvet cloak, dying of heartbreak, coughing up blood between the odes. Felix's suit and shaven face didn't fit the picture.

But Herbert showed no surprise: 'Not much joy in that, is there?'

'Joy?'

'Call it what you like, it comes to the same in the end. You meet all sorts. If you don't stick them first, you may as well jump off Battersea Bridge.' Herbert dodged and skittered, resting nowhere for more than a moment. 'Profit . . . commission . . . fees . . . the wherewithal, the ready, the necessary, the what-have-you – it makes no odds, it's filthy lucre whichever way up. There's not a lot in it, is there – not in poetry?' From his raincoat pocket he brought out the hand that wasn't holding a glass of rum and rubbed the fingers together, stroking imaginary money.

'I've never heard of one becoming a millionaire.'

'Ah, that's another thing – a millionaire. For many are called, but few are chosen. Which is no bad thing, if you take my point. As the man said, money's like muck – no good unless you spread it. The way I see it, we have our limits, each and every one. It's all according.'

'According to what?'

'To your lights. Or your luck. A bit of one, a little of the other, a touch of the third. Not too much of anything. That's the secret, in my humble opinion – when to stop.'

'Go on with you, Herbert,' Violet said. 'You never stop, you're always on the go. Here one minute, and the next you're off on something else.'

'Second-hand cars,' Baxter said.

'You being funny?' Herbert drew his hand back into his raincoat sleeve and returned it to the pocket. 'Who wants a car with the petrol ration what it is? – enough in a month to go from Hammersmith to Marble Arch, and back next month.'

'So what is it – old furniture? antiques?'

[147]

'You learn to shop around. A penny here, a penny there.'

'Black market?'

'My friends,' Herbert said, 'there's no call for getting personal. It's hard times for all of us, without the bombing. You keep your eyes open, front and back. Look after Number One, yours truly. Take what comes, or someone else takes it.'

When the Café de Paris reopened and Violet and Baxter went to work there, Herbert Robinson surprised them: 'What d'you think of our Leo?'

'Leo Robb at the door?'

'Sergeant Robb as ever is, to give him his due.'

'You know him?'

'I'll say I know him. Have done for years. My dad was married to his mum once, for about a week. Ten years they lived together with never a bad word between them, before they went into the registry to make it decent. It was like a curse put on them. Came out shouting and screaming – you wouldn't know them for the same. Punch and Judy wasn't in it. Tooth and nail, day and night. One week and they'd had enough. On top of a bus riding down Oxford Street, going at each other, swearing to make your ears drop off, when up comes the conductor and asks them kindly to get off, it's agitating the passengers. Which they oblige. And walk away from each other like two strangers at the bus stop, without so much as good-bye. Leo and I – we had to laugh.' But it was hard to think of Herbert opening his mouth for more than a snigger, or to light another Gold Flake.

'That makes you Leo Robb's stepbrother,' Baxter said.

'Step up for one, step down for the other – look at it whichever way. As the man said, everything's got a moral if you can only find it. It's all according.'

Felix wrote a poem about Herbert Robinson – the elusive, bloodless figure on a bicycle steering a nearly straight course across Pimlico, his tyres fixed in a private groove.

[148]

The world was going mad, London was being bombed to bits, but one man would go pedalling on through the ruins, vanishing round the end of the street, bent on some unobtrusive profit.

29

Eunice tastes the champagne; nods to the waiter, then watches him pour more into her glass – rising to the brim, sinking a little, always sparkling. More fizz is what the world needs. Her life would have been flat enough if she hadn't blown some bubbles into it.

The waiter puts the bottle back in the ice-bucket, hangs the napkin over the edge, leaves the cork wedged under the handle. In the top of her stocking Eunice still has the cork shot at her by the Canadians. She can see them at the table, her own table, near the band: James the First and Second in kilts and their two nurses, Cathy and Liz, trim and alert on coming to the war. Nice people, like everyone here, with a lot to celebrate: their first day in England after crossing the Atlantic in a convoy and the engagement of two of them at sea. She likes to see new figures, lovers especially, in the old haunts. They were right to choose the Café de Paris, the only place these days – smart and expensive but elegant, unique in London. The food, decor, music, the shimmering hubbub, the tinkling variety, the champagne zest – it deserves applause like a woman who has taken trouble with her face, and tonight it is getting it. But there is a brooding sadness to the joy, because of its butterfly brevity: a terrible vulnerability in the air which you would notice even if you didn't know what was going to happen.

The Canadians' Atlantic voyage must have been very different from Eunice's before the war in the *Queen Mary*, working her passage with lonely men. She would like to tell them about it; about meeting Baxter and her week of lust with him, and introduce them. Perhaps they have noticed him already: the stunning Jamaican on the alto saxophone. He is just in view from here, and at the sight of him a strand of anguish, stretched like elastic between yearning and jealousy, snaps in Eunice. She scorns nostalgia, she is free of self-pity, but she is near to panic for a moment. She would like to scoop them all up – the four Canadians, and Baxter and Violet from the band, and dull heroic Lionel and lovely tin-hatted Celia from the dance floor, and the luscious cigarette girl and the sombre Charles, and the young naval officer with his widowed mother, and dear Felix from the bar upstairs with Guy who may join her soon for dinner and stay all night, and Betty and Humphrey who haven't arrived yet but who will be here in a minute, in time for the show with luck – scoop them into a glorious party round her, of ecstasy and despair.

Suddenly the band breaks into *Happy Birthday* with Violet's voice cutting through the rest. It stings Eunice – the anniversaries notched up, the years going down the drain – and she flinches. At first, like Guy, she thinks it must be for Felix, but there is a big party at a table in the corner, standing up with their glasses and bawling, '*Happy birthday, dear Jennifer!*' The singing is led by a young captain of the Irish Guards with a handsome military face that could belong to any generation of the past century: keen eyes, black moustache, a look of health and confidence and natural command. Jennifer, the birthday girl, is beside him and he makes a little speech, taking from his pocket an enormous gold key on a ribbon which he solemnly gives her. The people round the table laugh and clap, and Jennifer glows with kisses and happiness. She is twenty-one today.

The name strikes a bell. Eunice knew a Jennifer once, a horrid girl whom she remembers with distaste and gratitude, and wonders if this could be the same. She can't tell in this light at such a distance. The blue dress and plain pink face and mousy hair are no help, but the age is right.

It was after returning from her flight to America with the runaway baronet. She was working as a fashion reporter on *Vogue*; having flying lessons at weekends, shuddering over the suburbs of her childhood in the open cockpit of a Gypsy Moth. Nobody had taken Baxter's place in bed. A journalist and an airline pilot and a cricketer and an absconding monk were given a chance – an audition, Eunice called it, amazed at the noises they made and wondering each time if she could endure it to the end. Then a breathtaking man called Lancelot carried her away from a party after the briefest words between them. They were hastened by that other Jennifer, the schoolgirl daughter of their host, all spots and sniffs, who introduced them and on some unholy impulse, seeing the instant success, stayed to watch. Nothing happened except the messages of surprise exchanged by two strangers who glimpsed the same bright promise. But at a signal they jostled the girl so that she dropped a plate of anchovy toast. While she was picking the mess out of the carpet they escaped. Lancelot had no place of his own, he lived mostly on a boat somewhere or stayed with friends, so they went to Eunice's flat. In bed, in a flash, she knew there could be no doubt this time. The performance, for its silences as much as its style, was faultless.

Next morning Lancelot said, 'Thank Jennifer for this.'

'She deserves to lose her spots.'

'What were you like at that age?'

'Good enough for the gravedigger's son, six feet down in the cemetery – a virgin in a grave.'

'What d'you want now?' Lancelot had a wife who would never divorce him.

'Anchovy toast.' Eunice was as close to tears as she had been for years.

'And after that?'

[151]

'The same as you, I guess.'

'I might break your heart.'

'Break it if you must,' Eunice said, knowing it was half done. 'But for God's sake don't waste my time.'

Later that day, fetching a suitcase, Lancelot appointed himself her permanent lover. It lasted four years and was happier than anything Eunice had believed possible. In time their child was born – Hugo. Pregnancy and motherhood were new to Eunice, she approached them with enthusiasm and the hope that they wouldn't happen often. But from the moment after birth when she looked into his froglike eyes and he looked back, Hugo turned out to be a friend: part Lancelot, part herself, but mainly an unknown original who dropped so perfectly into her life that she wondered how she had avoided him so long. She was surprised by their tenderness together and unhinged by their fragility.

Lancelot worked as yacht skipper, boat builder, photographer, printer, rent collector, barman, cook, apprentice verger in Westminster Abbey and fishmonger at Harrods. Variety was his nourishment, repetition his dread. He held no job for more than two or three months. He had held no love, till meeting Eunice, for any longer. She too drifted in and out of work – from fashion reporter to fashion model, from art gallery receptionist to airline stewardess on the daily Paris flight. Sometimes, hilariously, their tracks crossed. On his way to negotiate a cruise in a French tycoon's yacht Lancelot was one of Eunice's passengers. While photographing beach pyjamas for Selfridge's he found she was his model. To impress a client of her gallery she took him to the restaurant where Lancelot cooked the sauces. Surprise and novelty marked their lives. The Bayswater flat, with Hugo in it later and a series of fugitive Irish girls to look after him, was the still centre of their orbits.

When the war came Lancelot, who had once been a naval cadet, was called back. No battleship could contain him for long; no routine could fail to catch him in some lapse. Thanks to a friend in the Admiralty he was sent to command a torpedo boat at Dover, a swashbuckling pirate's role. He grew a beard, ripped the stiffening from his cap, wore an Icelandic sweater with pyjamas underneath and a silk dressing-gown on top, and cultivated a casual sloppy air as defence against any hint of bravery.

Nobody enjoyed the early months as he did, driving his little ship at forty knots and extending the patrol to include some of the best restaurants along the French coast. Once, before the war got dangerous, Eunice came with him – smuggled aboard in Dover and emerging on the bridge when they were out to sea. The crew could expect anything from their skipper and plied his beautiful passenger with cocoa, sausages and rum. All day they cruised through the minefields, watching for the enemy, spoiling for a fight. It never came. Lancelot was glad, Eunice sorry. But the empty winter was brightened by the lobster they ate that night in Boulogne and the love they made in the captain's cabin on the way back to England: something to remember when the Germans broke into France and there was less fun.

At Dunkirk Lancelot made many trips to the beaches and back with a deckload of soldiers. One of them was Lieutenant Guy Ronson, who became a friend. Eunice liked him at once: debonair in a more innocent, less picaresque way than Lancelot. To save her from her nightmares she saw that he could be useful. Guy was clever enough, or enthralled enough, to see it too.

Soon the French coast was in enemy hands, the Germans were working from harbours close to British convoys, an invasion was expected. Lancelot was often in action, quick and violent and fought at close quarters; and earned a medal from the King and a gasp from his flotilla for slipping at night into Dieppe, sinking two ships with torpedoes, raking the harbour with machine-gun fire while the Germans struggled out of their shock, then switching on his

[153]

loudspeaker and leading his crew singing *'We're sure to meet again some sunny day'* full blast in the dark, before slipping back to sea.

It couldn't last long. Lancelot escaped to London whenever possible to be with Eunice and Hugo. They laughed, played games, walked in Hyde Park, pretending that nothing could wreck their lives and knowing it wasn't true. Lancelot made a toy torpedo boat for his son, driven by yards of rubber band, which they sailed on the Round Pond. It ran out of power in the middle and they watched it drift all afternoon. A keeper said he would rescue it when it came ashore, but he never did. They had uproarious tea parties, inventing a private language to deflect their thoughts from Lancelot's departure. When he had to go Eunice and Hugo watched from the window, waving as he walked lightly down the street to get a taxi. It was the only time Eunice wished they were married. Lancelot's wife, who had taken herself to the safety of Cornwall, would be the first to hear bad news and could be trusted not to pass it on.

Alone in the flat with Hugo, frightened as she had never been before, Eunice held her breath through the hot summer weeks; watched her child – the exquisite joy of growing and discovering; tried hopelessly not to look for omens in the lonely days and nights. The lingering smell of Lancelot in a pillow, the piercing likeness of Hugo's movements to his father's, the jaunty stride of another naval officer with his girl seen from a bus, the cry of seagulls on some silly radio programme, the heavy August green that hung like mourning in the chestnut trees – each was a sign, yet told her nothing. But the agony was a kind of truth, a creed, a devotion that could sustain if not console.

It was Guy who broke the news – thoughtful, selfless Guy – as Eunice had foreseen. The telegram would have gone to Lancelot's wife whose first thought would be of her widow's pension and second, probably, of a way to hurt

Eunice. Through friends, Guy made sure he was told before Eunice could find out casually. He went straight to her flat on the grim mission. Lancelot's torpedo boat had been in a duel with an E-boat off France; had been hit by a shell in the fuel tank; had blown up and sunk with no survivors. It was a fair fight and Lancelot had lost.

Alone at her table Eunice drinks a little champagne and watches the young naval officer with his mother. A naval uniform still cuts a hole at the root of her stomach, though it is six months since Lancelot was killed. Six months of numb horror. After Guy brought the news she clutched her sorrow, hugged it and Hugo together in a bundle of sobs and laughter for the happiness that was gone. She had never thought she was a woman to grieve. In the flat she set a plate for Lancelot on the table for a meal, briefly disbelieving or just forgetting; then put it back in the cupboard. She walked alone through the streets and across the park, with Lancelot keeping step in the empty space beside her. She slid into the big cold bed, daring herself to feel insulted but not demolished by this swipe of death. She woke in the night, hearing a door close quietly somewhere or someone breathing, and cried his name into the dark, only waking Hugo.

She wonders what ship the young officer is in. Something big. He isn't a little ship man, he has the shine of discipline on him, scrubbed and holystoned like a quarterdeck. A cruiser, or a battleship like his father's that went down at Jutland twenty-five years ago. Eunice smiles at the fable she has told herself, confident that it is true. Nothing else is possible.

The band starts playing *Oh Johnny!* Eunice hates this tune – inane, repetitive, futile. But it has nothing to do with the war, which is why it is popular, and perhaps Snakehips Johnson feels it is vaguely about himself. Violet stands at the front of the platform with the silver microphone clenched between her breasts, belting out the words.

[155]

Eunice smiles again, at the thought of Felix's weekly affair with a Jamaican and wonders how long it will go on.

This must be the last dance before the show. More people are coming downstairs. Others leave their tables to join the pack on the dance floor, pressed together, jigging a few inches this way and that. No space for anything ambitious: cheek to cheek, chest to chest, hip to hip, all the way down. Hems are trodden on, toes get scuffed. Jennifer, the birthday girl with her gold key on a ribbon round her neck, is led away by the Irish Guards captain who runs his eyes, then his fingers, round her waist before slipping with her into the lazy, rhythmic shuffle. A beautiful woman at their table, very tall and thin with grey hair and huge green eyes who might be thirty but is probably fifty, stands up and with the softest, most compulsive smile summons one of the party, a sun-tanned little man in a white tuxedo, to dance with her. But the four Canadians haven't finished eating, they will sit this last one out.

The young naval officer draws on his cigar, blows smoke over the table at his mother and smiles. He will give her a dance later, after the show. Just now, as Eunice sees, he is imagining what the cigarette girl will be doing with herself when the Café de Paris closes in the early hours. Whatever it is, he would like it to be with him. He regrets the chance he missed of stroking those network tights and looks round to see where she has got to, weaving among the tables with her tray on a silver chain. To Eunice, her legs are a perfect pair but oddly artificial, like the mole on one breast, as if she hired them from an agency for limbs: pedestals for the purple tutu on which her incredible body rests. She stops to sell a box of black, gold-tipped Sobranie cigarettes to an admiral of the Dutch navy; then moves on across the restaurant, a lone puppet on a random path.

The Dutch admiral and his wife have been served with mushroom omelettes and are about to eat.

'*Oh Johnny!*'

30

Leo Robb was forty-eight when the war began: twenty years since he had left the army, discharged without a pension. He had shrugged off the dishonour, though never lost the marks stamped on the shoulders of Trooper Robb, and got a job with a Fulham coal merchant. He was strong, he could shift a ton from the bunker on to his cart and into a coalhole faster than the other men; and shod his horse, fed and watered and groomed it fit for a cavalry parade-ground.

Through the nineteen-twenties Leo lived with the smell of horse and tarred coal sacks. In the streets of Fulham and Kensington his black face cracked into a grin for any child allowed by its nanny to give the horse a sugar lump; then into a whistle for the nanny's legs. With tips on his wages he made two pounds a week, which left enough for the Saturday races, till he saw a pretty parlourmaid called Eve while delivering a load of coal and got her knickers off in the scullery. When Eve's mistress found she was pregnant and sacked her she came to live with Leo in the mews where he kept his horse and cart. He made plain that she would have to earn her living once the baby was born, but he didn't count on his love for the child, a daughter by the name of Lily.

Eve went to work in one of the Kensington stores: a tempting figure with a knack for moving it that drew the eye of the manageress, who put her on her list of 'late-night extras'. Eve knew the future would be tough and this was a chance to make it easier. A job for a late-night extra came up once or twice a week and earned two pounds, with commission to the manageress. The clients were rich young men or their even younger brothers. Nothing was surrendered more happily than a schoolboy's pocket money, with his virginity, to his mother's former parlourmaid.

When Leo saw that Eve was earning more than he was, he tried to catch up – cheating with the weight of coal, selling the surplus. Such a cheerful coalman, so good to his horse, fond of children, always whistling: nobody guessed. When Lily was bigger he took her up on the cart beside him, riding through the streets. This man could never be a crook. He was only caught when someone wondered where he got the racing money. In court he heard the judge tell him he was a disgrace to his old regiment, nothing new to Leo, and in prison he worried about Lily. When he came out in 1933 there were two million unemployed. He would have liked to emigrate, but with a prison record he couldn't get a passage. He shifted from job to job, from bookmaker's ticktack man to Hammersmith street-sweeper, often on the dole, going to prison again for living off Eve's immoral earnings.

'You're no good to me,' she said, 'you've got no class,' putting on a starchy parlourmaid's accent. Sometimes she practised a French one on Leo, and asked for any words he had picked up in the Amiens brothels. She was now fully professional, controlled by a Maltese who gave her a flat and a maid of her own. Leo lost his room in the mews when he lost his job as coalman and moved from one lodging to the next, trailing Lily with him. The less Eve cared for the child, the more Leo loved her. His terror was of losing her to Eve's vicious world, or to the bureaucrats and steel-eyed officers of charity.

Racehorses, his next delight after his daughter, were his bane. Once he borrowed five pounds from a barman and put it on the Derby favourite. The race was won by an outsider, an Irish horse owned by the major who had ordered Leo's flogging more than twenty years ago. Hatred and disgust boiled in him. When the barman insisted on his money, Leo grabbed Lily and fled from their lodgings, not knowing where to go. At Earl's Court station he felt a hand on his shoulder. He shrank under it and turned cold. He thought he had got away.

'It's a small world, my brother boy,' a rasping, just familiar voice said. It was Leo's stepbrother, Herbert Robinson, with his bicycle. 'What's the urgency?' Herbert asked through the Gold Flake stub in his lips, looking at Leo's old suitcase. 'Time for a cup of tea if nothing else, is my opinion.' Then he saw Lily: 'You can introduce me to the lady.'

They went to a café, Herbert taking charge, Leo glad to put off deciding where to buy a ticket to, and Lily bouncing at the thought of an ice-cream soda.

'Hopping along, weren't you?' Herbert said as Leo's troubles came out. 'The lodger's bunk, the morning flit. Speaking as a landlord –' He took out the Gold Flake and lit another with it.

'Horses,' Leo said. 'I lost a packet, we had to move.' He watched his daughter dipping into her soda.

Herbert watched her too, with a glint in his narrow eyes: 'As the man said, let not poor Nelly starve.'

'Lily,' she corrected him.

'If you walk down Piccadilly with a poppy or a lily,' Herbert hummed; then removed the glint and said to Leo, 'You came to the right address. Landed on your feet, I'd go so far as saying.' He had backed the Irish horse and won a hundred pounds. 'We'll make arrangements, you and I, for old time's sake – in memory of Mum and Dad. How about that, my brother boy?'

'Meaning what?' Leo had done two spells in prison, he wouldn't risk another. 'I've got the girl –'

'First on the menu is a place to live.' In his unhurried way, the way he bicycled, Herbert went without deviation to the point: 'I have a property in mind. The basement of a

[159]

house I'm interested in. Does that sound the kind of thing?' He looked at Leo, then at Lily.

Leo shook his head: 'I've got no money for the rent. No work.'

Lily said, 'I love vanilla.'

'A penny bus from the House of Commons,' Herbert went on. 'Ditto the Abbey. Useful for Buckingham Palace. Easy reach of the Tate Gallery. You have it all. Politics, religion, society, culture –' He ticked them off on his fingers. 'Leaving one for luck. In short, the back end of Victoria Station.'

'Handy for the trains,' Lily said, licking the spoon.

'Handy's the word, madam. On your very doorstep. Passing your window, one a minute. Through the room, you feel – the Brighton Belle, no less. A close view of the Southern Electric. Fast and frequent service, level with your eyes. Worthing, Bognor Regis, Bexhill-on-Sea – reach out and touch them. As premises go –'

'I'd never pay the rent,' Leo said.

'As the man said, we'd all be idle if we could. Nothing payable till you find a job, my brother boy. We might arrange something in that direction too, all in good time, to suit your fancy. Meanwhile, some light employment as you please. Dustbins, the doorstep – you can mend a fuse? Touch up the paint? You're the man for me.'

Leo and Lily moved in that day. They never knew where Herbert lived. He bicycled away down the street and round the corner, not saying where he went or what he did there.

'I've struck a bit of luck,' he announced one day, 'on your behalf.'

'A job?' Leo had surrendered to his stepbrother's manipulation, his sinuous feelers and contacts.

'The Palais de Danse,' Herbert said with the faintest triumph. 'Only the very best for the very best – is that your line of thought?'

[160]

Lily clapped her hands: 'The Hammersmith Palais?'

'As ever is, young lady. Nothing like going for the moon. The manager and I are – shall we say business friends? We had a natter on this and that and the other thing. A vacancy at the door, he said, and you sprang to mind, my Leo boy. He was in accord. A fine figure of a man is what he's after, and I knew the very object of his search. Hot-foot from the King's colours, I said you were. The glory of the flag – not to overstep the modesty of nature, as the man said. St Peter at the Palais gates, if you'll pardon the humour. You'll do it nicely.'

'Chucker out?'

'Commissionaire's the title – more airs than commission, if you'll pardon once again. Tailor made, no question of it. Report for inspection Friday, start Monday and call yourself a lucky man.'

The last two years before the war were a happy time. Outside the Palais, implacable but benign, Leo saluted and stamped a little stagily, and got greetings from people in the street and toots from passing cars. Not many recognized the coalman, and nobody the cavalry trooper.

In their Victoria basement, once they got used to the trains, he and Lily made a cheerful home. Lily shopped on the way from school, cleaned, cooked and sat up for her father to come back to supper. Eve faded into the dark reaches of London, appearing sometimes at a police court before returning to the shadows. The last they heard of her was when a doll came for Lily, three weeks late for Christmas.

'She bought it in the New Year sales,' Herbert Robinson told her. 'I know the breed – mean as a duchess.'

'D'you know any duchesses?' Lily asked. It didn't seem impossible.

'The Duchess of Clarence down by Vauxhall Bridge. And there's the old Duchess of York in Battersea. But the beer's gone off, they never clean the pumps.'

[161]

'That's a nice name for my doll,' Lily said. 'I'll call her Duchess.'

In August 1939, after two years' watching the trains roll past their window to the coast, Leo took his daughter on one to Littlehampton. It was her first time away, and beyond her dreams: the fruit gums her father bought her, the sliding doors in the corridor, the carriage with upholstery and seaside photographs, the brief sight of their basement window – Lily half expected to see herself looking out of it – the roar as they crossed a steel bridge over the Thames and the fortress power station on the other side, the lurch and crash of the points at Clapham Junction, the stations and cemeteries, the first cows, woods, cornfields, the silhouette of Arundel castle, the immensity of countryside – this endless England where she lived, so foreign yet her own – and the terminus at Littlehampton where the train stopped a yard from the buffers, with a short walk to their lodgings through this unimaginable, magic town.

It was a wonderful week. Leo wouldn't bathe, not wanting Lily to ask about the funny marks, but he watched her sidle into the water and shriek for the cold as it gripped her thin blue legs. They built sandcastles. They hired a fishing-rod for sixpence and dug up worms in their landlady's garden and stood all afternoon on a breakwater, knocking limpets off and popping seaweed, but catching nothing. They saw a little coaster shoot out of the river and steam away over the swell, trailing smoke; and a liner with three funnels creeping like an insect along the horizon. They pushed pennies into slots and sucked toffee apples and bought a china rabbit to take home and watched Punch and Judy, watching each other with delight and fear.

'Is Brighton as nice as this, Dad?' Lily asked, slipping her hand into his.

'Nothing like – it's a waste of time.'

'So let's come back next year.'

'Next year never comes.' Leo could feel the danger of losing her.

'Silly Dad.' She too was jealous, seeing how he looked at women and they looked back – this fine big laughing man with only a schoolgirl daughter for company. She wished they could see him in his Palais uniform, and was glad they couldn't.

They went shopping for postcards and threepenny souvenirs; and sat in a cinema and saw *The Ghost Goes West*, twice through; and chose a different place each day for their fish tea. Even when Lily didn't put her hand in Leo's she curled it under his arm, or stretched over a table and tickled the hairs on his wrist. He couldn't take his eyes off her, she was prettier than Eve could ever have been, though cruelly like her. He tucked a lock of hair behind her ear and had to restrain himself from kissing it; then he didn't restrain himself. His daughter! He put himself in a young man's place in six years' time, and thought of Eve. Hell no – in four years, three years. Lily being enjoyed by a man half Leo's age: a soldier or another coalman. And enjoying it too.

They went home, glowing like lovers. Three weeks later, two days before the war began, Lily went on her second train – evacuated to Wiltshire with her school.

The sudden good-byes and surprise of travelling again, the thrill of fleeing from the bombs, dissolved at the other end. In a village hall they were met by a row of women who ladled out plates of mince. Tired and terrified, in unsuitable clothes, they clung to each other, to gas masks, labels, teddy bears, while the billeting officer arranged their homes. Their reputation had gone ahead: they used foul language, had lice or scabies, didn't blow their noses, lied and stole, never washed or wiped but always wet their beds. Forced to take them in, people came to sift the tolerable from the impossible, the disagreeable from the disgusting.

It was swift and heartless like a slave market. Families

were divided, enemies thrown together. Children screamed, kicked, bit. Some were put back in the train to be taken elsewhere, anywhere. Lily found her hair, ears, fingernails being examined by a woman who said she had never seen such a swarm of little monsters. A pack of thieves, her husband called them. 'This one's the cleanest,' the woman said, twitching her nose at the choice. 'And looks healthy. What's your name, little girl?' They signed for Lily, put her in the car and drove away. The man said, 'You can only trust your luck.'

The Griceleys had no children. They were impelled by patriotism and a wish to do good, mainly to themselves. England would be better with more Griceleys, and they set about making one. The more they heard, the more convinced they were. The child was conceived in a scullery. Bastard daughter of the doorman of some low-class dance hall and a parlourmaid turned tart. Lived under a railway, without light or air or proper food. Couldn't tell a blackbird from a thrush. Vulgar accent, atrocious grammar, morals sure to decline. Didn't know the first thing about manners, let alone what to do in church. But it wasn't her fault and she was quite pretty for a Cockney. Showed willing, seemed bright, might be rescued, given a chance. A firm hand would do it, if nobody interfered. A clean break with the past. Leave it to the Griceleys.

'My bedroom is in the attic by the cook's,' Lily wrote, a month after Littlehampton, 'and there's a picture of Jesus. You can't hear the trains because it's six miles. I like porridge now. I get dinner at school and tea in the kitchen except on Sunday I have it with Auntie Gee and Uncle Gee which is how I call them. They say you are not to write much because it makes me cry. Auntie Gee took away my Duchess and gave me one who shuts her eyes. Hot water comes out of the tap so you don't have to boil. Uncle Gee says it's rude to say pardon. There's a cock on the chimney which tells the way it's blowing. Soon we will have autumn when the leaves come off and the gardener says I can sweep them. Uncle Gee says I mustn't say crikey because I don't know what it means and he is going to give me a penny when I don't all week and piano lessons perhaps.'

Each word was a needle in Leo's heart. They would make her into a lady. Teach her smart talk and drawing-room tunes and her place in society, and theirs and his. She was being rescued from her father by stuck-up prigs who thought they knew better, because they kept a house full of servants without working for it.

'You want to strangle them,' he said to Herbert Robinson.

'That's the song I like to hear,' Herbert said. 'A man of spirit, who's not going to be trodden on by a pair of fancy high heels from Bond Street. Not scared to stand and fight. We've got another war on, not just Hitler's – that's what they forget. And brother boy, we've got everything on our side.'

Lily's letters became fewer, with sentences that didn't sound like hers. When Leo sent a three-shilling postal order for her birthday it was returned by Mrs Griceley with a note that the girl was getting the right pocket money and more would spoil her. On Christmas morning he took a train to Wiltshire and walked the six miles carrying a doll's pram, second-hand but nice. At the front door he was told by a maid that the Griceleys were at church with Lily. Leo once had a way with maids and nearly told this one what was coming to her. But behind her he saw a Christmas tree with a doll's pram under it, bigger than his and new. She said he couldn't stand there, he must go round to the back.

'It doesn't matter, Dad,' Lily said, fresh from church and standing at the kitchen door. 'Anyway I'm getting too big for dolls.' It was true, she wasn't the child of Littlehampton. She couldn't ask him in, they were too busy with dinner.

'We could go for a walk,' Leo said, without hope. 'Just in the garden.' He longed to take her hand.

Lily looked at her shoes: 'They mustn't get muddy and it's almost dinner. Auntie Gee says I'm having it with them because I stirred the pudding. It's a shame –' She stopped, and looked wildly into her father's eyes and up to the rooks' nests in the leafless winter trees, and rushed on: 'But they'd let you have some in the kitchen, there'll be enough.'

If only one of them had cried, or laughed. Leo left the pram on the doorstep – like a dog, he felt, leaving a bone at someone's feet – and saw Lily throw her melting smile.

'Happy Christmas, Dad!' she said, quickly turning into the house: into her world of other people's carols and candles and crackers.

He walked six miles back. But he oughtn't to mind, it was best for her. Give her a leg up. Alone with him, it wasn't right for a girl. She would do better for herself, brought up by the Griceleys. Stand a proper chance. And it was healthier in the country. Safe from the bombs. Safe from Eve. At the station the Christmas trains were running at long intervals. He had missed one, and had to wait three hours. The pub was shut, the afternoon grew dim.

'Come and listen to George!' the ticket clerk called through the window.

'George?'

'Albert Frederick Arthur George,' the clerk sang to the tune of *Good King Wenceslas*. 'Defender of the faith, emperor of India, squire of Windsor, your sovereign lord and host if you've been in the nick, glasshouse, clink or quod.' He couldn't know that Leo had spent three Christmases in prison, none of them as unhappy as this. He pulled up chairs to the fire – a shiny rubbery man who bounced off everything he touched – and they listened to the radio.

'The festival which we know as Christmas,' the King began, 'is above all the festival of peace and of the home.'

'You got your own family at all?' the clerk enquired.

'Yes – yes, I suppose.' Lily would be listening to the King

[166]

in the Griceleys' drawing-room, her eye on the doll's pram.

'Lucky for some,' the clerk said.

The King said, 'True peace is in the hearts of men.'

'Myself I'm a bachelor, hence this merry day of duty.'

'The men and women of our far-flung Empire –'

'Speak for yourself, your majesty.' The clerk boiled a kettle, whistling *Once in Royal David's City*, and made a pot of tea. 'Not quite Windsor Castle, but in our own small way –'

'The great family of nations –' The royal voice was strained and thin, filtered through the radio.

'You hold with that sort of thing?' the clerk asked.

'After a dinner like the one he's just eaten –' Lily and the Griceleys had eaten one too. Leo had had nothing till this mug of tea.

'I believe from my heart that the cause which binds together my peoples –'

'Believe what you like, George,' the clerk said.

'Through the dark times ahead –'

'Darker for some. Try cycling home through the blackout with a puncture.'

'I said to the man who stood at the gate of the year –'

'Jesus wept, what's coming next?'

'"Give me a light that I may tread safely into the unknown." And he replied, "Go out into the darkness and put your hand into the hand of God."'

'Put it where it suits you, George.' The clerk switched the radio off.

The Griceleys would never switch off the King. They would stand for the national anthem and speak with reverence of the royal family, as holy as the one at Bethlehem. The Princesses were about Lily's age, so now they had one of their own. Soon they would be cutting the Christmas cake. Leo didn't envy them, he was happy by the fireside of this friendly railway clerk, though he ached for his daughter; and knew as the train carried him to London, full of soldiers singing in the half-lit carriages, that he was leaving her for ever.

'Poor Dad in London,' she wrote in the spring, 'because Auntie Gee heard a cuckoo yesterday and I did today. It goes cuckoo like anything.'

Leo didn't want her pity. He wasn't sure what he did want: the best for his daughter, but nobody told him what it was. He missed her fiercely; cooked the meals she used to give him; watched the girls coming in and out of the Palais, wondering always about Lily.

'Uncle Gee says it's good I was evacuated because the war is getting worse and Hitler wouldn't waste bombs on here because he'd only kill some rabbits.'

Uncle Gee could stuff himself, with his three-piece suits and condescension. Likewise Auntie Gee, the dried-out fleshless old bag. They could do with a bit of bombing. Leo had never seen them, but could imagine. They were contemptible, not just dangerous. Feeding Lily with ideas, never mind the asparagus. What was wrong with a working man's food – a bit of haddock and boiled potatoes, or beans and rice pudding from a tin?

'Except for the war,' Lily wrote, 'we'd be going to Torquay in the summer which is bigger than Littlehampton, but we're to stay at home and I'm to help in the harvest which is when they cut the corn.'

Home, she called it. Fourteen years old and teaching her father about the harvest. Next thing, she'd be sending food parcels to help out with his rations. She had better be careful. In the paper the other day a man got three months for selling hams on the side, from his own pigs.

The next thing, when it came, was worse: a letter from the Griceleys to say his daughter was fourteen, as if he didn't know, and should leave school. But the teacher said she was a clever girl, as if Leo didn't know that too, and deserved better than becoming a shopgirl or housemaid or munitions worker. She could be saved by going to a boarding school and the Griceleys would like to pay, but wanted something in return. They had consulted a lawyer and understood there was no obstacle to adoption. A court would view it with favour. They only needed the father's consent.

Leo was nauseated, then turned wild. Kidnappers! Murderers! Plotting to turn Lily into something she was never meant to be. Using influence, money, class, to work their poison. Bringing in the law. Hinting at the broken home, the background, the bombs. No mention of love. Nothing about their feelings. They hadn't got any. They were cold, hard. No wonder they had no children of their own – they couldn't do it, they were sterile, impotent. So they stole someone else's. Too easy. Take a man's daughter. Pick a good one, bright as a pin. Train her up. Teach her the tricks and make her grateful. Show her off, acting the little pet. Never mind the father. He can rot in his hole under the railway. Let the bombs fall.

'Calm yourself, my brother boy,' Herbert said. 'Get what you can out of them. There's always profit if you know where to look.'

'Profit! In losing Lily!'

'Time's on our side, I always say. Keep your eyes open, then step in and take the pickings.'

Leo wasn't so wise. He started drinking at lunchtime, before going to the Palais. When the manager caught him insulting a customer who arrived with a chauffeur Leo recognized the signs. He was on his way down. This time it wouldn't end in a flogging, but would be just as wounding. Drink was the best pain-killer. He took ten minutes off in the pub at six o'clock and again at eight. They could do what they liked. It was August and the Battle of Britain was on. Hitler had called for surrender, Goering had promised to destroy Britain, the sky was full of Germans. Leo had fought them before, and they hadn't beaten him and wouldn't this time. But he had learnt since then. Your

[169]

enemies aren't just the ones you're told to shoot at. They're all round you, they're even the ones who tell you to shoot. Because of their rank, money, class. It's a lifetime's battle and they have all the weapons. You can put up a fight, but they get you in the end.

He was given two weeks' pay and told not to come back. The money went in a week, on drink and horses. In the second week the Palais closed, forced by the war: Leo would have lost his job anyway.

'Lie low,' Herbert advised. 'Keep your head down so they can't snipe.'

'They'll get me, I'm finished, I'm too old.'

'As the man said, if you believe that you'll believe anything.'

The first round was lost, Leo knew. He would surrender Lily. With the war going the way it was, and himself without work, it was mad to think of having her back. The Griceleys had got what they wanted, he only hoped Lily would remember him. At least she was getting the chance he never had, and was safe.

When the raids began, his windows were blown in. The rain followed, washing away all trace of Lily. He hated the place now. Soon he was sheltering in Hyde Park Corner underground. He hated that too. People came from the East End every night, burrowing under London. They crowded the passages, slept on the platforms, filled every arch and stair and corner with bodies. Before the last train, children took rides up and down the line. Leo couldn't watch them without thinking of Lily. Lovers lay under newspapers, old people stretched out as if already dead. Draughts of soiled air blew down the tunnels. The smell was terrible. Smart West End people seldom came down here: this was a sewer, these were the rats. The danger wasn't of being bombed or buried or getting cholera, but of turning into something else. Another species would emerge on the surface tomorrow morning, or at the end of the war: pale

[170]

and blind, speaking a new language. Leo was glad that Lily was spared.

'Not to worry about the rent,' Herbert said, 'till we fix you with a job again. Mind you, times aren't easy.' The Gold Flake drooped on his lip, but never came unstuck. He got on his bicycle: 'Through all the changing scenes of life – we'll get by, you'll see. Till then –' And pedalled away.

They got Leo to sign the papers easily enough. The trick was to offer him ten pounds not to contest it. A court case would cost twice as much, so it was a saving all round – Leo's time and the Griceleys' money. Typical of the way they went about things: haughty, confident, successful. Anything to suit themselves. They'd get their reward when the revolution came. They had twisted the rules, cancelled the elections till the end of the war. Putting off their downfall, hoping for salvation, keeping the war going to save their skins. The end of the war! – the war to end wars. Same as last time. Fighting to make a world fit for heroes. Heroes' graves, they meant, in rows and rows with the Griceleys dancing on top. Ten pounds was the price for a man's daughter. He should spit on it and throw it back. But ten pounds was a month's wages. With no rent to pay, thanks to a stepbrother, and no family to keep, thanks to Eve vanishing with her Maltese pimp and Lily being sold, Leo could live off the money through August and September. Perhaps till October.

In October the Café de Paris, shut since the beginning of the Blitz, was reopened. Herbert heard the news and made arrangements: 'Don't let me down again, brother boy,' he said. 'It's an ill blitz that blows nobody good. Doorman in the West End isn't something to drop on you every day. You've got the experience now, not just the face and figure. And you'll get a better quality of customer than at the Palais. Could be useful to yours truly.'

Leo was pleased and grateful: 'Just see me bowing

[171]

them over the pavement,' and performed a courtly little mime.

'As the man said, all of us are in the gutter but some of us are looking at the stars.' Herbert's quotations, like his information, came from odd places.

Trooper Robb was made a sergeant, with 'Café de Paris' on his cap and three medal ribbons on his chest. He stood at the door, greeting customers on arrival and ushering them away on departure, till Saturday the eighth of March 1941, the night the bomb fell.

31

When the band begins *Oh Johnny!* Felix and Guy have ordered their fifth martinis. They met a few hours ago, there is much to find out. For Felix, to discover a stranger is to discover himself.

'I've never been in battle,' he says. 'It's something I've no idea about – my own resources. Do I fight or run away? Or stand there giggling?'

'You were in the Blitz, you behaved –'

'Not the same. Not the hand-to-hand stuff. You can't see the enemy. You can't hit back, you can only survive.'

'That's all I thought about in France – will I live or won't I?'

'When you know you won't, how d'you behave? Going down on the *Titanic*, what d'you do? Shut your eyes and listen to the band play *Nearer my God to Thee*? Head for the bar and swallow everything in sight? Grab the nearest woman and have her pants off, so you drown together, screwing to the end? Or d'you stand up on the poop, watching the tilting deck and the rising water, asking the same old questions you've been asking all your life – who am I? why am I here? what's the point? where the hell am I going? – knowing that nobody's going to tell you, ever?'

'You rush around being a hero.'

'I couldn't be brave, I'm a compulsive coward.'

'Saving the women and children, getting the boats away, heedless of yourself.'

'It's a thing I dream about. The stern's right out of the sea and I'm up there by the rail, being lifted higher and higher before the plunge. The funnels are going under, one by one, with a hiss as the water gets to the boilers. I love it, it's a marvellous moment. The last great ecstasy. I want to keep it for ever. And that's the terrible thing – it's like the insect that makes love once and dies. I know it can never happen again and I won't be here to remember it.'

'So you can't write a poem about it?'

'It's why anybody does – to preserve the moment.'

'For yourself?'

'And to tell other people. To sing a song.'

'So you need someone to listen.'

'You need a language, that's all. Then retire into your-self –'

'Because our self is all we have in common?'

'Creep into your hole and you'll find everyone is there.'

'Your oyster's the world?'

'The nucleus we share.'

'It sounds like a signalman flashing messages through the dark.'

'Sorry.' Felix sips his martini, afraid of getting pompous. These sudden wartime encounters are to be relished and he loves to try out his words. But they can sound false, however fragile. He doesn't want to frighten Guy away.

Guy asks, 'So that's the answer?'

'Recognize the moment and surrender.'

'You can't stop them. Moments by the million, tumbling over each other – how d'you choose?'

[173]

'Pick the one that suits you. Try it on, see if it fits, don't let it go.'

'Can't anyone have it?'

'Make it your own. Do it well, and you get the others envious.'

'It was available to them?'

'So simple, they let it pass.'

Guy wonders whether to go down and join Eunice for dinner. It is nine months since Lancelot brought him back from Dunkirk in his torpedo boat. Six months since Guy told Eunice that Lancelot was dead. He sees her often and knows she wants him for her lover, though he is much younger. He isn't sure himself. But their friendship is secure and this new one with Felix is tender, it could expire tonight if he isn't careful. He is enjoying it, he won't risk losing it. Like the moment, it is something to preserve. He says, 'You make it seem like luck.'

Felix says, 'Mostly it's knowledge.'

'And talent?'

'Talent is common. What's rare is knowing what to do with it. How to tame it. Make it do what you want. You brought it from the jungle we all came out of. It's up to you, and you're on your own. But you haven't got long, you can't waste time.' Felix stops abruptly: 'Time – it's food and poison, the giver and taker, all the clichés in the book. The moments keep coming, in all sizes – happy, sad, precious, useless, pelted at you faster than you can cope. You catch one and give it the best you can, while more fly past and get lost, wasted –'

'What a fate.'

'You can be saved if you surrender to the moment.'

'With conviction.'

'And honesty. Then any subject will do – anything you like.' Felix looks up from the bar, round the glittering spectacle. *Oh Johnny!*, turned up to full volume by Snakehips' band and Violet's microphone, comes flooding

[174]

through the circular hole of the balcony – like the sea, you may think, into a sinking ship. 'But the picture's shifting, and your judgement's all you've got. Plus your conscience. Go through that with a comb. Pick out the nits, watch for grey hairs. Unless you've pawned it for a ticket to one of the clubs. Paid your money and said your prayers – then it's easy. You get your subject through the letterbox with the gas bill, signed by whoever you fancy – Marx, Rousseau, Gandhi, Churchill, the Archbishop of Canterbury, the Pied Piper of Hampstead –'

'You need commitment?'

'Concern is enough.' Felix rolls his drink round in the glass, swilling it up the sides. 'But your conscience is vital. Sell it, lose it –' He is preaching, he must stop.

Guy says, 'Cynical, it sounds.'

'Only sceptical. Leery of the systems.'

'Withdraw into your private world, hoist an aerial and transmit your poetry to anyone who cares to pick it up.'

'It's not in code. I read the papers, I keep up. You must, to get through. Be involved. Be affected. Laugh and cry, and love. It's a matter of generosity, to balance the arrogance. Be susceptible. Poetry isn't a refuge, not something outside life. You can't escape the nightmare, you only find consolation . . . briefly . . . with friends, lovers –'

'With yourself.'

Something comes back to Felix that he once said: 'A poet's an ordinary man, more ordinary than most.' He repeats it and the words bring back the occasion: fifteen years ago, to Bunty in her Irish castle.

'*Oh Johnny, oh Johnny, how you can love!*' Violet sings downstairs.

It will be another four hours before she and Baxter can get away: four hours at the bar, for Felix. He might ask Harry for the pack of cards, when Guy leaves him to join Eunice. There is a hand that Miriam used to try for – all the aces – testing her chances, hoping it wouldn't come: it meant

[175]

failure, imprisonment, danger, and she never got it. Felix might try, teasing himself with memories and luck. Or go for a walk when the raid is over, along to Leicester Square and Covent Garden. If tomorrow wasn't Sunday there would be a pub open all night for the market workers. The smell of onions and spring cabbages. Carthorses snuffling in their nosebags. The first daffodils up from Cornwall. There are already some on the Café de Paris tables.

But he will stay here, feasting on the lovely picture. The scene is irresistible, definitely one of the Impressionists. The shimmer, the translucence, the marvellous explosion of blue light that suddenly, magically breaks over the balcony . . .

'Don't you think –?' Guy begins.

'Oh Johnny!'

32

'Give me the wide open spaces,' Celia says. She pushes her tin hat to the back of her head, letting her red hair float from under the brim, and laughs at Lionel laughing at her. They are crammed together, clutching each other for their lives. Other dancers laugh with this lovely girl in a tin hat, shuffling round the crowded patch of parquet.

'Oh Johnny, oh Johnny, how you can love!'

'I'm not complaining,' Lionel says into Celia's ear. 'If it wasn't such a squash we'd need some fancy footwork.'

'I bet you're brilliant.' Celia shouts to be heard. 'A real wizard.'

'I'm not Fred Astaire.'

'You've got the figure.' She was hugging it. 'An absolute partner's dream. I can see you. Breaking away. Tearing all over the place. Leaping on a table. On the piano. Up and down the stairs. Giving the girls a thrill. Me, anyway.' Celia's blue eyes, flapping between each gasp, get bigger every time. They will have to burst.

'I can't tell a rumba from a tango. I don't know what this is, except it isn't a waltz. I'd be falling down without the people. They're holding me up.'

'Certainly dense. And piping hot. I'm something in a stewpot.'

'Watch out, I'm hungry.'

'Vegetable stew. Because meat's rationed. Very thick. Nearly cooked. Being stirred. Round and round. Mustn't spill over. Mostly potatoes. And onions. I'm a bean. Getting nice and tender. You're a carrot. Soon we'll be done.'

'I can't wait.' Lionel wriggles in his RAF uniform.

'Don't you wish you were in the sky? Alone in your Hurricane. Being a bird. Nobody clinging to you.' She clings harder. 'Must be beautiful up there. Up in the sun. All to yourself. The rotten old world below. Free to go anywhere. No cares. Nothing to bump into. Nobody in sight.'

'Till the Messerschmitts come at you.'

'Hide-and-seek in the clouds. Don't pretend it's not exciting. One of the few.'

'You don't want to swallow that stuff.'

'You saved us. Everyone knows. Not just Churchill. If you heard what they say in Fighter Command.' She rubs her chin on Lionel's medal ribbon.

'It's not like that.'

'Let's have it, Lionel. The unvarnished truth. The naked facts.'

'You're on your bunk in the hut, having a cigarette, reading the paper, joking –'

'Telling dirty stories. Comparing women. Leering at the pin-ups. Don't tell me. RAF men are all the same.'

[177]

'In ten minutes you'll be dead, screaming down in flames.'

'You baled out last time. Lived to fight another day.' Celia presses closer.

'Another day I won't be so lucky.'

'You always will. I'm positive. Winners and losers. You're a winner. Remember that. Next time you see Jerry coming.'

'You want to fly away, but there isn't time.'

'He's terrified too. He wants to get back. Same as you. To his pin-ups. Big fat German ones. Bosoms out to here.' Celia shows him.

'You don't think of that. He's not a man at all, he's the enemy and he's trying to get you, and you've got to get him first.'

'Oh Johnny, oh Johnny, heavens above!'

Celia tosses her head and the tin hat nearly falls off. She catches it and puts it on Lionel. A fighter pilot in a tin hat. Together they dance on, moving slowly round the floor.

'I love you in a tin hat,' Celia says. 'The warrior in his armour. Oh Lionel –' She would unbutton his tunic if she could. She slides a hand under it, round the back, creeping up his shirt to feel the knuckles of his spine. 'Too much bloody armour.'

The four Canadians, eating at their table near the band, call out to Celia and Lionel as they pass, but the words are lost.

'What shall we do when the show starts?' Lionel asks. 'Sit with Eunice? Go up to the bar, to Felix and Guy?'

'We'll watch. Sit on the staircase. Grandstand view. I'll fix it with Charles.'

The head waiter is half-way up the stairs, posed like a statue. His ivory face is unflickering, an allegory for satisfaction. He has played his part, there is nothing left for him. You want to pinch him into life, but he has moved beyond.

All the tables are full. Charles is pleased with the scene, he couldn't have arranged it better.

Celia and Lionel reach the platform: step by step, pivoting and jigging along in front of the band. Snakehips, conducting with his back to the musicians, lifts the tin hat off Lionel's head and crowns himself with it.

'*Oh Johnny!*' Violet, her eyes wide open and fixed on some vivid Caribbean scene – a chocolate piccaninny rolling in the surf, a grizzled old man lying in his hammock, a mud-caked pig snorting in the shade, a pomegranate sun dropping through the palms – breaks into a loving, yearning smile which the dancers believe is for Snakehips. They cheer and stamp with the song. After a dozen bars Snakehips taps the tin hat with his baton, takes it off and lays it on Jennifer, the birthday girl with a huge gold key on a ribbon round her neck. She wears it briefly before giving it to her partner, the young captain of the Irish Guards. But he doesn't want it, it diminishes his rank. With a cry of 'Ma!' he puts it on the beautiful, tall, grey-haired, green-eyed woman from the same party. So she is the captain's mother. And something, a tiny dart from the past, tells you that you have seen her before.

'She's more sporting than Mummy,' Celia says. 'Gone to ground in her Welsh hotel. Fingers crossed. Thumbs twiddling. Tongue wagging. Telling everyone to make stinging nettle soup. Carrot jam. Toadstool salad. Never touches them herself. Rationing means nothing. She lives in the clouds. All wrapped up and nothing to do. Except send panic telegrams. To her daughter in the front line. Don't go out tonight.'

'Who knows? – perhaps she's right. You're in mortal danger, you'll be assaulted by an airman.' With one hand in the small of her back Lionel leans his thighs on hers: grey trousers against turquoise dress. The other hand is in her armpit, working towards the front. 'You'll wish you'd stayed at home.'

[179]

'That's not what Mummy meant. She remembers the last war. She had her fun. Quite naughty in her day. She knows I can defend myself. If I want to. I wasn't born yesterday. All the same. She gets these funny dreams. Like last night.' Celia laughs: 'I'll send a reply in the morning. "Not to worry, Mummy. Thanks for warning me. I took a tin hat. Wore it all night. Nothing else."'

The tall thin woman, with her soft smile, slips the tin hat on top of the sun-tanned little man in a white tuxedo she is dancing with, who reaches up in turn to place it on a woman with a fussy heap of curls that won't stand the weight. Shrieking, she lets a South African naval surgeon snatch it for his own partner, an Australian nurse, who surrenders it to a colonel of the Polish cavalry.

'Where shall we go afterwards?' Celia asks.

'Not far.'

'All the way, for me.' Her huge eyes fill with lust.

'Regent Palace is closest. You can get a room after midnight – the second shift.'

'You seem to know.'

'Twenty-four hours off?'

'Back on duty tomorrow night.'

'Me too.'

'All yours till then.'

'Enjoy yourself.'

'I shall.'

'How's the air commodore?'

'Looking for his ballerina.'

'Suits me.'

'You jealous, Lionel?'

'Just sorry we aren't at the Regent Palace.'

'After the show.'

'Leo Robb can get a taxi.'

'Quicker to run. Do it in two minutes. Through the bombs.'

'The raid will be over.'

'Get my tin hat back.' Celia, her arms round Lionel, draws tighter to him and rubs herself across his trousers, feeling for the bulge.

'Oh Johnny!'

Looking down from the balcony you can watch Celia's tin hat being tossed from head to head. It becomes a symbol, a sacrament for Lionel from his red-haired lover, but passed on gaily, promiscuously. It goes to a bald dome, a greasy scalp, a blue rinse, a permanent wave, a temporary blonde, a probable wig; to white strands and black tresses and golden ringlets and scurfy locks; to heads from Norway, New Zealand, Belgium, Denmark, Newfoundland . . .

It is a child's game – Old Maid or Musical Chairs. Who will be wearing the tin hat when the music stops? A pale unhappy woman with a double chin puts it on a laughing wounded marine with no chin at all, who puts it on a girl in a crêpe de Chine dress, who puts it on a boy in a blue suit, who puts it on a fat man in a velvet dinner jacket, who puts it on an officer in Free French uniform, who puts it back on Celia where it belongs, the heroine of the dance who . . .

'Oh Johnny!'

33

Eunice looks at her watch. Nearly ten to ten. What has become of Guy? The show will be starting any minute. And Betty and Humphrey should be here, or they will miss the fun. You may think that they should be warned to keep away, but Eunice can do nothing now, only wait and drink champagne. The taste – of wine and of the moment – is delicious.

34

'Don't you think –?' Guy is asking.

But he must be drunker than he seems. Five martinis on top of what he had at Eunice's. He slides off his stool and collapses on the carpet where he lies quite still, face upwards with a puzzled milky look in his eyes and a smile on his lips left by the unfinished question.

35

The waiter comes back to fill Eunice's glass. He lifts the bottle from the ice-bucket and wipes the drips. Then for some odd reason of his own, instead of pouring it out, he lays the bottle on its side on the tablecloth in front of her. Saying nothing, unless the little gurgle comes from him and not the bottle, he folds himself up and falls clumsily, like a bad actor, to the floor.

To Eunice he looks like an Italian, but most of them were interned last summer. Possibly he is Greek.

'Bugger,' she says aloud, to herself as much as to the lunatic man.

36

'Oh Johnny!'

'Oh Lionel!' Celia tosses her head and the tin hat falls off again. It won't stay on. She will do without it, and begins to put it back on Lionel. Tosses her head once more as she does so, to let her red hair float free. Sinks slowly, burying her face in him, like an imploring mistress in a melodrama – like a shot bird or a spent firework or a severed flower – down his front. Kisses her way down the buttons and buckle of his tunic and the aching promise in his trousers, still hardening as she passes. Sinks to Lionel's feet and stretches out on the polished dance floor, crowded now with the dead and wounded.

37

'Bugger,' Eunice says again: at the waste of champagne that comes frothing in gollops over the tablecloth. The waiter is flat on the floor beside her. Something else in gollops is coming through his shirt. 'Bugger' for that too. But mostly 'bugger' because the show has begun without Betty and Humphrey. They are on their way from Quaglino's, they have missed the start.

The drummer launches into a terrific roll. This is the way it always begins. The lights go out except for a single beam and the glow from the bar upstairs, where Felix and Guy are drinking. 'Bugger' for Guy also, for not coming down to join her. Now there will be a crescendo on the drum and a clash on the cymbals and the lights will come back, bursting over the chorus girls. Percussion. Dazzle. And an instant of dead silence caught between the last bang and the first applause.

'Wonderful!' someone whispers in the first dim silence. The whole band – Snakehips, Violet, Baxter and all – has vanished in a blue flash and smoke. This is something new. The greatest show in town. Trust the Café de Paris. You knew it was going to be good. You never expected this.

Snakehips is famous for modulation. His last is up to standard. Life slips into another rhythm. With hardly a jerk *Oh Johnny!* is transposed into a song without words, a lament without music. Snakehips is dead. So is Violet. This time the band doesn't play on while the ship sinks, but survivors from the *Titanic* would recognize the scene.

38

Felix feels something heavy on his head. A sandbag. He reaches up, but there is nothing.

'Eunice! Eunice!' Betty and Humphrey come running down into the foyer from the street: the two who went to Quaglino's.

As they pass, Felix says, 'She's having dinner,' and watches them run to the balcony. He doesn't understand. He remembers thinking of Degas or perhaps Renoir before the sandbag came on his head. A bomb doesn't occur to him. He has been hauled into the painting he was looking at. Floundering in pigment. Bits of wood and glass and canvas over him.

Then he knows what it was, though he can't remember

an explosion. The noise was too loud to hear. His nerves were spared, he was drugged by a gland that restores consciousness by degrees, gauging his strength to bear it. He has never been so close before. He will recognize the symptoms in a minute. The thing is not to panic. To keep calm. It isn't easy with a dead man on the floor, knifed in the back by a blade of glass.

39

Baxter remembers hearing a thin twang like a piano wire snapping. Into that tiny noise his sister disappeared. He brought her from Jamaica for this: to be blown to bits in front of him in the middle of a song. He is too numb for grief, incapable of an emotion. Snakehips too – butchered where he stood at the platform edge. They've stopped that wriggle of the pelvis for ever. Made a mess of him. They'll have to clear it up themselves.

But the rest of the band has survived. One man has both legs broken. Another holds out his clarinet for blood to dribble from the end. A third sags over his trombone, winded by blast. The drums have been blown against the wall. The double bass lies smashed under a beam. The piano has been brought to its knees like a hamstrung animal. There was once a bear pit down here, and the ghosts are still around.

40

Opening her mouth to gasp, Eunice dimly sees the young naval officer check the time on his watch. Then he looks at his mother. Then he screams. The woman's head is still on her shoulders, but her face has gone. Simply wiped off. Darkness and smoke and the young man's screams. At first Eunice thinks it is herself screaming, and shuts her mouth to stop. But it goes on. She wants to say 'bugger' once more for the screaming man, but can't do it. Her voice is locked. Her eyes are clogged with dust, her ears blocked to everything except the screams. The faceless woman, who danced here twenty-five years ago and was going to dance again tonight, nods her head twice as if saluting her two partners – the husband drowned at Jutland and the son screaming across the table – before toppling forward into her coffee cup. She would never scream, she would rather die.

Someone flicks a cigarette lighter on.

'Bloody fool!' a man shouts. An officer, by the sound of him. The young captain of the Irish Guards who was dancing with Jennifer. 'Put it out, damn you – there might be gas!'

It was like this in the trenches, Eunice thinks. *Journey's End*. So this is what happens. The screams subside into low cries. Groans and whispers come from the dark. Shadows wave across the one bright light, streaks of paleness hover in the glow from upstairs, phantoms harden into living figures as the dust settles.

'Eunice! Eunice!'

Someone is shouting, again and again.

'Eunice!'

[186]

She can't think why the word is so familiar. The voice too. Is it herself out there in the dark? Has she departed from her body and is searching for the exit? A way out? Where to?

'Eunice! Eunice!'

Two voices. Betty and Humphrey back from Quaglino's, of course. They got here in time, after all. She can see them on the balcony, or what is left – half of it has fallen to the floor below. Two friends up there. Shouting for her. Peering down. In coats over their evening dress. Staring into the mangled, bleeding rubbish. So they didn't miss the show.

'Thank God you made it!' Eunice shouts back, glad to find her voice unlocked. 'It's incredible!'

They tumble down the wrecked staircase – past the place where Charles was standing a minute ago – and reach Eunice's table. The three hug each other.

'Join the party,' Eunice says, and picks up the champagne bottle.

Half of it has drained away, but the glasses are still standing. Betty and Humphrey can share the one that was meant for Guy. He doesn't deserve any. As Eunice pours out the wine the froth rises with a layer of dust on top. She says 'Bugger' again, and wipes it off with her finger.

41

It was only a fifty-kilo bomb, much smaller than the ones that the Germans had been dropping lately, that fell at ten minutes to ten. It slipped clean through the building above, avoiding the Rialto cinema on one side and Lyons Corner House on the other, aiming for the centre of the balcony ring, and exploded at waist height in front of the band. A second bomb followed without exploding; merely broke open on hitting the floor and spread its disgusting

chemicals over the mess left by the first. Thirty-four
people were killed and sixty badly injured.

During the next hours you may believe that the whole
night is a piece of art. Details fall into place, there is no other
way they can go. There is a rightness in each line, shadow,
stroke of paint. A horrible perfection has been reached,
which you see could never be otherwise.

A few people, shattered but annoyed at being cheated of
the show, sum up the destruction: there is no future down
here tonight. They pick their way up to the street, reeling
figures in evening dress or uniform emerging on the pavement from a scorching underground ordeal, to be stared at
like freaks by the pitiless gang that gathers at the sniff of
blood; and go home or to the nearest pub, astonished to be
alive.

For the rest, for many reasons or for none, it is impossible
to leave the dead and wounded. If you stay you will see
some odd behaviour, to hearten or depress or only to
perplex you.

42

Felix drops from his stool and kneels beside Guy; watches
in surprise his own blurred tears fall on the lieutenant's
uniform. He didn't cry for Diana, the Brigadier's daughter,
but he does for this young man, a stranger till this evening
and now a stranger again. Surely the face can't stay like
that. The eyes will blink and smile, the lips finish the
question: 'Don't you think –?' Think what? Felix shakes him
by the shoulder and hears the suction, the ooze of blood
seeping on the floor. But the flying stiletto left only the
neatest hole.

The sense of weakness is overwhelming. Wooden beams

and steel joists slant from the walls, blocks of masonry smoulder with powdered plaster, beds of glass glitter dimly in the corners. The plants in pots along the balcony have been stripped like bushes by a plague of locusts. A chandelier, collapsed like a crinoline, lies in a heap. Dust fills the place, solid curtains of it hanging from above. Through it comes a bitter smell to choke the lungs of anyone who breathes. The silence grows into a murmur of stifled human noises, then a chorus – coughing, moaning, sobbing. What can a man do but wonder why he lives, and weep for this insult to his friend?

Other men are doing things. That frightened military voice cuts through, shouting about the risk of gas. Now there is another, quieter and closer, pulling Felix out of his shock. Somewhere behind the bar. Speaking into the telephone. Good man – he knows what to do. Call the wardens' post. Get the system going.

'Direct hit, I'd say,' the man is saying, urgently into the telephone. 'Quite a slaughter. Nasty – very nasty.'

Felix can see him. It is Leo, the doorman. Trooper Robb. Smart soldier. Transformed. Deserves to be promoted. Something has been switched on in his eye. The light of battle. All that training years ago is paying off. The sergeantly figure in maroon, so formal but also false as he sweeps guests in and out of taxis, has been fired into action: the trigger sprung. This is Leo's moment, he will rise to it. The salt of the earth. Never at a loss. He was up at the street door when the bomb fell, he came doubling down to the bar to call the warden.

'Very nasty indeed, I'd say. Hop on your bike, boy.' They will be here in a minute. Ambulances, fire brigade, heavy rescue squad. After six months of this they have the drill worked out. Leo puts down the telephone, takes a quick look round the scene – this hell down here – and doubles back upstairs to his post.

Felix is impressed, but doesn't move. A minute, two

[189]

minutes, five, have gone since the bomb. He has done nothing but weep over a corpse. As air-raid warden he leapt into each incident, enjoying his own energy. But here as victim, a poet at the bar with a lot of gin inside and a dead friend at his feet, he is useless.

43

Baxter fingers the keys of his saxophone – all he has left; wipes the dust off it, opens the drain, blows the spittle out, fixes the cap over the mouthpiece, packs it into its case. This war is nothing to do with him: a silly joke between white men, a typical plot. They drop bombs on each other, and black men get killed. And a black girl. They called her the hottest singer in town, they said they loved her. Call that love.

Nothing counts, nothing has a meaning without his sister. He doesn't care what they do next, he won't wait to see. No bacon and eggs tonight. Pack up and go away. Go round to the Boogie Woogie Club, where Violet used to sing. Good friends there – not the kind who murder in the middle of a song. This slaughterhouse. Things will be warming up at the Boogie Woogie. Go there for the sake of sanity. Have a blow and think of Jamaica. The butterflies, the indigo hills, the shining teeth, the girls with upturned hopeful breasts. Play all night at the Boogie Woogie. By morning he might be fit to face himself again. To face Sunday on his own.

Like a sleepwalker Baxter steps off the platform on to the mess of flesh and debris. Yellow treacle is spreading over it from a thing like a broken oil drum, smelling of poison. People are pulling themselves out, brushing themselves down, catching up with life. Baxter stumbles to the foot of the staircase and sees Eunice Fancourt at a table, drinking with two friends. Her red dress, her luminous vitality. Another plot. They kill a man's sister without looking up from their champagne. Baxter won't bother, either. Eunice has forgotten that once she was screwed by him for a week, and loved it.

He starts up the ruined staircase. At the bottom the sun-tanned little man in a white tuxedo is whimpering like a child in the lap of the tall woman he was dancing with. Higher, Baxter reaches a sheaf of menus on the carpet and remembers Charles standing there: the ivory-faced manipulator, the black-tailed enigma. He has vanished from the world, ushered himself out, not even leaving a last sepulchral smile, only his menus dropped in the haste of going. At the top another waiter, buried to the chest in plaster, lies hoping for release. His silence makes the screams from others louder. Let them scream. Baxter crosses the foyer.

At the bar Felix Bayne is sitting on a stool: Violet's lover who comes every Saturday for his pleasure. A glass in his hand, a dead man beside him. They have no hearts, these whores and pimps. They can tidy up their own filth, bury their own bodies. Violet's too. Baxter isn't going to help. He goes on upstairs, making for the street.

44

'Thank God you came,' Eunice says.
   'Should have stayed at Quag's,' Humphrey says.
   'Thank God, thank God.'
   'This is where the action is,' Betty says.
   'Thank God.' Eunice pours out the rest of her champagne and they drink, it is the only thing to do. No comment is

adequate for this. They have been flung into a dream, they must act as dreamers till they wake. In time they will get busy with something, but they can't see what it will be. Let the dust settle, the screams stop, the dying die.

The dust: the choking dust that drifts through the twilit restaurant. People blow and cough, wipe their plates and cutlery, flick their napkins – spectres moving in the mist. And the screams: the young naval officer can't keep it up, it doesn't put back his mother's face, but from everywhere come wails of misery, howls of pain. And the dying: some have finished; have got it over without fuss like Eunice's waiter, stretched beside the table with the blood turned off, ready for a coffin. Others are doing it in less hurry, with heroism or terror, surprise or irony. A few will spend the rest of the night and all tomorrow dying.

'What amazes me is –' Eunice begins, but forgets what it is.

'That you're alive,' Humphrey says: a lean man with a doggy face, a City broker doing well out of the war. Soon, you may think, he will be called up into the army and get a staff job if he isn't rejected as unfit.

'More amazing to be dead,' Eunice says indignantly. Being killed is ridiculous.

'Funny it hasn't happened to us before,' Betty says. 'It's always in the next street. Or while one was out. Or un-exploded.' She is Humphrey's wife, chirpy and crisp and impatient. You wouldn't give their marriage a chance, you can see Betty going off with a man in battledress when it suits her.

'We still haven't been hit,' Humphrey says, as if it is inescapable one day.

'My God!' Eunice cries, jumping up.

The naval officer, having spent his screams, can only press his fists into his face to make sure it hasn't gone like his mother's. Between extraordinary little noises he appeals to Eunice: 'She's all right, isn't she? She'll be fine, I know

[192]

she will. She's perfectly – I mean, it's nothing deep and they can do wonderful things, can't they?' But the woman is appallingly dead, slumped over her coffee, faceless and still. The mess is beyond the mind's acceptance, therefore tolerable.

'Humphrey,' Eunice says briskly, 'we'll get her on that bench.' They lift the woman off her chair and lay her on a velvet settee against the wall. Betty spreads a tablecloth over her and the son sits by his mother's head, wailing. Eunice simmers with rage: 'Good God, man, what sort of sailor are you? I had one last summer, the best in the world – blown up and sunk. What d'you expect?' She feels tears coming for Lancelot and this dead woman.

'It's my fault.'

'This is war.' Eunice is boiling over. 'What's your name?'

'John.'

'John, of course.' It is obvious, it couldn't be anything else. A brave, wholesome name. She needn't have asked.

'We changed places.'

'Yes, I saw.'

'To let her see better.'

'I was watching. You were being thoughtful, you're not to blame.' Eunice hopes he can hear the sarcasm. 'Then you were going to dance.'

The young man chokes: 'You know?'

'She danced with your father here before he was killed.'

'You know everything.'

'It wasn't difficult, John. It was written all over you. Following in his steps, weren't you?'

'He was killed in action.'

'She was so proud of you.'

'We shouldn't have changed places.' He has been jolted towards recovery by this stranger who knows so much. 'It was supposed to be me. I was always meant –'

'Nobody's meant to get killed.'

[193]

'I was expected . . . I was told as a boy –' He breaks down and starts to cry.

'For God's sake.' Eunice leaves him.

It is getting lighter as if the Sunday dawn, taken by surprise, is creeping in too soon. Torches sweep round the ruin, looking for horrors, for hope, for a gap in the present chaos to glimpse the future. In places a match or cigarette lighter spurts brightly and the young captain shouts to put it out: captains can't help shouting, it is their function. Candles are lit, bringing holiness to the hell. Someone produces a hurricane lamp, someone jams open the doors to the kitchen where the lights still work. From the bar upstairs a pallid moon-glow falls on the scene.

The closeness of destruction to survival is weird. Eunice's waiter has been blown dead by blast, though he has no damage. The soothing incorruptible Charles, who directed other fates, has been whisked from the staircase into oblivion with only his menus to mark the spot. The cigarette girl has been raped and abandoned, her legs left on the floor in their network cage, more false than ever and detachable, as Eunice guessed: above the purple tutu her gorgeous body has been sliced off. The Dutch admiral who bought a box of Sobranies from her is under his table among plates, spoons, bread rolls, spring daffodils, sending out distress signals in Dutch and English. Above, his wife is eating her mushroom omelette while it is hot.

'Everybody report to me!' the captain shouts, taking command of others when he can hardly control himself.

'Everybody ignore that idiot!' Eunice shouts back, sorry that she has to shout.

The tall green-eyed woman, more unearthly since the bomb, leaves her sun-tanned little man still whimpering and approaches Eunice: 'My son gets nervous, I'm afraid.'

Slipping off his dinner jacket and bow tie someone says he is a doctor, and collects a party of helpers who move with

[194]

him into the kitchen. But nobody can stop the captain: 'Casualties not to be moved till the ambulance –'

'Bertie, darling, please!' his mother says. 'Do shut up or you'll start a riot.'

In a haphazard way a sort of order forms itself in the wreckage. The shattered restaurant assumes another purpose. Tables are piled away, chairs and benches turned into beds. Eunice, with Betty and Humphrey and the tall woman, begin bringing in the dead and wounded from the battlefield. The kitchen becomes a hospital. The band platform, clasped in the broken arms of the gold and crimson staircase, is a morgue. Its first two bodies, being nearest, are Violet's and Snakehips Johnson's.

45

'Nasty, very nasty,' was what Leo called it on the telephone. The rescue people should be here, they aren't usually as slow as this. But the Café de Paris isn't the only incident in the West End tonight. The services must be badly stretched.

In time Felix is stirred by Leo's example and Guy's death. He straightens the body, closes the eyes, puts his own coat over the face. He has done this before, but never for a friend. He has never made and lost a friend so quickly: three hours since they met at Eunice's.

Nasty is an understatement. Felix is frightened by the helplessness. Smashed bottles lie under a coating of dust, Harry's cards have been blown across the bar. Felix looks for the aces, but a whole pack of them wouldn't be bad enough for this.

In the foyer people rise from the ground like sleepers waking; stretch and rub themselves, blink and cough and blow their noses; pick up their lives to see the damage. They are too tender to make decisions. The first to act are the ones who stumble to the stairs up to the street, and Felix nearly follows. London is up there: buildings, shops, traffic – friends of his, allies against this nightmare. Tomorrow the buses will be running as they did today. London will go on.

Down here you can't be sure. Felix crosses the rubble to the balcony and looks over: a slag heap covering the dance floor under the hole in the ceiling made by the bomb. Wood, metal, bricks, glass, a mass of fabrics; furniture broken up and scattered. But at the back some tables are intact, where diners sit in a trance among the crockery and food.

'Felix!' Eunice calls from below, helping the tall woman extricate a waiter.

'Not Felix Bayne?' the woman asks, speaking more to herself, her green eyes lit with curiosity. She watches as he comes picking his way down the staircase, like a mountaineer down scree. 'The poet?'

'You know him?'

'He won't remember.' She lets a small laugh escape: a laugh, even at such a time, is a way to mark this fluke of life.

Felix says, 'Guy's dead,' when he reaches them.

The famous mirrors and ornate panels have been splintered into darts. You may not have known that beauty can be destroyed in one rending moment. At least the *Titanic*, except for the iceberg hole, kept up her appearance till she sank, as lovely as on her launching day. Here you can see undamaged bits of flotsam – an unopened champagne bottle, a trolley of *hors d'oeuvres*, Violet's microphone – but they enhance the ravage. And the destruction of material is a puff of dust, a scrap of plaster, to the outrage of a sudden death.

'Guy's dead.' Felix looks hard into Eunice's eyes, sealing the end of a man's life into her mind: 'A piece of glass.'

'Guy's dead?' Eunice is saved by disbelief. The speed is

an anaesthetic, the switch of life to death too shocking to be felt. Guy and she would be dining now and he was coming home to bed, the first since Lancelot. 'Guy Ronson –' she says softly, shutting her eyes to keep him: the young lieutenant brought back by Lancelot from Dunkirk; shy and boyish, difficult to imagine leading a platoon of soldiers in the retreat from France; fighting on the beaches, embarking with his men; tactful, truthful, the obvious choice for a messenger to bring news of Lancelot; the choice too, though less obvious because he was much younger, for her next lover; but chosen now by death. Tender for his age, Felix called him this evening; breakable, soluble, brittle. Too right! Too bloody right! Too breakable and he broke just now, aged twenty-four, sitting on a bar stool with a poet and a dry martini. Rescued from Dunkirk for this. Eunice clenches her eyeballs to squeeze the grief, to clutch the monstrous obscenity of a random bit of glass that can do what no bullet ever did. Pierce Guy's uniform and reach his heart.

There is so much to be done: the trapped to be freed, the wounded taken to the kitchen, the dying eased, the living encouraged. Beams that supported the balcony must be lifted, fallen ceilings pulled away, chairs broken up into shovels. Fingers get cut by glass, feet sink into cavities, shoes fill with rubbish. The yellow sticky stuff oozing from the second bomb, to redeem itself for not exploding, stinks of murder.

The Dutch admiral, the cigarette girl's last customer, is still under the table. His wife has finished her omelette and begun on his. There is a peppering of dust on it but she won't waste anything, she needs food. The admiral sees that nobody will answer his signals, in whatever language, and he will have to save himself. He grunts his way out, and stands up.

'Good,' he says, scanning the view as if emerging on his bridge to find the fleet sinking round him; unsteadied by the explosion but excited at the disaster, if excitement can touch such a stolid man. 'Good,' seeing the cigarette girl's legs cut off above the tutu. 'Good,' at the dance floor piled with wreckage and bodies. And 'Good,' finding that his wife has eaten both omelettes. He opens the Sobranies and lights one.

'Good,' the wife says. It is their favourite word, it folds them in goodness. He watches her lay down her knife and fork, swallow her wine, hold her stomach for a moment's flatulence, before they go to work: staunching wounds with napkins, tearing up tablecloths for bandages, dabbing at cuts with champagne, loosening collars and belts. With the fewest words they rouse the cooks and dishwashers, and organize a system for the doctor's team. A hand has been sliced, an eye stabbed, a face riddled with glass: 'Good.' The Dutchman and his wife welcome each new case. They never expected to finish up like this tonight, but they aren't put out. In these unpredictable times it seems a proper way to end.

The Café de Paris makes a stylish setting. Patients are laid out on the draining-boards, splints are made from wooden spoons, saucepans and mops and ladles are used for surgery. The stirrings of life, like objects in a lifting fog, penetrate the chamber of death. Beauty will prevail through the ugliness. A vision of truth emerges as the dust settles. The wrecked restaurant recovers an elegiac version of its elegance, nobler in calamity than before.

Lionel is next with news of death: 'I thought someone had thrown their drink in my face. Squirting from the balcony. We were dancing and it came splashing down. I felt it trickling, Christ –' He is alone.

'Celia – ?' Eunice asks cautiously, knowing the answer.

'All because of that mummy of hers, having a dream. Sending a telegram, Christ –'

'Celia –' The beautiful Celia is dead, the ordinary Lionel

[198]

alive. To Eunice it is a private insult. She never liked Lionel much, but loved Celia more than she knew.

'It's coming back,' Lionel says. His uniform is torn, showing blood on his shirt. On his head is Celia's tin hat. 'She was sinking out of my arms, I couldn't hold her up, Christ –' This man killed Germans in the sky; saw his Hurricane plunge in flames as he dropped on a parachute; was saved by his Mae West and picked out of the sea; has survived this other battle with a German airman, under ground.

'Sit down, have a drink.' Felix finds a glass for him.

'She was lying on my feet. She wasn't wearing her tin hat, she took it off. Gave it to someone. Or it fell –' But seeing Eunice and Felix look up, feeling it on his head, Lionel puts a hand up to touch it: 'Christ –'

'Here, drink this.'

'Tonight –' Lionel's voice is crackling like a fighter pilot's on the radio, coming through the clouds. 'Tonight –' This isn't what Celia promised. They were going to the Regent Palace, she was going to wear the tin hat and nothing else all night, and send her mother a telegram in the morning. 'She said I'm always a winner. Christ –'

The young captain comes blustering up. 'All medical staff report to the kitchen.' But nobody obeys. His authority has lost its ring, like a cracked bell, and no longer works. 'You there,' he says to Felix, faltering before an older man: 'You –'

'Bertie darling,' his mother says, 'don't you remember your tutor – Felix Bayne?'

'Well, for heaven's sake!' Bertram's face splits with laughter at this escape from duty, the relief from being a captain. He holds out his hand: 'It's a tiny world. What a place to meet! After all these years. Who'd have thought – ?' The platitudes come tumbling out.

Felix finds himself taking Bertram's hand, reaching back to touch a boy in an Irish castle and returning the convention: 'Nice to see you again.' But he is more shocked

[199]

by this than anything tonight. The greetings of people who haven't met for fifteen years, framed in such disaster, are indecent as no death or laceration can be. And what happened to turn a child on a pony into this dreadful officer?

'This calls for a celebration,' Bertram says.

'Well, hardly –'

But formalities may be the best refuge from the enormous force that is possessing Felix. For the first time since the bomb – ten minutes, two hours, two years ago – he can feel his unique existence, the diamond at his heart, whole and undimmed and giving joy, not just in being alive but in the point of life. He knows he is lucky – there is no logic in survival – but a climax has occurred tonight, a pattern has been completed. The appearance of Bunty and Bertram, impossible yet natural, has closed a gap.

'"On a poet's lips I slept."' He remembers the way Bunty's voice can lick the air, uncoiling as she herself uncoils and touching only the person it is meant for, like a blessing. This woman gave him something that has infused his poems. There is no generosity in him that wasn't planted by Bunty. He looks at her now; watches her as they work through the night with Eunice, the Dutch admiral and his wife, Betty and Humphrey and Lionel, fumbling in the chaos, jiggling the disorder to make some sense.

46

The four Canadians are dead. They crossed the Atlantic in a convoy, docked this morning, reached London this afternoon to fight for England; to die on their first night, having dinner. Eunice remembers her brief rage at finding her table taken. She would have survived anyway, even there, and saved the Canadians. But danger was what they came for, they said: 'Be seeing you!' James the First's kilt has been blown off, he is wearing nothing underneath. Eunice has never seen such a cock, lying useless on his thigh. With admiration and sorrow she lays a napkin over it and helps Felix lift the body to put with the others on the platform; then James the Second and the two nurses. She can't remember their names or which of them got engaged at sea, but they died drinking champagne.

In the top of her stocking Eunice has their cork. She pulls it out, presses it softly in her fingers – a bequest from four dead strangers – and slides it back, knowing that she will keep it. She says to Felix, 'It's the mystery that I can't cope with.'

'Why some people – ?'

'I wish I knew.'

'It might be terrifying.'

Some people who are scarcely hurt believe they are already dead. Some who are dying are certain they have escaped. The sun-tanned little man in a white tuxedo who was dancing with Bunty is still whimpering at the bottom of the staircase, as if offended that he has no battle scars to show. The birthday girl, Jennifer, who was dancing with Bertram, has been stripped except for the big gold key. Felix has a vision of the photographer in Berlin, beaten up and left in the street with nothing but his Leica round his neck. Jennifer's forehead is torn open, her face is a mask of blood with holes cut for eyes and mouth. Felix and Eunice wrap her in a tablecloth and sit waiting with her.

'Sorry about this.' Jennifer can turn it into a mere accident, a problem of her own, nothing serious. 'Silly of me – really, you mustn't bother.' She might have upset her wine, she hates being a nuisance. 'I've seen you before,' she says to Eunice.

'At a party.' It is the same Jennifer, and Eunice peers into the mess to find a schoolgirl's spotty face.

[201]

'I loathed myself, I was so gauche.'

Eunice laughs: 'You had a tray of anchovy toast.'

'And dropped them on the floor.'

'You did me a lovely favour.'

'Tell me,' Jennifer says. An imminent calm lies beyond the agony.

'That man you –'

Jennifer swivels the eyes in her terrible mask to look at Felix. He can only watch the last awful, inspiring moments of an unknown life. She called herself gauche and she may have been till now, but grace transfuses her.

Eunice says, 'It was fatal.'

'I saw the way you clicked. He was my god, I was so jealous.'

'You hung around, you wouldn't leave us.'

'I hated you.'

'We made you drop the tray.'

'I cried all night,' Jennifer says, a smile invisible on her face except in the bright eyes.

'We blessed you.'

'And lived happily ever after.'

'We had a son called Hugo – he's three.'

'Lucky you.'

'Thanks to you.'

'I'm lucky too.' You may not agree: this mangled girl on her twenty-first birthday, on the fringe of life. 'All of us are lucky.'

Eunice thinks of Guy and Celia, Snakehips and Violet, the four Canadians; and Jennifer being laid beside them. 'The ambulance will be here,' she says, hating her dishonesty.

'I'll be all right. Bertie can take me home.' A pulse of torture shoots through Jennifer's body. When it has passed she asks, 'Where is he?'

'Fixing things,' Felix says. 'Organizing people, taking charge.'

[202]

'Good for Bertie.'

'Have you known him long?'

'He needed another girl, it's all I'm ever asked for – to make up numbers.' She sounds muted and remote, talking from another room. 'Someone said it was my birthday, so he gave me this silly key and we were dancing and all his troubles came out. He's been in the army since school, but never in battle. Never fired a shot in anger, he was saying, when it all blew up. It's what he always wanted.' There is a trace of mockery in this dying girl. As she moves away her fading voice gets sharper.

Eunice, assailed by the need to distract her, says, 'Felix was Bertie's tutor once.'

'We met again just now,' Felix says. 'Bertie was a boy –'

As if hearing his name Bertram appears: 'How's my birthday girl?' But he can't bear the sight, he won't stay long.

Frantically Eunice says, 'It's Felix's birthday too.'

'Happy birthday, dear Felix,' Jennifer sings, tunelessly from the distance.

Bertram joins in loudly and finishes the verse; then exclaims, 'What a night of coincidences!'

Jennifer begins to say, 'It takes a bomb –' but another convulsion severs her words.

In embarrassment Bertram says, 'Not much longer now – the chaps will be along.'

In the destruction of her face, darkening as the blood dries, Jennifer's eyes are on Felix, but her mind is hard to follow: 'In Ireland, was it? . . . your tutor, d'you remember? . . . she's your mother, the tall lady . . . she was ravishing when she was young . . . d'you think they were lovers? . . . tutor and tutoress . . . now she's got that funny little rabbit in a white coat, I wonder why . . . good-bye, and thanks for asking me . . . silly of me to drop the tray . . . what a mess . . . don't bother, please, I'll pick them up . . . thanks so

[203]

much . . . I'm tired, I'll find my own way home . . . any time you like . . . a spare girl . . . I'm always free . . .'

Bertram is keen to get away: 'This is the limit, I can't think what's stopping them, I'll go and reconnoitre.' He must be busy, he won't wait for anyone who can't keep up. A soldier is meant to advance, not stay and tend the wounded.

Jennifer goes on talking, while Eunice and Felix try to catch the retreating words. Soon her voice, getting thinner as it stretches to reach them, will snap.

Eunice knows she must fill the remaining minutes. Her inadequacy alarms her. But nothing can frighten Jennifer, this mutilated girl whom now she loves and weeps for, forgetting the uncouth schoolgirl. She looks at Felix, and suddenly he takes Jennifer's hand and begins to speak.

47

Looking down from the tottering balcony twenty minutes after the bomb you may notice the normality, the sense of this being nothing exceptional. Londoners are used to it, they aren't going to make a fuss. Only Bertram's voice rises above the murmur of people who are calmly rectifying the mess, though few have done it before. Shock is followed by an instinct to continue, not to be checked but to move on into the night, towards the morning.

You may be surprised at the imperturbability, the famous British phlegm. People who would rage at being given a chipped teacup keep their tempers at this disaster. It was nobody's fault, it couldn't have been prevented, it must be taken into stock and absorbed with other trials.

You may be surprised to see Herbert Robinson at work down there, a nimble figure in the twilight, nursing the wounded, propping up the dying, carefully lifting the dead. This is what the Blitz has done for Londoners. Everyone is in it together. The famous wartime spirit. Churchill's inspiration. The bulldog breed. People passing in the street, hearing of the bomb, have come down to help. They got here first, before the ambulances and rescue squads, and waste no time. Blood is draining away, hearts are stopping. Speed is vital. Herbert's stub of Gold Flake is missing from his lip, but he still wears his green pork pie and hasn't taken off his trouser clips. You would never guess he was a man to hurry, ready with a deft pair of hands to offer a glass of water or a tourniquet, but in these strange times you can expect anything.

48

Holding Jennifer's hand and hardly taking breath, releasing words like an impromptu prayer, Felix says, 'You got it right, we were lovers in that castle and here we are, blown together by a bomb, otherwise she'd have gone on dancing with her little white rabbit and I'd be up there at the bar, the same as any Saturday, not giving her a thought though she's never far away, she was my first love and the keynote to the rest, the note they start from and return to, always sounding somewhere underneath, telling me it all began with her . . . Jennifer, we've never met before and I'm bursting with the luck that puts me here, holding your hand and I don't want to let it go, your hand or the chance, because *carpe diem* is my motto, seize the day though I haven't always done it, I hate to think of the days I've missed . . . Grab the day and hang on to it and to hell with the future, don't trust the future, it's a sham, it's put there by the enemy, it lets you down though it's too late to tell you . . . When I was a boy I wrote a poem about a statue with a clock for a face, watching the people pass, and they smashed it so as not to see the hands go round but it went on ticking in their ears . . . I know you're not a child, you're twenty-one today but I feel the same as I used to with my son when he was small and couldn't go to sleep . . . It's a privilege because already you've gone further than any of us, you can hear the answer to the secret, you've got there first and it's like being with my son when he was still close to the darkness he came from . . . He hadn't lost touch with the mystery and magic and simplicity and I held his hand and sang a stream of nonsense and looked in his eyes, hoping he'd shut them and go to sleep and let me write a poem or open a bottle or peel his mother's clothes off yet hoping he'd stay awake because I might see through his eyes into the dark and find the secret there but he drifted into the light when he grew up and now he's like the rest of us . . . We can't turn out the light and go back into the dark, it's only when we're with someone near the beginning or the end that we feel it again . . . If that sounds sentimental it's too bad but don't get me wrong, Jennifer, I love the bright lights as much as anyone, I'm a sucker for the cheap thrill and the easy option and the short cut and the quick return, the tricks we play to dodge the pit . . . If you're listening you'll think I contradict myself but I have no theories, not even principles, I've avoided them . . . I catch myself saying something I don't believe because I want to test myself and try out a new thought and put it into words and look at them and listen and if I like them it's good and if I don't it's good too, good practice and the words aren't spoilt or wasted but I can't always get them right first time . . . I've never done this before, talked against the clock, talked a life away and I'm sorry if it's clumsy like you with the anchovy toast but perhaps you can't hear me, you've slipped away, I don't blame you . . . What I want to say is I do believe there's a law, not like the ones that rule the tides or planets but something impalpable and personal though universal, a kind of inner justice that we obey or you could call it integrity and it's dishonest to pretend we're free . . . Truth is a better word, not the lawyer's truth because you see, Jennifer, I'm not being fair, I'm on the poet's side every time and that's one of the contradictions . . . If you're a poet you're only living more intensely, trying to point to something, make suggestions, ask questions but not give answers, you aren't God, you're as fallible as anyone, frightened and uncertain, you're the most human human but perhaps that's what God is after all . . . I wrote a poem about a man at a swimming-pool who hopes every day that he can dive off the top board but before climbing up the ladder he thinks of all the reasons not to try, he tells himself the water's too cold today or he's not feeling his best or he had a nasty letter from the bank this morning or his wife wouldn't make love last night or there's someone on the diving board who might be put off if he went up too so he slips into the shallow end without getting his hair wet . . . There are temptations everywhere and it's easy to surrender to the kisses, the hot-water bottles, the soothing honeydrops that save you in the night when you lie disgusted with yourself and the world and everyone in it and the black days when you think only of failure and the time you fritter away when you ought to stand up and do, act, create, discover, anything to be true . . . You're living more acutely too, you're out on the frontier, the explorer who pushes the big experience a bit further with no regrets and only a tiny flame in your dubious heart . . . But it's dangerous out there, it's not everyone's idea of fun, you've got to be mad and reckless and desperate and not mind the loneliness though you still need your friends and family and lovers, you need the critics too, the war correspondents who go up to the front and send back reports telling the world where you've gone wrong and how it should be done, saving their own skins though they know in their

[207]

hearts that life will have its answer, there's no escape from the terror and boredom and the best and bravest thing is to out-talk the bastard even if you only talk about yourself, a load of egoistic crap . . . Someone said that art is made by the alone for the alone and I've found it's true, I'm never so much myself as when I'm alone and I'm never so alone as when I'm writing because I can only be truthful when I'm alone . . . But now when I'm talking to you I fail myself, I lose the truth and become a liar though in lies there's a truth to discover or rather two of them, one truth in the lies and another in what's hidden under the lies I choose so I . . . But Jennifer, you're doing the right thing in the right way . . . Most people spend years doing it, they wander away down dead ends with dead hopes and dead habits and they call it life but they don't know what real life is nor real death . . . But Jennifer, Jennifer, you're not listening, you didn't hear a word and you're absolutely right, it's crap, you didn't miss anything, I swear.'

Felix watches Eunice close the girl's eyelids in the appalling face, shutting the secrets in.

'It takes me back,' she said, thinking of the General Strike fifteen years ago when she worked in a mortuary. 'I can cope with the living and the dead, it's the ones between that I find –' She looks up: 'Thanks, dear Felix.'

49

Herbert Robinson has been in the business too long to overplay his hand, though he works quickly. Never look a gift horse in the mouth, even a dead one. The pickings of a lifetime. Just when the Blitz was letting up and profits dropping. There were some useful incidents in the early days – often a shop wrecked with the week's takings in the cashbox, not difficult to find. But last month a gang was netted and given long sentences. Herbert must watch his step. Good job he fixed up Leo Robb, it's paying off.

A little butter – there's a whole week's ration on each table – and the rings come off a lady's fingers nicely. A bracelet can be slipped from a corpse with no trouble at all. And no trouble to look as if he's tending the wounded, tidying up the dead. In a sense, he is. Loosen that choker round the throat, remove those heavy ear-rings – it's a kindness. And people are very trusting, they expect the best from everyone. The public has got a name for good behaviour, the stories are all of honesty. Looting has been hushed up, for morale.

A pearl necklace, a sapphire brooch, a pair of gold cufflinks, a silver cigarette case. Emergency lights will be brought in soon, when the rescue men arrive. Till then, Herbert is safe enough. Watches, bangles, handbags. As the man said, riches grow in hell. Fill your boots, boy.

50

Overwhelmed less by grief than fatigue Eunice has to stop: 'I need alcohol, I'm finished – this will go on all night.'

Somewhere Felix finds a bottle of gin and tumblers. It may look obscene to sit drinking among the havoc and slaughter, but anything is consistent with this evening's erratic show. Each turn follows from the last. Mistakes are not wrong, but only items slipped into the programme, all the better for being unrehearsed. You can gasp at the variety, applaud the versatility.

'Happy birthday,' Felix says wanly, lifting his glass. 'St Felix's day.'

'What a fucking life.' Eunice feels tears pumping back.

Sorrow, after all, must penetrate exhaustion. She pours gin down her throat and chokes. 'It's the degradation. Why do we –?'

'Why do we what?' But Felix knows what. Why go on? Why bother? Why believe it can be anything but this?

'My little Hugo's never known anything but war,' Eunice says. 'And it'll be years before it's over. He's got to go through the whole long story. Learn the same old lessons as if they were new, cliché by cliché – all for this.'

'Being dead is no alternative.'

In the half-light they watch the Dutch admiral and his wife with Betty and Humphrey carrying the naval officer's mother slowly across the dance floor, with the son following the little cortège. Felix wants to grab a drum from the wreckage and beat a funeral march. For Snakehips too, and Violet.

'Hugo isn't you,' he says to Eunice. 'And Peter isn't me. They're someone else, their life isn't ours. Nothing's the same unless we want it. But too often we want it over and over again – never trusting ourselves with something new.'

'Better safe than sorry. Safe –!' Eunice looks around: 'The safest place in town, Celia said, and she died here.'

'Leaving Lionel sorry.'

'Sorry for himself. Cheated of that bedroom at the Regent Palace.'

'Eunice, that's not fair.'

'He's one of the takers. Puts his hand out, expects people to cough up and they do. Celia was a giver. Even at the end she gave, and Lionel took.'

'Difficult to feel generous in a Hurricane, fighting for your life. And difficult when you're told you're a hero. You can't blame them – those pilots deserve the prizes.'

'Celia was a prize all right. So was Guy. And Lancelot.' Eunice helps herself to more gin. 'And Violet.'

Felix can say nothing. Nothing of the immense pity, the

consuming dirge that fills him. He loved Violet for a year and a half, he will love her always with the same fresh excitement; will look back on her as one of the great treats of life. In time it will assemble into words and come out in a sustained lament for her or in casual moments of elegy to punctuate the future: the brittle Sundays ahead, the hollow echoes of a song of hers sung by someone else. Till then he will nourish it inside with dreams and tears.

Eunice puts her hand on his: 'Think of the people we could do without.'

'The dodgers? Passengers – who get a place on the raft while others drown?'

Eunice says, 'I had a husband once. Unbelievable now. But I see why I married him. My father –'

'Was a crook.'

'He was your father's churchwarden. And my mother –'

'An Egyptian whore.'

'They were going to turn me into a respectable daughter.'

'To bring redemption.'

'They held it over me. A home and husband, a son-in-law for them –'

'A garden full of grandchildren.'

'I met him at the dramatics society.'

'Stage comedy husband.'

'An estate agent on his way to the top. Town councillor, freemason, Conservative candidate – now he's a planning chief.'

'Faceless, hidden in blueprints.'

'I was a step on the way up, another diploma he'd got – you're better qualified with a sexy wife, you feel envied. We lived in a little Tudor mansion.'

Felix can see it: 'Gables and spinning wheels and horse brasses – he bought it from a catalogue.'

'We went to bridge parties and dances at the golf club, and copulated in a four-poster bed – that's the only word. We did it as a social move, the right thing.'

[211]

'Trying out a new golf shot.'

'I laughed in the middle. I knew the fun it could be and saw us bucking up and down. He bared his teeth and snarled – I wasn't being serious.'

'Making a joke of his performance.'

'Marriage became irrelevant, like lunch – some people have it, some do without. I had to cheat the future. Play along with it for a time and one day scuttle out of the act.'

'Stage comedy wife.'

'I gave him his breakfast and walked out, hoping to God I wasn't pregnant.'

'Leaving him hiccupping among the apostle spoons.'

'He'll always come bubbling to the surface. He floats naturally, he can't sink – I knew it that morning when I walked away across the lawn.'

'Mown in stripes, two shades of green.'

'He stood in the porch, wiping the toast crumbs off and waving his napkin at me. Not waving good-bye –'

'It never entered his head you might be leaving him.'

'But furious – I should have walked down the path, not over his precious grass.'

'Leaving footprints in the dew.' Felix remembers the footprints in the snow at Cambridge – how long ago?

'But it's odd – I'd put so much into the act, I couldn't take it all away. So there's a bit of me I left behind, that belonged to the cosy life, the coffee mornings –'

'Not your biggest bit, Eunice.'

'But all my own, and it stayed with him in that phoney Tudor house after I'd gone.'

'Haunting the inglenooks. Twanging the springs under the four-poster.'

'We collided once in Piccadilly, in the blackout. He mumbled something but didn't recognize me, probably he'd forgotten. I was the failure of his career, best wiped out. He had another woman with him.'

[212]

'Yourself – the bit you left behind, the woman you would have become.'

'She smiled and I smiled back.'

'You had the same secret.'

'She took his arm and they slipped away into the dark. He'll slip away from anything, bombs and all – he doesn't have to try, he's a chronic dodger.'

'Who's a dodger?' Bunty asks, sitting down with Felix and Eunice in the devastation.

'Not you, thank God.' Felix pours some gin for her.

'I'm lucky, that's all – horribly lucky.' Bunty's huge green eyes are only slightly faded, though her copper hair is now a burnished grey, oxidized by the long moist Irish years. Not much else has changed: the white skin, slender figure, lustrous height, the liquid voice. She says, 'We're all lucky, we don't deserve it.'

'It's more than luck,' Eunice says, remembering that Jennifer also called herself lucky. 'It's not even fate. It's a kind of role we have to play. Being killed would be out of character.'

'Isn't there a mad scheme in it?' Felix suggests. 'I can't believe it's haphazard. It fits into a plan somewhere. Nothing is random. Bunty and I –' He hasn't seen her since the day he took Francis out on his motorbike – the day Francis died. Now he strains to catch in her the dim pictures he has kept since he was nineteen, before they dissolve at this sudden encounter: standing at a fireplace in a straight black dress; sitting at the end of a long dining-table; twined in bed with *Prometheus*; galloping on her horse. He says, 'I often wondered –'

'I had more to go on,' Bunty says. 'You're public property, I could scoop up the fragments as they dropped.'

Felix is glad she knows nothing else. His life is in his poetry, she can read him and know it all. Intuitive, sympathetic – she needs no more.

'I'm a fan of yours,' she says. 'Book by book I've

[213]

shadowed you. Cambridge, Berlin, Dunwich, Belsize Park
– I've kept track. And the Café de Paris follows the theme. I
wasn't lying in wait here, but perhaps I was expecting –'
    'Nothing you don't know about him?' Eunice asks. She
can claim priority, her own friendship is twice as long.
    'Nothing important. It's there, laid out on the page.
Hints, clues –'
    'I hope you're right,' Felix says.
    Eunice asks, 'You have no life outside your writing?'
    'Not one that matters. Life is unreal. Look at this down
here, the stupidity, waste – d'you believe it?'
    'But you say it isn't haphazard. Anything with a shape is
real.'
    'Perhaps only the shape is real – what you see and feel,
what you make of it.'
    Bunty says, 'Like Keats – nothing becomes real till it's
experienced.'
    'You don't exist?' Eunice touches Felix's hand again.
    'I have to prove it. So I write, and that's real.'
    Eunice says, 'Life is for living,' remembering Jennifer.
    'Living?' Felix considers it.
    'You put it in a poem,' Bunty says. 'There was someone
living your life, but you knew nothing about him. You
watched him as a stranger.'
    'I am my work, I'm nothing else.'
    'One of your best, I thought.'
    'Thanks.' But though Felix likes the compliment and is
curious to know more, he deflects it like a blow. The
response must come from himself, and at each turn of
thought and tick-tock of conversation a new image forms.
The old is finished, he must move to something fresh.
Already he is impatient: 'An idea I've got – of a man, a
popular writer who is a recluse. A compulsive disappearer,
though he's a big success. Everyone reads him, nobody
knows him. Who is he? How old is he? Is he married?
Where does he live? But these things are nothing to him –

[214]

they're empty, vain. He won't have a photo on his book or sign copies or go to parties or play the publicity tricks. Every book is a best-seller, but he cultivates obscurity. There are rumours – he drives a taxi, he lives in a windmill, he was seen in Birmingham, he's a monk, he's a maharaja, he's a woman – but they're false. Or true, if you like. They're wrong, they're right, he's none of them, he's all of them – it makes no difference. More and more is irrelevant as he flees from his own fame.'

'To write his famous books,' Eunice says.

'They sell in millions while he retreats further towards vanishing point, always ahead of the hounds. In the end they give up. They've driven the story to death and they leave him in peace.'

'Where he rots,' Eunice says. 'And never writes another word. Extinguished. Obscurity has won.'

'It's for a novelist,' Bunty says. 'A novel's about people, a poem's about yourself.'

'Perhaps this is about Felix.'

'The old dilemma –' Bunty says.

Felix takes it up: 'The need to speak, but the fear of being found out.'

'You want to hide, yet you give yourself away.'

'So,' Felix says, abruptly switching, too spent to sustain anything. 'How about you? The castle, the Major – fill me in, I'm out of date.' The bomb has blasted the years apart and let them fall into a different order. The explosion, the shock of death and survival, the martinis at the bar and now more gin between spells of rescue work – Felix is overloaded.

'Ah, the castle and the Major.' Bunty's voice encircles them both, the building and the man, lapping to Ireland and returning with the news: 'They're still there, just the same. The Major in his castle, the fish swimming round the moat, the huntsmen galloping down the drive – they're getting a little ragged, they need clipping.'

[215]

'The Major is –?'

'Blissful. He's given himself a knighthood and normally wears one of the suits of armour from the hall.'

Eunice erupts: 'Normally! Your husband in armour!'

'He fell off, out hunting before the war, and got concussed. Slight brain damage, but he's very happy. Just rather hard to live with. Like the ancestor who built a castle on top of a house – it runs in the blood. Mortimer looks after him – you remember old Mortimer? They get through barrels of brandy between them. The other servants have drifted away, they couldn't adjust to the Middle Ages.'

'*Droit de seigneur* among the maids!' Eunice claps her hands, she is enchanted.

'The hounds were let loose. Sometimes they break into the kitchen, and there's a pack roaming in the park – it keeps the Republicans away. The cars were sold, and the horses, except one – the Major's big hunter which was brought into the castle. He rides it up and down the stairs and along the corridors, clanking in his armour. Swiping at whatever he fancies with a sword. You remember those stuffed wolfhounds and racehorse paintings? – they're being massacred. Mortimer follows behind to clear up the mess.'

'Don Quixote and his faithful squire,' Felix says. 'I might have seen it coming.'

'At night they roast huge joints of meat –'

'Mortimer turning the spit?' Eunice is enjoying the picture. 'Your husband telling stories of chivalry? Sometimes singing a ballad?'

'More or less.'

'Tossing mutton bones to the dogs? Go on.'

'That's all there is. Mortimer has slipped into the act – it was that or a dungeon, and the brandy helps. I didn't take to it, though in an odd way I love my husband more like this. Now he's mad, he's less ridiculous. But I was expected

[216]

to languish in one of the towers, playing the harp or doing needlework, chaste and weeping.'

'So you were rescued by a prince.'

'I'm fifty, I had to take what came.' Bunty looks towards the ruined staircase where the sun-tanned little man in a tuxedo is still nursing his indignation. But now he is standing up, he has been given a drink. In time he may rejoice to have no scars. She explains: 'He's American, a professor of medieval warfare – he knows more about battleaxes than anyone in the world. Last summer he heard that the Home Guard were getting pikes to defend England –'

'And came charging over the sea,' Eunice says, with appreciation, 'in support.'

'Then he heard about an eccentric cavalry officer in an Irish castle. He turned up in a taxi and when I saw him tripping across the drawbridge I knew he was my hope – our first visitor for months. But I had a job to get him away, even when the Major threatened to put him on bread and water if he didn't wear chainmail. I had to bribe him. Not just the lady in distress story, though he loves a legend, a bit of minstrelsy –'

'A lay in every sense,' Eunice says under her breath, swallowing her gin and choking.

'Alas, he'd never think of that. His passion is weapons. I told him he could cut some wood from the yew hedge, the hindquarters off one of the horses that wouldn't show, and make it into long bows. Now we have a studio in Notting Hill where he chips and chamfers as if we were arming for Agincourt. I can't escape the period, can I? Or the lunatics. But there's a lovely bonus – it's sent me back to Chaucer.'

'Wow!' Eunice exclaims. 'It's an epic.'

Felix says, 'And Bertram?'

'Bertie's in the Irish Guards – over there.'

Bunty's son, having failed to get obeyed, is helping to clear the staircase; prop it with tables to make a passage for

[217]

stretchers. Ambulances have at last arrived, and loaded up and gone away. More are wanted. Though the doctor's team in the kitchen is doing heroic work, other lives can be saved if aid comes quickly. But nothing is happening quickly. After the first paralysis people were stirred into activity, useful or futile, but with the dust clearing and more lights brought in they are settling into a slow rhythm. No jerk, no haste, almost no sound to spoil the mood: a funeral ballet without music. The least nod or whisper is enough. Cries and groans have been silenced. Figures – Bertram among them – move like dancers, careful not to break the trance.

Bunty says, 'He hasn't got the family streak. It may come out one day. Perhaps he'll become a friar – he's very dim. I watch for signs. I should be grateful he's so ordinary, instead of wanting to be shocked. But Felix – you've got a son too, he comes in the poems. The unknown person in a cot, your invention but not your possession. And the bubbling child in your arms, careering down Hampstead Heath. And the father split by joy and agony, watching his son. He must be six, seven –'

'He and I were friends,' Felix says. 'Quite an addiction – but we'll have to do without, till after the war. By then we may have lost the habit. Like other nice things that stopped – avocado pears and silk stockings and the rest. I tried to tell him the world is horrible and the secret is to know it. Face it. Feel it – then you can begin, just begin, hoping to be happy. I'm not sure I still believe it, I just don't know –' Suddenly Felix is very tired. He can't think. He has nothing to tell anyone. He remembers someone – the old Brigadier? Churchill? – saying that war is the ultimate reality. He might repeat it. 'It's the thing we have to live with.' But he only hears himself say weakly, 'Eunice has got a son too.'

Then he hears another noise.

A shout.

'God!' it might be.

[218]

Or, 'Stop!'

Or, 'Look!'

It comes from himself. His own voice. He hardly knows he is shouting, but it is nobody else.

'Look!' It comes again. A blast of rage, disgust, shame.

Someone shouts back: 'What?' A woman. Close to him. Eunice. Or Bunty. They are both staring at him. Fright in their eyes. 'Are you mad?'

'Look!'

But he doesn't know what to look at. Or what he saw. He has lost it.

'Stop!' The ballet stops, the dancers freeze.

'Look!'

He sees it again. The trouser clips. Then he loses them in the fog of gin and exhaustion and grief and more gin. And finds them. The clips on Herbert's trousers. They start a dreadful thought. Running like poison through him. Nasty, very nasty. Who said that? Who was Leo calling on the telephone? Hop on your bike, boy. Herbert knows the streets, he wouldn't waste time getting here. Pedalling through the air raid. Weaving through the shrapnel and broken glass, careful not to burst a tyre.

'God!'

That explains it. That's why the ambulances and rescue squad were so long coming. Nobody called them. All the horror of tonight is fixed in this one vile thing. Herbert's trouser clips. Hop on your bicycle.

Felix moves fast. Through the tables, kicking a chair over, across the dance floor. Stumbles and falls, his foot through a hole in the boards. The old bear pit down there. Picks himself up, races on over the debris.

Herbert is faster. Vanishes with his pockets full of loot snatched from the dead and dying. Up the staircase. Springing through the foyer. Wreckage everywhere, fallen chandeliers, slashed upholstery, shattered mirrors. The bar where Guy died. Too many martinis tonight. Herbert must have gone this way unless he knows a back exit. Dashing for the stairs up to the street.

Leo Robb at the door.

'Steady there, sir! – not so fast.'

The phoney sergeant in his maroon overcoat, on sentry duty. Medal ribbons on his chest. The ballad of Trooper Robb. Too much juice in him, the Major said.

Felix trips again, on Leo's boot. Down on his face, down on the pavement. Up again.

'Steady, steady!'

A hand shoots out to grab his shoulder, but he dodges it. Out into Coventry Street, out from that hole down there, out into the night. Left or right? Leicester Square or Piccadilly? People are standing at the Café de Paris door. Scavengers, carrion crows. The usual callous idiots, bloody jackals. A woman laughs, a taxi honks. No bicycle anywhere. Which way?

Felix turns right. Running through the blackout. Gunfire in the sky. A glow of fire behind him. Like that night in Ireland, running for his life. But then he was fleeing, now he is chasing.

A man can get lost in the blackout, no problem at all. Melt into the dark. Bolt into the underground. Most stations are public shelters, he can sink into the crowd down there. London is infinite. A city with a giant's maw. Herbert would be sucked through the tunnels, absorbed into the bloodstream, spewed out of the pores elsewhere. A short start and he has gone. No hope of catching him. A rat gone down his hole.

Knowing it is useless, Felix runs down the steps into Piccadilly station. The ticket office is shut, the trains have stopped. Two policemen stand by the shuttered news-stand, another at the top of the escalator with an air-raid warden. The machinery has been switched off, the stairs are motionless.

'Did you see –? Did he go –?' Felix looks down the empty

[220]

silent slope. Nobody in sight. A long way to the bottom, to the platforms crowded with campers, refugees from the bombs. 'A man with a green hat . . . a pork pie . . . trouser clips . . . bicycle clips –' He sees how futile it is.

'No pork pies been this way,' the warden says, and winks at the policeman. 'On a bicycle or otherwise.'

Felix goes to the men's lavatory, bursting and out of breath. Big china niches all round the walls for men to stand in. Most are empty. A smell of urine and carbolic, a noise of water flushing through the pipes from London's own vast bladders somewhere. Notices on the white tiles, warning of venereal disease. A bucket clashes and echoes, a man sloshes water over the floor with a broom.

Herbert is in a corner niche, his back to Felix. A rat in a corner. Felix runs and skids. Crashes to the wet floor, picks himself up, muck on his hands and clothes. Slips again, but saves himself and is about to shout. Will it be fists? He has never had a fight, only watched Reuben.

But it isn't Herbert, it is more like Francis, killed in Ireland fifteen years ago. A sad beguiling face, a girlish appeal in the eyes. A question – friendship? money? love? – crosses the young man's lips. The simplicity and beauty of a summer afternoon by an Irish lake. Certainly it won't be fists.

Felix turns away; climbs the steps back into the street; goes slowly back to the Café de Paris.

51

Eunice was standing outside. She had followed him out and was waiting on the pavement, not knowing where he had gone. She saw without asking that he hadn't caught Herbert.

'I feel terrible,' she said. A mist lay in her eyes, of rage and love but mostly loss. Her red dress was torn down the front, her fur coat dusted with plaster, her hair filthy. Dried blood had formed a scab across one cheek, the other was smudged with grime. Her beauty was clotted, tangled.

'Taxi!' Felix called into the blackout. He had no coat, he had put it over Guy's face.

A single bomber throbbed faintly in the east, returning empty to Germany: to come back another night. A searchlight scanned the sky, gunfire rumbled down the Thames. The raid was finished, the all clear would go before dawn. The late-night milk bar in Leicester Square was shut. Only the entrance to the Café de Paris defied the darkened street, a bright door into the hell below, ringed by its little gaping crowd. With gas-mask cases slung like cameras over one shoulder, they were tourists of a morbid kind. 'What's going on down there? What happened?' They had missed something, they wanted to make sure of every thrill, every free show, on a Saturday night out in the West End. People in evening dress, emerging bruised and bandaged, got a clap and a cheer like marathon runners at the finishing line: they had won. Stretchers got a shameless gasp and were taken away by ambulance: 'Anyone famous?'

The dead were laid out on the pavement, to be removed later. Pale and quiet, their fine clothes covered in dust or tablecloths, they looked like beautiful dolls destroyed by a child and left on the ground in rows: a still life but more living, more stained with the restlessness of life, than the bunch of gawpers. You might, in the middle of that scarred and distracting night of early spring, have been tempted to lie down beside them.

A taxi swung into the kerb. Eunice opened the door, Felix spoke to the driver. But looking at them closer the man said, 'Not in my cab, thanks – I'm not having no blood in here,' and drove away.

They would have to walk, Eunice to her flat in Bayswater, Felix to his near Tottenham Court Road.